Praise fo...
Marla M...

POISON SLEEP

"[A] wonderfully whimsical urban fantasy." —*Publishers Weekly*

"Pratt's second book featuring bad-girl sorcerer Marla Mason is just as awesome as the first volume, if not better."
—*Romantic Times* (4.5 stars)

"It's the little differences—like the third-person narratives, the novels being self-contained, the strong supporting characters, the plot manipulations, the inventive magical concepts, et cetera—that really separate both *Blood Engines* and *Poison Sleep* from the competition.... One of the first[series] that I recommend to readers wanting to discover great urban fantasy."
—FantasyBookCritic

BLOOD ENGINES

"A fast-paced, thoroughly fun, satisfying read."
—Kelley Armstrong, author of *No Humans Involved*

"*Blood Engines* wastes no time: by page three I knew I was reading an urban fantasy unlike any I'd previously encountered—the characters and world are real, immediate, and unapologetically in-your-face, throwing you into a story that trusts you'll keep up with the fast pace without flinching. It charges along with crisp pacing, a fascinating range of secondary characters, and a highly compelling lead in Marla Mason—her ruthless pragmatism gives her a completely different feel from her fictional contemporaries. I genuinely look forward to the next book!"
—C. E. Murphy, author of *Coyote Dreams*

"Pratt is a deft storyteller whose blend of suspense, magic, and dry humor kept me entertained and turning pages. *Blood Engines* is one of the most absorbing reads I've enjoyed in a long time, gluing me to the couch. I adore Marla, her done-at-all-costs character is someone I can relate to and want to cheer for. Best of all, I didn't figure the ending out until I got there. It's a book widower, and I can't wait for the sequel."

—Kim Harrison, *New York Times* bestselling author of *For a Few Demons More*

"Brain-twisting, superb... Amazingly strange, fascinating ideas spring from the pages, one after another with surprising frequencies, blending a dozen or more schools of magical thought into a psychedelic tapestry of unexpected depth.... I've read a lot of urban fantasies, and believe me, *Blood Engines* is new and different and not to be missed."

—SFSite.com

"The first of what promises to be an exciting and compulsively readable new urban fantasy series. Pratt has a deft touch with characterization and plot, fusing magical elements with more mundane details easily and seamlessly."

—*Romantic Times* (4 stars)

"Strong overtones of both noir and steampunk... [and] the darkly witty dialogue is like what a reader might expect if Howard Hawks had written urban fantasy, where the only way to tell the good guys from the bad guys is that the good guys get even sharper dialogue. In addition, Pratt plunders a plethora of pantheons and perspectives on magic, ensuring that the magical San Francisco is just as diverse as the nonmagical version, counting amongst its citizens silicon mages, biomancers, and metalworking artificers, not to mention shamanistic sex magicians (who are well worth mentioning).... I would recommend *Blood Engines* to anyone who loves a fun and fast-paced fantasy adventure."

—*Green Man Review*

"An entertaining romp featuring a kick-ass heroine, a distinctive magic system, and lots of local color."

—*Locus*

ALSO BY T. A. PRATT

Poison Sleep

Blood Engines

DEAD REIGN

T. A. PRATT

BANTAM SPECTRA

DEAD REIGN
A Bantam Spectra Book / November 2008

Published by
Bantam Dell
A Division of Random House, Inc.
New York, New York

Bantam Books and the rooster colophon are registered trademarks and Spectra and the portrayal of a boxed "s" are trademarks of Random House, Inc.

ISBN 978-0-553-59135-4

Printed in the United States of America
Published simultaneously in Canada

www.bantamdell.com

OPM 10 9 8 7 6 5 4 3 2 1

For Greg,
who would make a ferocious zombie killer,
if it ever came to that

In their last sleep—the dead reign there alone.
So shalt thou rest, and what if thou withdraw
In silence from the living, and no friend
Take note of thy departure?
—William Cullen Bryant, "Thanatopsis"

1

Marla Mason sat in the branches of an ancient oak on a ridge, spying on the moonlit cemetery below. A tall elderly man with a walking stick stood near a freshly disturbed grave, supervising a pair of homeless ordinaries armed with shovels. A black goat chewed peacefully on the grass near the grave, tethered by a length of twine to the stone cross of a neighboring headstone.

"I can't believe we're sitting in a tree," Rondeau said, shifting on the branch next to her, but remembering to whisper, at least. "I'm ruining my pants."

"At least it's summer. Be glad we're not sitting in an ice-covered tree in winter. I told you we were doing a stakeout tonight. It's not my fault you decided to wear a leisure suit." She glanced at her morose colleague. "That shade of green doesn't even blend in with the foliage. I'm not sure that shade of green even exists in nature." She looked back down on the scene below. The tall man paced around the gradually emptying grave like an expectant 1950s father in a waiting room.

"Why do I have to be here again?" Rondeau said.

"Stakeouts are boring. You make them slightly less boring, what with your amusing complaints and comical discomfort."

"Wonderful. Remind me to cultivate greater dullness. I don't see why we need to spy on Ayres. We're in the business of hassling crazy people now?"

"We're not hassling Ayres. He doesn't even know we're here. We're just going to enforce the terms of his parole. Unless you want hordes of zombies running around all over town?"

"Fast zombies or slow zombies?"

Marla scowled at him, but he didn't take much notice. "What?"

"Well, the classic George Romero *Night of the Living Dead* zombies, shambling around slowly, there could be a certain pleasure in dealing with that, you know? Taking them out using shotguns and baseball bats, whack whack whack. Killing zombies is like killing Nazis. You don't even have to feel bad about it. It's like shooting rats at the dump. Very cathartic."

"You're a sick bastard, Rondeau."

He shrugged. "Fast zombies, though, like you see in movies nowadays, those are scary."

"Ayres makes real zombies." She considered. "Well, not actually like Haitian Vodoun zombies, either, I guess. He animates corpses to do his bidding. Not like movie zombies anyway."

"Oh, so the zombies aren't even contagious? I mean,

if they bite you, you don't rise from the dead with a craving for brains? Hell. Those would be easy."

"Under the terms of his release, Ayres isn't supposed to practice necromancy. I insisted on that. And unless he's gotten into garden-variety grave-robbing, he's about to break his agreement."

"Why the restrictions, though? Dr. Husch said Ayres is cured. He's trying to become a contributing member of our little underground society again. I think you just have an irrational hatred for necromancers, ever since that guy Upchurch raised Somerset from the dead and you got your ass kicked."

Marla punched Rondeau in the arm, making him grab wildly for a branch to keep from tumbling out of the tree. "My ass was only kicked provisionally. I beat Somerset in the end. No, I've got personal reasons to want Ayres out of the picture."

"Why don't you ever tell me anything?"

"Sorcerers have secrets like surgeons have scalpels, Rondeau. Tools of the trade."

Marla didn't look at him, but she could *sense* Rondeau rolling his eyes. "Okay, whatever. So what's the goat for?"

"Sacrifice. Necromancy runs on blood. To make the dead speak, a few drops of the sorcerer's own blood will suffice. To raise a fresh human corpse, you don't need much blood—just a rat or a pigeon. To raise older corpses or get a skeleton walking around, you need more blood, bigger sacrifices."

"That looks like a fresh grave they're digging up, so why's he going to kill that cute goat instead of a rat?"

Marla shrugged. "He's an old man, and it's easier to buy a goat than catch a rat? Or maybe it's because he's been out of practice for fifteen years? I don't know. I'm not a necromancer. Smelly, ugly business."

The men at the pit hauled the casket up out of the hole with ropes. Ayres paid them, and they left, brushing grave-dirt off their already filthy clothes. The necromancer watched them depart, then opened a satchel and drew out various jars and candles. The goat watched him with interest. Marla let him pour out a few lines of sand and powder on the grass, getting well into his ritual, before saying, "Okay, let's go break up this shindig."

She dropped out of the tree, her black cloak flapping behind her. She'd permanently retired her signature magical purple-and-white cloak—she preferred using magic that didn't actually drive her insane, and this new cloak was purely decorative. It had silver trim and everything. Still, style counted for something, and at this point most of the denizens of Felport's magical underworld had a visceral reaction to the sight of Marla Mason wearing a cloak—pretty much the way a field mouse reacts to the shadow of a hawk on the ground.

Rondeau came down after her, rather less gracefully, but he managed a lazy saunter by the time they were halfway down the hill. "Hey, Ayres!" Marla shouted. "You've been a bad boy!"

"Miss Mason," Ayres said, his voice about as sepulchral as could be expected. He rose from his preparations and hobbled toward her—was he making a bigger show of being frail now that he knew she was watching?

"I . . . am surprised to see you here. I would not think my actions would interest you."

"Rondeau, go untie the goat, take him back to the car, would you?"

"You're going to put a goat in the Bentley? I think the owner's manual advises against transporting livestock. It's bad for the leather."

Marla shooed him, and Rondeau complied, untying the goat and leading it away. The nibbles it was taking out of his pants would annoy him, once he noticed.

Marla turned to Ayres. "Of course I take an interest. You were clapped up in the nuthouse until a few days ago. Your release had one condition—don't mess around with dead bodies—and here you are, up to your armpits in dead people. Metaphorically. I can't have a rogue necromancer with mental health issues running around my city raising the dead unsupervised. It's bad for business. And morale. And tourism. And hygiene." She sat on the headstone, after glancing at the inscription to make sure it wasn't anyone she knew. Ayres had probably just picked the freshest-looking grave.

Ayres lowered himself carefully down to sit on the unopened casket. "I require a servant." He was unapologetic. "I'm an old man, and I need assistance."

"You can't raise the dead in Felport, Ayres. If you leave the city, you're out of my jurisdiction, and you can do whatever you want. Go down to Mexico—there's lots of call for necromancy down there, I hear. Or fly up to Detroit. That lunatic Nain Rouge who runs the place could always use another corpse-grinder. But you can't do it here."

"This is my home. I helped make this city great. When Somerset ruled, during World War II and afterward, Felport was a colossus. What have you done?" He sneered. "Under Sauvage's reign, under yours, we've lost industry, the bridges are rusting, the bay is polluted, shipping has fallen off—"

"That's not us, that's just the economy." She scowled. "Sauvage and I held disintegration at bay, damn it. Factories are leaving this country in droves, but we've turned Adler College into a world-class institution of higher education, we're cleaning up the parks, we're bringing in biotech companies and research firms and—" She stopped. "Why am I justifying myself to you?"

"When the factories ran, when the smokestacks darkened the sky, when metal was forged and things were *made* here, Felport was a place of power, and Somerset tapped into it, he grew strong as the city did. What power can you draw from research, from ordinaries studying their incomplete histories in ivory towers? Bah."

"We do all right. It's a different world now, Ayres."

Ayres started to rise, then made a visible effort to remain calm, sinking back down. "I beg you to reconsider. I served the previous two administrations, and I could serve yours. I understand you have no necromancers of note in the city now, merely half-trained *ronin,* men who should be apprentices but lack masters to teach them."

"The city coroner, Dr. Matte, can coax a murdered corpse into telling us who killed him, and that's about all the need we have for necromancers these days."

Ayres leaned forward, his professional pride clearly wounded. "Those who communicate with the dead have far more uses than solving the petty crimes that afflict ordinaries." His voice had the reflexive contempt many old-line sorcerers exhibited when talking about mundane citizens, the great mass of people going about their lives unaware of the magical men and women and things in their midst. She didn't appreciate the attitude. Ninety-nine point nine percent of Felport's populace consisted of just such ordinaries, and Marla was sworn to protect the *whole* city, not just the sorcerers who lived there. Besides, she'd been an ordinary herself once, before being initiated into the mysteries. It was an argument she'd had many times with Felport's other sorcerers, who variously saw ordinaries as obstacles, experimental subjects, means to make money, or nuisances.

"Like what?" she said. "The *last* powerful necromancer we had in town, Upchurch, brought back the most horrible tyrant in Felport's history. He raised Somerset from the dead, and Somerset killed him for his trouble, before going on a crime spree and trying to take over the city. You know how hard it is to kill an undead sorcerer?" She shuddered. She'd developed a gut-deep hatred of the living dead in all their incarnations during that nightmare.

Ayres shifted under her gaze. "I knew Upchurch. He was my apprentice, and when I . . . became ill . . . he took over my position as Sauvage's advisor. He chose to resurrect Somerset for his own reasons, I'm sure. But think of it, Marla. I can call the shades of the city's great past leaders to consult with you. I can shield you from death, and call you back to life if you should die. If the city is ever threatened, I can raise an army of undying warriors to fight by your side. I can communicate with inhabitants of nether dimensions, and they have resources we can scarcely comprehend. I can be of *use* to you, Marla."

She took her dagger of office from the sheath at her belt and held it up to the moonlight, watching the reflection of light on metal. The dagger had a shining blade eight inches long, with a handle wrapped in alternating bands of white and purple electrical tape. The dagger never needed sharpening—it was magical, passed from chief sorcerer to chief sorcerer over the decades, and could cut through anything, material or ethereal. The sight of Marla holding the dagger tended to unnerve people. "Nobody's doubting your qualifications. But you've been locked up for fifteen years. You just got out of a hospital for the criminally insane. It doesn't look good on a résumé."

"I am fully cured. Dr. Husch can vouch for my—"

"Ayres, you thought you were *dead*!" Dr. Husch had told her the condition was called the Cotard delusion. Those who suffered from the syndrome genuinely believed they were dead. Sometimes they thought they were being tormented in the afterlife, or believed they were wandering the world as ghosts, or thought they were zombies. Fifteen years ago Ayres had begun his constant complaints about the stench of rot, but at first, people thought it was just a side effect of his business—it was too late when they realized he thought his *own* flesh was rotting.

"That was then. I now know I am very much alive." He tapped his walking stick on the grass, but that was his only sign of agitation. "Dr. Husch's therapies were most effective."

"You thought you were in Hell. You killed three innocent people because you thought they were demons!"

He bowed his head. "I know my crimes. I regret them deeply. I have paid for them. You cannot imagine the suffering I endured, Miss Mason. Aware of my own putrescence, smelling my own rot. Convinced I was dead and trapped in a Hell that simulated the streets of my beloved city, tormented by monsters who wore the faces of my friends, beasts with false smiles. Trying to play along with the charade of life, lest I be sent to some even more horrible and explicit Hell. That is penance, Miss Mason."

"Yeah, well, screw all that," she said, twirling the knife. "The real reason I won't give you a job is because you betrayed my city by raising Somerset from the dead."

He flinched. "I was imprisoned at the Blackwing Institute when that happened. I only heard about it secondhand. Upchurch was responsible—"

"Upchurch was a hack. He wore a top hat, and white greasepaint to make his face look like a skull. When somebody tries that hard, you know they don't really have the chops. He was your apprentice. You told him to raise Somerset."

"You have no proof of these allegations."

She shrugged. "You were in low security back then, because Dr. Husch had decided you weren't a threat to others. You were allowed to walk the grounds at Blackwing, with supervision. You were allowed to have visitors. I know Upchurch visited you several times in the weeks before Somerset was resurrected—I checked the logs. I don't know what you *talked* about, but I can guess. Somerset killed Sauvage. That guy was my *friend*." Sauvage was her predecessor as chief sorcerer, and they'd gotten close back when she was a freelancer living by her wits and her steel-toed boots. "If I hadn't stopped him, Felport would be a little piece of Hell on Earth now."

"Somerset was a great leader. Strong. Sometimes ruthless, it's true. I served him until he died, and then I served Sauvage, who was barely half the man Somerset was. He had no vision. But still, I worked for him loyally."

"Until he had you locked up, right, Ayres? That must have pissed you off. Somerset wouldn't have put you away—he didn't care if the occasional ordinary got killed in the course of business. They were never part of his *vision*."

Ayres took a deep breath. "As I said, you have no proof. Your accusations are baseless."

Marla looked him over. He was old, yes, but far from broken. She'd hoped he would confess, but really, did it matter? "True. Upchurch was torn to bits by Somerset, and Dr. Matte couldn't put his skull back together well enough to make him speak after death. So yeah, all I've got is suspicions. But they're strong suspicions. If I had proof, you'd be dead by now. Dead for real."

"I could have brought Upchurch's shade back to answer questions," Ayres said, a trifle smugly. "You see? You could use someone of my talents."

Marla snorted. "I'll pass. Get out of here, old man."

He blinked at her. "What?"

"Beat it. Get lost. This is your one warning. If I catch you trying to practice your craft in my city again, I won't have you committed—I'll just strip you of your property and banish you."

"I've done nothing wrong. I deserve—"

"You deserve whatever I want to offer." Her voice was low and dangerous. "I don't even need reasons. I'm in charge, and you're out. If you want to retire and spend your days yelling at the kids on your lawn and playing Bingo, great, you're welcome to stay, and I won't say boo to you. But your time as a sorcerer is over. I won't have you bringing any more dead monsters from the past to life."

Ayres slumped his shoulders, and the light left his eyes. "I cannot change your mind?"

"Please. You're lucky I gave you one screwup for free."

"I will be on my way, then." He started to gather his candles and powders.

"Leave that stuff. Consider it a donation to the city."

Ayres didn't even object, just nodded and walked away, leaning heavily on his stick as he went.

Marla opened her cell phone and called her consiglieri, Hamil. "Can you send a couple of guys with shovels down to the Browne Memorial Cemetery? I've got a coffin that needs burying. Or rather, reburying."

"I don't even want to know, do I?"

"Probably not." Marla didn't tell him about her suspicions regarding Ayres. She couldn't prove anything, after all. "Nothing to worry about."

"You're still going to see the Chamberlain tomorrow about the Founders' Ball?" Hamil said.

"Yeah, yeah, you've reminded me a thousand times." Marla hung up.

She should get back to the car. Rondeau could get into all kinds of mischief by himself, and she shuddered to think what he might accomplish with the help of a small goat. But being in a cemetery made her melancholy, and she wanted to shake that off before she rejoined the company of others. Marla wasn't far from the grave of her friend Ted, who'd died last winter, and she walked toward his modest marker. She also wasn't far from the grave of her onetime lover Joshua Kindler, the man who'd killed Ted, and the last person to die at Marla's hands. Marla wasn't comfortable with killing people—from a purely pragmatic standpoint, murder incurred a deep karmic debt, and could eventually have dangerous consequences for a user of magic. As she looked down at Ted's dark gravestone, set flush with the ground and inscribed with only his name and dates, she thought about other graves she'd filled. Three here in Felport. Two in San Francisco, though one was just an unmarked hole in Golden Gate Park. One back in her hometown in Indiana. Too many deaths. Most were situations where she'd had no other options, but some of them . . . some of them could have been different, if she'd been brave enough or smart enough or, though she hated to admit it, a little less sure of her own righteousness.

Marla shook off the weight of her regrets. She had things to do in the here-and-now, and the past was better left buried. On her way out of the cemetery, she paused by the casket Ayres had exhumed. A couple of Hamil's apprentices would be along shortly to bury it. She patted the coffin's lid. "Sorry we disturbed you," she said. "Rest well."

The next morning, Ayres sat seething on an iron bench on the esplanade, staring at the deep blue waters of the bay. Yes, he'd helped raise Somerset from the dead, though the Somerset that came to life was not the fearless visionary Ayres had expected, but a monster rendered insane by too many years of death. Ayres regretted his part in the affair, but Marla's arrogance was insufferable. Ayres had been a prominent sorcerer in Felport when Marla's *mother* was in diapers. He'd been born and raised in this city, steeped in the magical subculture from his earliest youth, when he'd first discovered the ability to speak to roadkill in the street and raise euthanized butterflies from the dead. Marla was an outsider who'd come to this city in her teens and stumbled into magic. Yes, she had a certain rough-edged charisma, and was said to be one of the most potent martial magicians the city had ever seen, but the ability to damage people physically didn't qualify one for leadership. She wouldn't even allow him to raise a servant. It was intolerable. He *needed* a servant—he was an old man, even by the long-lived standards of sorcerers, and he couldn't very well scrub his own toilets and carry his own burdens or conduct his own reconnaissance. But what Marla didn't know . . .

He rose and began walking, every step easing his stiffened joints. Once, he'd believed that stiffness was rigor mortis setting in, but he was *alive,* he knew, and the pains were only encroaching age. It would be a waste of time to try exhuming another corpse. Marla was surely having him watched. Fresh corpses were easiest to raise, but in truth he would prefer a nice mummy or bog-man, a corpse that had been preserved by the old methods. They flaked a bit, but didn't fall to rot and wormy ruin as other corpses did. There was a mummy in the natural history museum, but he couldn't spirit that away without being found out. He had to act in secret. Perhaps there were other options. He had some connections from the old days who might help. Somerset and Sauvage were not the only masters he'd served. He'd sometimes consulted with Hamil, but the man was Marla's lapdog. Ayres needed someone he could get leverage over, who could be convinced to defy Marla. . . .

He stopped. He smiled. He twirled his walking stick, feeling almost jaunty, and set off for one of the access points to the secret catacombs beneath Felport, the tunnels and caverns and vaults hidden to even the most seasoned of sewer workers, known only to sorcerers like himself. He went down a crumbling concrete stairway that led to the bay. The tide was out, revealing a strand of rocky beach. Ayres picked his way along carefully, the stink of low tide reminding him of his own rotting flesh—no, no, he was alive, still alive, he'd never died! After a while he reached the spot he remembered and slowly clambered up a few slick boulders, working his way carefully up to the face of the sea cliff. He used his stick to clear away hanging curtains of seaweed, revealing a mossy iron gate, which he pulled open, the hinges squealing and protesting from years of disuse, and he wondered if anyone else even remembered this passageway. Well, Viscarro would, of course—Viscarro was Felport's subterranean sorcerer. He'd been here for as long as anyone could remember, carving his vaults beneath the street, drawing magic from the darkness, raising mushrooms with peculiar properties, hoarding gold and stranger treasures. He had a little bit of everything hidden away, it was said . . . and Ayres knew a secret about him. For sorcerers, secrets were power, and Ayres knew more than a few.

Ayres entered the stinking passageway, stepping around puddles of pooled filth. Soon the concrete walls turned to brick, and farther along to the black stone of natural caverns, walls furry with mold. Ayres finally reached a modern gate of steel bars, where a cadaverously pale attendant sat in an illuminated booth behind a Plexiglas barrier, his head resting against one wall as he dozed.

Ayres rapped on the Plexiglas sharply with his stick, and the attendant shot up. "Very shoddy," Ayres said, leaning close and shouting through the cluster of holes punched in the glass to allow communication. "Does Viscarro know you sleep on duty?"

The boy—he was perhaps in his forties, and to Ayres, any man who wasn't old enough to be dead of natural causes was a boy—sputtered, "I . . . no one has come to this gate in years!"

"I need to see Viscarro."

The apprentice frowned. "Who may I say is calling?"

"Ayres, the necromancer."

The boy scribbled something on a sheet of paper, tucked it into a glass-and-brass cylinder, and shoved the whole thing into a pneumatic tube, where it was whisked away to some deeper place in the vault. "It'll be a few minutes," he said, not quite apologetically. "I'd offer you something to drink, but, well . . ." He gestured at the bars that cut him off from Ayres.

"Viscarro's hospitality is as fine as I remember." Ayres leaned patiently on his stick.

A few moments later a cylinder dropped in the pneumatic tube. The boy unrolled the note inside, frowned, and said, "Viscarro sends his apologies, but he can't see you right now. He suggests you come back next month, when the moon is new."

This was not totally unexpected. "Tell him to see me now, or I'll reveal his deepest secret in a way calculated to cause the greatest possible damage."

"What secret is that?"

Ayres just stared at him. The boy sighed, scribbled a note, and sent it up the tube. After another interminable wait, a return note arrived. The attendant glanced at it and pressed a button, sounding a buzzer and making the metal gate swing open. Ayres passed through the opening and followed the apprentice to a solid-looking metal door. Beyond the door, Viscarro's lair looked like something between a bank and a university archive—a series of rooms with low ceilings, crammed shelves, and endless rows of filing cabinets and desks, all lit with hideous fluorescent lights, with industrious men and women poring over heaps of papers. They walked past dozens of vault doors, all shining metal with enormous handles shaped like ship's wheels and complex locking mechanisms that combined technology, magic, and sheer dense physicality. Viscarro was a hoarder, and he'd been under the city for a long time. Whenever a sorcerer in some faraway place died, Viscarro sent his agents to attend their estate auctions or—it was rumored—to simply steal their treasures. He'd raked in whole libraries and art collections over the years, and his horde of apprentices went through them diligently, sorting the genuinely valuable items from the frauds and trinkets and objects of merely sentimental value. Viscarro made a good living as an antiquities dealer, but his real wealth was here, in the vaults. In addition to countless charmed, enchanted, cursed, and haunted items, Viscarro was rumored to have half a dozen genuine magical artifacts—those strange items of intrinsic power, of mysterious and ancient origin, which sometimes seemed to have minds of their own.

Ayres had only ever seen one artifact up close, and that was the dagger of office that every chief sorcerer of Felport inherited in their turn. The stories said the dagger could cut through anything, and that if wielded by a hand other than that of its rightful owner, it would turn and kill the holder. Ayres wondered about that last part.

It sounded like apocrypha meant to scare would-be thieves. Artifacts were items with *motives*, though, so who could say? Marla was said to possess another artifact, too, a strange purple-and-white cloak with powers of healing and devastation, though Ayres had never personally seen it, and she was reportedly reluctant to wear it anymore because of the damage it did to her psyche. Which just went that much further toward proving her unsuitableness to rule Felport. If Somerset had possessed an item of such power, he would have used it to expand his control of the city, make it into an empire. He'd been a ruler with *vision*. Viscarro was no better, though—if he got his hands on the cloak *or* the dagger, he'd just shut it away in some deep vault, thrilled by the mere fact of possession.

"The master is through there." The apprentice gestured to an office door marked "Management." Ayres went to the door, knocked once, then stepped into the dim office beyond. The room smelled of sweet spices. Viscarro sat behind a large antique desk, illuminated by the glow of a banker's lamp. The skin of his bald head was so white and papery it made his apprentices look tan in comparison, and his ears seemed subtly wrong, too pointed, perhaps. He looked up from the papers on his desk, the monocle in his left eye catching the light and glinting, and offered Ayres a brief, toothy smile. "I should have you cut up into food for my worm farm. To come here and threaten me with nonsense about secrets?"

Though he hadn't been offered a seat, Ayres sat down in the leather chair before Viscarro's desk. "It's good to see you, too, old friend. It's been too many years. I understand you could not visit me during my time in the hospital—I know sunlight and fresh air do not agree with you—but you might have sent a letter."

"We are not friends," Viscarro said. "You were a tradesman. You *worked* for my friends."

Ayres sniffed. "I was one of Somerset's closest advisors."

Viscarro laughed. "Nonsense. Perhaps it amused Somerset to let you think so, or perhaps your delusions extend beyond the belief that you're dead and rotting, hmm? You were a vassal, Ayres. You should leave your betters alone."

"These pleasantries *are* nice, after so many years in the low company of mindless homunculus orderlies at the Blackwing Institute, but perhaps we'd better get to business? I need a mummy."

Viscarro cocked his head. "Are you still here, O defiler of corpses? Perhaps my suggestion that you leave was too subtle for your vulgar senses, so now I say it directly—be gone, or be fed to the worms. Some of them are very big worms."

"You wouldn't have let me in to see you if you weren't worried about the secret I know."

Viscarro leaned forward. "Understand this, unclean man—I am the master of secrets. I do not fear secrets. Secrets fear me."

"It's said two can keep a secret, if one of them is dead." Ayres was enjoying himself. "But, of course, I can speak to the dead, so no one can keep secrets from me. If you are so unconcerned, you won't mind if I go see Marla Mason, and tell her one of the ruling cabal of Felport is an undead monster. Good day." He rose.

"You lunatic. You say *I* am dead now? I see your madness has turned outward. Say what you wish, no one will believe you."

"Oh, really? You don't think Marla will investigate? You think she'll come down here and check your pulse personally? You know how she feels about dead things that don't lay down. Ever since Somerset's return to life, she's had a certain . . . understandable prejudice. And you, sir, are just such a creature."

Viscarro sat very still. "Your allegations are ridiculous."

"You're a lich." Ayres leaned forward and put his weight on his walking stick. "Because of some horrible genetic quirk, the normal life-extending spells wouldn't work on you. So you cast a dark magic and allowed your body to die. You are little more than a spirit haunting the shell of your corpse, like a ghost haunts a house. Your soul is locked away in a phylactery somewhere in these vaults, probably a jewel, knowing your tastes, and as long as it's protected, you are immortal. But you know Marla's beliefs—a spirit in an unliving body begins to curdle like milk, the humanity sours, and eventually only a monster remains." He shrugged. "When she finds out you are such a monster, masquerading as a live man, she'll kill you as she would a dangerous animal, and your treasures will be scattered to buy the loyalty of her other lieutenants. Now, about that mummy . . ."

"It will not be a quick death for you. Those who threaten me die slowly."

"I'm not new at this, Viscarro." Ayres was growing exasperated. A bit of sparring was all well and good, but he was too old to muck about with posturing all morning. He had dead things to raise. "If I do not return home in good time, several letters will reach Marla Mason, detailing exactly what I just said to you. Can we please move beyond the threats and denials? Somerset told me about your . . . condition, your inability to extend your life by normal magical means. As I said, I was one of his closest counselors."

"I—that's not—"

"Somerset helped you become a lich," Ayres continued. "He cast the spells, and wielded the enchanted blade that drained your life. Who do you think he came to for advice about the process, you fool? Who do you think showed him the rites and incantations? You owe your unlife to me. Besides, I'm a necromancer—I can sense the dead, and *you* are dead." Once, that boast had been true, but now living people often seemed dead to Ayres, or like figures carved from wax, poor imitations of the living. All part of his illness. He knew the delusions were false, but sometimes they still troubled him. Viscarro needn't know that, though. "I smell the spices you've used to preserve your body, to keep rot at bay. This is my area of expertise, Viscarro. So shut up and give me a damned mummy."

Viscarro rose from his place behind the desk. He didn't say anything for a long time. Finally, he nodded.

"One mummy. And you'll keep your . . . wild speculations . . . to yourself. Your allegations are untrue, but it would be inconvenient to have you spread such lies about me. Understood?"

"Oh, I think we understand each other beautifully."

2

"I can't believe I have to do this," Marla complained as Rondeau eased the Bentley through the crowded summer streets. "In the past few weeks I've dealt with the return of the beast of Felport, a crazy blonde in a leather catsuit who thought she was a superhero, and a godsdamned attempted invasion by interdimensional hedonists."

"They were elves," Rondeau said helpfully. "From elfland. Or faeries, from faeryland."

"There's no such thing as elves." Marla scowled at a cab turning left through a red light. "If stupid people want to call those creatures elves, I can't help that, but I'm not going to. Anyway, my point is, things have been busy, and the last thing in the world I want to do is plan a fancy dress ball. I don't *do* balls. Or cotillions. Maybe, occasionally, a kegger, but that's about the extent of my party-planning expertise."

"Eh, it's only once every five years, and it keeps the

ghosts of the founding families from destroying the city, right?"

"I think the Chamberlain made it all up just because she likes parties. Why doesn't she plan the thing? I mean, she's the presiding sorcerer up on the Heights. The ghostly ancestors of Felport's upper class are her responsibility, not mine. Let her keep them entertained!"

"She does keep them entertained, except for one day out of every 1,826."

"Stop being reasonable, Rondeau. I count on you to share my outrage. Five years ago I wasn't even invited to the Founders' Ball."

"You were a badass freelancer with a scary reputation back then. Nobody knew you were going to kill Somerset and become the big boss of Felport. Besides, we had way more fun at the block party."

"Well, yeah." Founders' Day had a strange magic in Felport—street parties and other celebrations broke out spontaneously among the city's ordinary citizens, a sort of magical-resonance response to the more stately revelry of the Founders' Ball. By the same magic, if the founding families were unhappy on Founders' Day, the populace of Felport would riot. It had happened once before. Historians called the events of that night the Great Fire of Felport. "Give me a monster to slay or a wall to knock down or an evil conniving bastard to outsmart, and I'm golden, I've got it covered. But I've never planned anything like this before. I'm gonna need, like, caterers. Waiters. Decorators. A whole party-planning squad. And they have to be people who won't freak out when ghosts start appearing, dressed like refugees from a costume drama, twirling around in a ballroom!"

"That's why we're heading up the hill, boss. The Chamberlain was pretty stoked when I called to set up this meeting. She said she was beginning to think you were going to hire a DJ and hang some crepe paper from the ceiling and call it a job well done."

"The Chamberlain always looks at me like I'm an idiot. Every time I see her I think about class warfare."

"She wasn't always so hoity-toity. She came to the city alone, working as a maid or some shit, right? But the ghosts took a shine to her, and now she's their chosen one. The two of you probably have more in common than you think."

"But she's the kind of woman who wears evening gowns and *likes* it. We're fundamentally incompatible, her and me."

"You're always telling me how rich people *got* rich, how the ruling class became the rulers." Rondeau honked the horn at a slow-moving flotilla of high school girls crossing against the light. "They were the meanest, smartest, toughest bastards around, and they killed and schemed and murdered their way to the top, right?"

"Yeah, and then those tough bastards had kids who grew up soft and spoiled, and *their* kids grew up even softer and more spoiled."

"Sure, but the founding fathers of Felport were those original tough bastards. Maybe their ghosts like dressing up in ectoplasmic tuxedos and listening to string quartets, but they started out backstabbing and scheming their way to power. Maybe you and the Chamberlain can relate, after all."

"Why are you defending her? Wait. You think the Chamberlain's hot, don't you?" Marla said.

"She wears high heels *all the time,*" Rondeau said, a little dreamily.

Marla grunted. They had to drive the long way around, because the rather redundantly named Market Street Market was in full swing, and that meant four blocks of prime downtown was closed to vehicle traffic and transformed into the weekly summertime street bazaar. The Market Street Market had started life as a farmers' market, but over the years had mutated into a strange hybrid of a swap meet and a county fair, where you could buy anything from heirloom tomatoes to motorcycle parts of questionable provenance to deep-fried candy bars. Marla loved the market, the press and jumble of her city's people afoot, and wanted nothing more than to walk there now, chatting with the guy at the carnivorous-plant booth, tossing a coin into the big fountain everyone used as a de facto wishing well (and which, local legend said, actually granted one wish in a million), drinking beer out of a plastic cup, and messing with the fake psychics. But she had to take a meeting. The Chamberlain had probably never even *been* to the Market.

Eventually they made their way through the clogged streets and crossed one of the iron bridges spanning the Balsamo River. Marla lived and mostly worked on the south side of the city, and they were going to the old city uptown now, to the neat, narrow streets of the original settlement on the river's north side. It was all Felport, and the whole city belonged to her—and she to it, for that matter—but she felt out of place up in the Heights, where the great houses of Felport's founding families stood alongside the mansions built by the nouveau riche. There were museums and art galleries there, and the Felport symphony orchestra hall, and the mayor's mansion, all places Marla mostly avoided, preferring to get her culture in nightclubs and beer halls and the little amusement park down by the esplanade with the Ferris wheel that looked like an exotic torture device. Despite the Chamberlain's humble origins, she was still a daunting presence, and seemed utterly at ease in exactly the situations where Marla felt most out of place. There weren't many people on Earth capable of making Marla feel inadequate—low self-esteem was pretty much something that happened to other people—but the Chamberlain came close.

"It won't be so bad," Rondeau said. He was worse at abiding a silence than Marla was. "It's not like you're having a seven-course meal with her or something. You don't have to remember which fork to use. It's just a little conversation. I'm not worried."

Marla snorted. "Right. That's why you're wearing a normal suit for once. Because you're so unworried." Rondeau's taste in clothes tended toward the vintage and the strange, and his closet was full of garish zoot suits, powder-blue tuxedos, and leisure suits in eye-wrenching shades. But today he wore a conservative black suit, utterly unremarkable.

"You blame me? The way she looks at you, it's like

her eyes are tiny lasers. And I notice you're wearing your fancy new black cloak, Miss Pot Calling the Kettle Black."

"Shut up. I like this cloak. It has lots of little pockets sewn inside, and it never tries to take over my brain and make me kill innocent people like my old cloak did." She looked out the window as the streets became narrower and more tree-lined, the shops going upscale as they headed farther north. They wound through a residential neighborhood where the houses got progressively bigger and set farther back on their lots, as black wrought-iron gates and stone walls rose up to hide the estates from prying eyes. Finally they approached the hill of the Heights, the highest point in the city, providing unobstructed river and bay views for the lucky few houses on its slopes. And the highest house, perched on the ridge, was the Chamberlain's, a gated mansion of ancient stone surrounded by acres of meticulously landscaped grounds. It was the largest private residence in the city, and the Chamberlain lived there all alone—or so most thought. As far as her ordinary neighbors knew, the Chamberlain—Mrs. Chambers—was an intensely private, incredibly wealthy black woman in an overwhelmingly white neighborhood. There were lots of rumors about her, Marla knew—she was a mad recluse, or she ran a highly exclusive brothel, or she hosted private orgies, or she was a senator's mistress, or, or, or. Most of the stories weren't even close to being as weird as the truth.

Rondeau pulled up to the front gate, and the uniformed attendant sauntered over and leaned down.

"Afternoon," Rondeau said. "Ms. Mason to see the lady of the house."

"She's expected. Go on up. Just park in the driveway."

The barrier lifted, and Rondeau eased up the curving road to the house, pulling around a large white fountain to park in the circular driveway. He cut the engine and they sat for a moment, looking up at the house. "It's like something out of *Jeeves and Wooster*," Rondeau said at last. "Some English country house–style shit."

"It is," Marla said. "One of the founders of Felport, Randall or Tennyson or something, I forget which, he got rich in the New World and decided to buy himself a lordship back home in England. Except even though he was officially Lord Such-and-such, when he got back to London, people still laughed at him behind his back and called him a jumped-up merchant, so he decided to piss them all off by shipping the big estate out of the country and reassembling it brick by brick in America. Left a big gaping hole in the middle of his newly acquired ancestral lands."

"Those old dudes knew how to be spiteful," Rondeau said, with a certain amount of admiration. "Guess we better go in."

Marla got out of the Bentley, and Rondeau followed her up the broad steps. The front doors were enormous, carved wood, with knockers shaped like lions, and Marla was rearing back her foot to kick one in lieu of knocking when someone opened them from the inside.

The Chamberlain stood in the entryway, beautiful as always, but Marla had never seen her like *this*—her cascade of dark hair tied under a kerchief, her fine gown replaced with an ordinary housedress, and inconceivably, a smudged apron. She was still wearing heels, though. "Welcome to my home, Marla." She gestured for them to enter, frowning at Rondeau. "Your associate can wait while we discuss things."

Marla bristled a little, but then the Chamberlain turned to Rondeau and said, "If you head to the kitchen, I think the cook's baking, and she may have something sweet for you."

"Much obliged." Rondeau ambled off in search of pastries before Marla could object.

The Chamberlain cocked her head. "New cloak, I see. Dashing. Does this one make you turn into a giant raven that eats the eyeballs of your enemies, or is it just for looks?"

"I don't need a magical cloak to eat the eyeballs of my enemies."

The Chamberlain smiled thinly. "I'm glad you called." She set off deeper into the house. "For a while I was afraid your pride would keep you from asking for help."

Marla scowled. "I wasn't sure you'd be willing to help."

The Chamberlain stopped, halfway down a hallway lined with portraits of plump dead white men, and turned, her eyebrows going up in surprise. "My dear, you're the chief sorceress of Felport. I'm at your disposal!"

"I've never been good at this double-talk bullshit." Marla crossed her arms. "You know, saying things that sound nice, but the words have razor blades hidden in them? I'm simple. I'm direct. Five years ago you were one of the three sorcerers who voted against accepting me as chief sorcerer, even after I saved the city from Somerset. We're not exactly allies."

"And what's happened to your other opponents among the ruling sorcerers, Marla? You tricked Susan Wellstone into taking over the city of San Francisco—"

"Tricked? The bitch tried to erase me from existence! She's lucky I found her another city to run and didn't behead her!"

The Chamberlain ignored the outburst. "And Gregor was killed by his own protégé, under orders from you. And now that protégé has taken a place among our little group, and is loyal to you."

"Gregor joined up with an evil lunatic who tried to take over the city." Marla forced herself to speak calmly. "He had to die. As for his protégé Nicolette being loyal to me, she's not loyal to anything but her whims. She killed her last boss—you think that makes me trust her?"

The Chamberlain smiled. Her teeth were even and perfectly white. "Nevertheless, your opponents have a way of reaching bad ends, or at least leaving town. Five years ago, when the matter came before us, I did not believe you were experienced enough to take on the burden of overseeing and defending the whole city, despite your success with Somerset. You have since proven yourself capable. I do, however, still find you rather unrefined. I was heartened when you called to ask for my assistance with the ball, as I believed it was a step in the right direction, showing an awareness of your shortcomings and a desire to address them. Was I mistaken?"

Marla opened her mouth, then shut it, then said, "Look, I haven't been pursuing some vendetta against the people who questioned my qualifications. Both Susan Wellstone and Gregor plotted against me, and they got what was coming to them—well, except Susan, may her new city fall off the continent in an earthquake, but anyway. You've never plotted against me." At least, not that Marla had ever heard about. "You keep to yourself. When I needed your help defending the city last winter, you summoned up your ghosts and did your part. I don't have a beef with you, but you look at me like I'm a dirty little commoner, you know?"

"You are a dirty commoner, Marla. As was I, once upon a time. Such people have their uses, of course. But I see more potential in you. You have a certain ferocious pride that could, I think, become dignity. Let me help you." She set off down the hallway again, though Marla wasn't sure whether they were done arguing or not.

"Yes, okay, I need a hand throwing a fancy ball. But, I mean, fuck it, a party? What's the point? Besides the need to appease the vanity of some overindulged ghosts?" Most ghosts were mindless repetitive shadows of themselves, but the spirits of some people retained consciousness, though they could never grow or change. The founding spirits of Felport were of the latter sort, and a powerful bunch, but Marla didn't particularly care if they had a nice party or not.

The Chamberlain slid open a door, revealing a huge ballroom in a state of great disarray, swarming with workers. Paint cans and ladders and scaffolding and drop cloths littered the place, and a servant on a high ladder meticulously polished the crystal chandelier. The Chamberlain took a deep breath, then turned on Marla, her eyes fierce. "Parties, Marla, are a social necessity. By the people you invite and the people you choose not to invite, you send certain messages. By speaking to some and snubbing others, you make certain agendas clear. You reinforce loyalties and show disapproval. You do *business*. How else do you get all of the most important people in Felport in one room without making them suspicious and putting them on their guard? Not just the major sorcerers—though we must invite them all, even the Bay Witch, even though she drips—but the powerful up-and-comers like Langford and Partridge and Beadle, and the leaders of the Honeyed Knots and the Four Tree Gang. You show off your wealth and power. You make toasts that are also promises and warnings. You give a speech and set the *policy* for this city. You show us your vision, and remind us why we accepted you as leader! My gods, woman, how can you not know this?"

Marla stared. "Oh. I never thought of it that way."

The Chamberlain's smile was perfect and insincere. "I thought perhaps you had not. That's why I was so pleased when you requested my assistance. Though, yes, satisfying the ghosts of the founding families is important, too. If they're unhappy, that unhappiness spreads through the city in waves. Citizens would riot, kill one another, destroy property. *Everyone* would be swept up in the frenzy. I know you think Felport is your city, and of course it is in many ways, but the founding families think this place is *theirs*. And if they aren't shown the proper respect, they'll make their displeasure known. But we can turn their demands to our advantage, too. Do you see?"

"Yeah, I see." Marla decided it would be best to start over. She stepped into the ballroom. "So you're helping with the cleaning?"

"You're surprised? You expected me to have an army of servants doing everything, while I reclined on a couch and ate grapes, perhaps? I'm not afraid to get my hands dirty, Marla, whatever you may think of me."

Marla grinned. "Look at you, being direct and saying exactly what you mean. I must be rubbing off on you."

After a moment's consideration, the Chamberlain laughed, and it sounded genuine; at least Marla was willing to believe it was.

"So you're going to give me a crash course in hospitality management?"

"Not at all. I'm far too busy. No, I'm going to give you someone who can help. I understand your last personal assistant met a bad end?"

"Ted. Good guy. He's missed."

"Then my man Pelham will be able to assist you in many capacities besides planning the Founders' Ball, I'm sure."

As if responding to a secret cue, a small, serious-looking man of middle years emerged from behind a wall of drop cloths, dressed in an immaculate if unassuming suit. He bowed to the Chamberlain and Marla in turn. "Pleased to be of assistance, as always."

"I don't understand," Marla said, though she was afraid she did.

"Pelham will be your valet, Marla. Call it a gift from me, to heal any breach between us. In the short term, he can help you plan for the party—though that is the least of his expertise. I'm sure you'll find him an invaluable addition to your household beyond that, too."

"My—you want someone who's loyal to *you* to be my, what, manservant?"

"A lady's maid would be more traditional, it's true, but you've never been one to care about such arbitrary gender demarcations. As for his loyalty, it will be to you, and you alone. Pelham comes from a long line of servants, from the days of the founding families. Isn't that right, Pelham?"

"Yes, madam."

"He'll be bound to you, Marla, not me, as soon as you accept him into your service. The constraints on his family line are very clear on that. No Pelham has ever had to serve two masters."

Marla shook her head. "Wait, he'd be bound to me? Like, magically? No, listen, I just need somebody to help me plan a shindig, I don't need a butler."

"I regret that I am not a butler, madam," Pelham said, "though I can fulfill the duties of a butler if required."

"He's a valet," the Chamberlain said. "He'll attend to your personal needs. Think of it as . . . eternal concierge service, plus a personal shopper, plus . . ." She was clearly groping for terms she thought Marla would understand, which annoyed Marla, because she knew perfectly well what a valet was. She'd been to the *movies*.

"I get it, and it's very generous, but I can't accept. I wouldn't know what to do with him."

The Chamberlain regarded her coolly. "Are you refusing my gift, Marla Mason?"

Marla went very still. Gifts were serious business. Refusing a gift was a heavy insult. By the same token, sorcerers didn't give gifts to other sorcerers without good reason. *Gods, is she* really *trying to make up with me? Giving me a valet the way I'd give her tickets to a hockey game?* "Of course not," Marla said. "I'm just . . . He'd be loyal to me? And he's not a . . . a slave or anything?"

"I know your views on compulsory obligation, Marla, fear not. He is a free man, and may leave your employ if he finds you unreasonable, and you may terminate him if he proves unsatisfactory—though that's hardly likely. You will, of course, have to pay him, and arrange for occasional time off, but he will be unable to spy on you or betray you. Such geas are laid on those of Pelham's line at birth. Pelham, excuse us for a moment, would you?" He bowed and drew back some distance. The Chamberlain sighed. "I know having such help is unusual for you, Marla. But just think of him as a personal assistant, if you must. One who knows and understands magic, and who can keep secrets, and who will eventually learn to tend to your needs before you yourself are aware of them. I'm afraid when the last of the living ancestors of the founding families left the city, Pelham was merely a child, and he's grown up with no one to serve, save me, and . . . well . . ." She gestured at the people cleaning and painting in the ballroom. "I have no shortage of help, and he would thrive in a more personal relationship. He could also help you navigate certain . . . social channels you currently find a bit difficult."

"Okay." Marla surrendered. "Thank you. It's a very generous gift."

"Think nothing of it. I'll see you at the party next week. Pelham will take you to Rondeau, and then he'll lead you out." She turned and charged off toward a stack of paint buckets, and just like that, Pelham was back, bowing to Marla and murmuring that she should follow him.

I can always fire him later, Marla thought, and went after him, wondering how exactly she'd become the kind of person who received a valet as a gift.

"You're going to raise the mummy *here*?" Viscarro said. "Really, I'd rather you took the thing away."

"Necromancy makes you nervous, does it?" Ayres grunted, marking the floor of the room with red chalk. "Funny, I'd think you'd love the stuff, as it keeps your bones from crumbling to dust."

"I insist you do your business elsewhere."

"Bah. Marla surely has me under surveillance in the world above. Here, I'm safely out of sight. You may leave. I don't need you here."

"You should treat me with more respect," Viscarro said stiffly.

"Bugger that. You're dead. Now shoo. Oh, and send in the other thing I asked for."

Viscarro spat at his feet—a sad little gesture, as walking corpses don't produce much in the way of saliva—and departed the storage room. It wasn't a proper vault; there were no magical items here, just curios and curiosities that Viscarro hadn't gotten around to selling yet.

Including the mummy, resting on a bed of straw in a wooden crate against the far wall. The preserved corpse was of relatively recent vintage, not Egyptian, or Meso-American, or dug up from some bog on the British Isles. The body was a leathery, crumpled, shrunken thing, dressed in the ruins of a black suit, with a few strands of dark hair still stuck to the stretched skin of the skull. The eyes were partially shriveled. "Who were you, I wonder?" Ayres murmured.

"We think that's the mummy of John Wilkes Booth," a tentative voice offered from the doorway.

Ayres turned his head and regarded the newcomer, a balding, nervous-looking man holding a clipboard. "Who are you?"

"Master Viscarro sent me to offer my assistance. I'm one of the researchers here."

Ayres laughed. "Viscarro sent you to make sure I didn't fill my pockets with stolen loot, you mean. As if there's anything of value here, apart from the mummy."

The man shrugged. "I just do as he says."

Ayres frowned. "Did you say John Wilkes Booth? Lincoln's assassin?"

The lackey nodded. "We don't have proof, but that's

the mummy that was *exhibited* as the corpse of John Wilkes Booth in carnival sideshows. Whether it's truly the assassin's body, well, we haven't done any tests to find out yet."

"I thought Booth was burned alive in a barn in Virginia by manhunters." Ayres didn't know much about the assassin, but he was fairly certain mummification didn't enter into the story.

"That's the official account. Some years later, a man out west told his lawyer, a fellow named Finis L. Bates, that he was actually John Wilkes Booth, claiming the man killed in Virginia was part of a cover-up. The 'real' John Wilkes Booth died in Oklahoma in 1903. Bates claimed his body, had it mummified, and toured it around the country as the Booth mummy. He even wrote a book about Booth's miraculous escape, to publicize the show. The mummy dropped out of sight, passed through various private collections, and ended up here years ago. As to whether the man was really John Wilkes Booth, or just a liar, or if the lawyer made up the whole thing, opinions vary."

Ayres grunted. "Should be easy enough to find out— dig up the body in Booth's grave and test the DNA to see if it's a match. Surely there are clumps of the assassin's hair and flesh still preserved?"

"Yes, and many have suggested such tests, but the family and the courts refuse to allow exhumation. The possibility that Booth escaped and eventually became this mummy . . . it's a fringe idea. Most historians don't take it seriously."

"Stranger things have happened," Ayres mused.

"Though more likely things happen far more often." He knelt to look at the mummified corpse. "Whether you were an infamous assassin or not, you're just dried meat and sinew now. I won't hold it against you either way. Whether you were a king or a pauper in life, you'll be my servant in death."

"Couldn't you . . . summon up his spirit?" the lackey asked. "Find out if he's really Booth?"

Ayres shrugged. "I could, though it wouldn't prove much. Spirits can lie as well as the living, and if he claimed to be Booth when he was alive, he might well make the same claim now, true or not. When I raise the spirit of a murder victim, they're usually happy to tell the truth, if it means they'll be avenged. Otherwise, the dead are no more trustworthy than you or I. Besides, I'm not here to satisfy your curiosity, only my own needs." Ayres was well over a hundred years old, and though he could still get around all right, he got tired easily. The mummy would ease his burdens, and wrapped in a simple glamour, it could even pass for human. Ayres had had better luck with life extension than Viscarro, but magic could take you only so far without inflicting serious psychological damage. He could try to make himself immortal—he knew the rituals, and though the success rate was low, it wasn't impossible—but true immortals all went insane eventually, and deep down he wondered if his Cotard delusion was the result of the steps he'd already taken to extend his life.

Like all necromancers, Ayres feared nothing more than death itself. He'd called on the lord of the underworld for help countless times, and owed the old dark god many favors, which would surely be called in during the afterlife. And now it was time to beg a boon of that god again. "Stand aside," Ayres told the lackey, and bent to chalk the final lines and diagrams on the floor. The design was his own—every necromancer had personalized rituals—but it incorporated vèvès from Vodoun, Gnostic imagery, and so-called Angelic symbols (though the beings men called angels were usually far more bizarre things). The markings were mere lines on a floor now, but when activated, they would become both a gate and a cage for a denizen of the underworld—or, at least, *an* underworld; some necromancers claimed there were many such places, catering to different types of the dead. Ayres could compel such creatures to do his bidding, and animating the corpse of a mummy was the least of their abilities. Being a necromancer was not really about being the master of the dead, it was about being the master of *entities* who were masters of the dead.

Once upon a time, a couple of dogs' worth of blood would have been enough to spark this ritual to life, even for a corpse this old, but Ayres had gone over fifteen years without casting a spell, and he wanted to buy his way back into the good graces of the underworld, which meant offering a *larger* gift.

Ayres rose, puffing, and leaned on his walking stick. He wobbled a little, cursed, and started to fall. The lackey rushed over and caught Ayres, stepping into the chalk design on the floor as he did so. "Thank you," Ayres murmured, and shoved a knife deep into the lackey's belly. The man's eyes went wide and he stumbled back, reaching down to stanch the wound with his hands. "You . . . I . . . Viscarro . . ."

"Viscarro sent you here for this very purpose. You must not be valuable otherwise. But don't worry. You're serving your master."

The bleeding lackey started to move out of the chalk design, which was no good, so Ayres cracked him across the face with his stick, breaking the man's nose. The lackey dropped to the ground, stretched out prone and unmoving, and the chalk on the floor began to glow. Ayres wiped his brow with a handkerchief—murder was exhausting—and listened to the distant howl that heralded the opening of a passageway. He'd always wondered if the howl was the sound of three-headed dogs bellowing, or souls in torment, or long black trains hurtling through tunnels beneath the universe. None of the denizens of that realm had ever cared to tell him. Ayres stared down, watching the floor turn to the blackness of deep space, bound by glowing chalk lines.

"Another dead man. Just what we need."

Ayres lifted his head. A young man, clean-shaven and lanky, sat on a crate next to the mummy that may or may not have been John Wilkes Booth. "Get out!" Ayres said. "This is delicate work, and you'll spoil it!" He assumed the stranger was one of Viscarro's men—he was pale enough—though upon closer examination he was dressed in an expensive-looking tailored suit, and was handsome enough to belong on a billboard somewhere, selling underwear or cologne. He wore eight rings, each glittering with a different gemstone, and when he stood and took a step closer to the glowing design on the floor he suddenly seemed wreathed in a dark aura of clotted shadows surrounding him, like the after-image that hangs in your vision after looking too long at a bright light.

Ayres whimpered. He'd seen such auras before. This was a being from the underworld, but any summoned denizen should have appeared *inside* the chalk design, bound there, unable to escape. Had he drawn it incorrectly, or was there a break in the chalk, or—

"Nice work." The man nodded at the design. "I was passing by, and saw you trying to snatch one of my servants. I thought I'd come see you instead. I presume you'd like a boon?"

"You . . . claim to be . . . what?" Ayres said.

"I claim nothing. I am Death."

"I have met Death," Ayres said, and indeed he had, long ago, during his initiation into the mysteries of necromancy. "He did not appear as you do now."

"Ah," the man said. "An older fellow, beard black as coal, forever sitting on a throne carved from a single enormous gemstone?"

"So he seemed to my eyes," Ayres conceded.

"Yes, well, he's out," the man said blithely. "Surely you know there are seasons in Hell. His season has passed. Even Death may die, little wizard. He was the old Death. I am the *new* Death. Some call me the Walking Death, for I am not content to molder in a throne room, attended by alabaster shades. I prefer to travel the vastness of the underworld, and occasionally venture above."

Ayres believed him. He knew power when he saw it.

He dropped to his arthritic knees. "My lord. I meant no disrespect. I knew your . . ."

"My father? Yes, well, in a way he was my father. Such a term is good enough for convenience."

Ayres had heard of such things, of incarnations of Death passing into some other state, dissolving or finding an afterlife of their own, and of new gods rising to take their places. Gods of death were tidal, seasonal, bound to the cycle of life and death and rebirth in fundamental ways. But Ayres had not expected such a changing of the guard to happen in his lifetime. "I dedicate myself to you, my lord, and ask—"

"Ask me nothing, old man. I'm not interested in granting you anything. Just because you were one of my father's lapdogs doesn't mean I want to scoop your shit or take you for walks."

Ayres looked up, frowning. "I have given many years of service, and sent many down to your dark lands. I deserve—"

"Oh, yes, because if there's anything we've got a shortage of in the underworld, it's *dead people*." Death rolled his eyes. "Well done. You mortals place such emphasis on death. I understand. It's important to you, and my father was happy to accept little gifts like this dead fellow on the floor. But from my point of view, well, I'm very young, as my kind go. I'm in no hurry. You'll all come to me eventually, and I don't care if you're hurried along at the hands of sorcerers or not." He flicked his fingers. "Find a new line of work. I don't trust anyone who was loyal to my father anyway."

"I can prove my usefulness," Ayres said desperately.

Death could cut him off, steal his powers, prevent his subjects from obeying Ayres. He *had* to earn the new god's trust. "Please, if you don't want sacrifices, then what? What can I offer?"

Death chuckled. "Nothing at all."

"I know many powerful people, and much lore. I have contacts, resources. Please, is there nothing I can offer?"

"Oh, very well," Death said. "There is one thing. I doubt you can assist me, and it's only a small matter, but it's something I've been meaning to investigate. Death once had a terrible sword, which dripped venom. It's said the blade can cut through anything, even memories, and lies, and abstractions. The sword was lost long ago by my predecessor in a game played with a sorcerer. It's only symbolic, that sword—I don't need it to call your spirits to the underworld when you die—but it would be nice to have it back in the family. I think I'd look dashing with it on my hip. I don't suppose you know where I can find that sword, do you?"

Ayres had heard legends about Death's lost sword, but had never really believed the stories, and he had no idea where such a thing might be found. "I'm afraid . . ." He paused. "Sir. My lord. I think . . . I may be able to find out. If you could give me a little time?"

Death lifted one eyebrow. "Oh, I've got nothing but time, old man. But that doesn't mean you should feel free to waste it." He tossed a small silver bell to Ayres, who fumbled and almost dropped it. "Ring that if you find my sword, and, perhaps, I'll grant you a boon or two, and let you into my good graces. But don't ring it otherwise, or you'll find there are things worse than death—namely, pissing Death *off.*" Death stepped into the glowing design on the floor, vanishing from sight, and all the magic in the room fled.

Ayres released a breath he hadn't realized he was holding. He grasped the silver bell tightly in his fist, afraid to ring it accidentally.

He hurried back to Viscarro's office, and the undead sorcerer scowled at him. "I need one more favor," Ayres said.

"You presume too much. I gave you a mummy, *and* a sacrificial victim I had better uses for, *and* some of my valuable time. I grow tired of your antics."

"Then I'm glad you're in no position to negotiate or retaliate. Listen: they say you know more about artifacts than any sorcerer on earth or under it."

"They speak truth, in this case."

Ayres lowered himself into the chair. "Have you ever heard of Death's sword? Supposedly won long ago by a sorcerer in a game?"

"Yes," Viscarro said. "I've heard it was a chess game, most often; at other times I've heard dice or cards. It's a potent weapon, though of limited use in ignorant human hands. The legends say the sword could kill anything, even abstract concepts—that it could be used to cut holes in time and space itself, to slice apart hope, to carve out memories. But most of those powers could only be accessed in the hands of a god, or someone with the knowledge of a god. When wielded by men or sorcerers, it's rather less impressive, though still a useful tool. Why?"

"Do you know where I can find this sword? Do you have it locked up here in your vaults, perhaps?"

Viscarro's mouth narrowed to a hard line. "You begin to tread in dangerous territory, Ayres. Asking for my material resources is one thing. But you're prying at my secrets now."

"This . . . this will be the last thing I ask of you under that particular threat," Ayres said. "I will swear the same in any circle of binding you care to draw, with any penalties. Help me find Death's sword, and I will never tell Marla Mason you are undead."

Viscarro considered the offer. "Fine. It is agreed." He rummaged around in a drawer until he found a thin glass vial, which he smashed on the surface of his desk. The walls of the office began to hum like a Tibetan prayer bowl. "This whole room is a binding circle, and now it is active. Breaking an oath made here, now, will lead to great torments, of the betrayed party's choosing. Agreed?"

"Yes." Ayres had made such contracts before. They were almost as common among sorcerers as paper contracts were among ordinary businessmen, though the penalties for violation were far more steep. "I swear I will keep the secret of your unlife from Marla Mason—"

"You will keep the secret from *everyone,* and never speak of it again," Viscarro interrupted.

"I will keep the secret of your unlife from everyone, and never speak of it again, in exchange for knowledge of the whereabouts of Death's sword."

"It is agreed." Viscarro smiled a terrible smile. "For all the good it will do you. Marla Mason has the sword."

"What?"

The room stopped humming, and Viscarro's dry laughter was loud in the sudden silence. "Her dagger of office. The artifact passed down from chief sorcerer to chief sorcerer since Felport's founding. It's the sword of Death, disguised as a mere dagger. In human hands, it keeps its edge forever, and can cut through flesh and ghosts and stone and demons, but none of the chief sorcerers knew its true capabilities, though I'm sure some suspected its provenance. I only know because, well, it is my business to know." Viscarro shrugged. "You have the knowledge now. Do with it what you will. Our business is done."

Ayres was stunned. When he told Death that Marla Mason had his sword . . . This could turn out very well. "May I use your storage room for another few moments? To finish raising my mummy?"

Viscarro sighed. "Go ahead. But when you're done, leave, would you? And don't come here again. Maybe you don't believe you're dead anymore, but I can make you wish you were."

3

Ayres rang the bell.

Death sauntered in from a shadow. "Oh. It's you. I've given out half a dozen of those little bells, most to rather fetching young women with a preference for black eye shadow and ankhs and unearned widow's weeds. Just my luck it would be *you* instead of one of them."

"Death is a great seduction for some, I understand." Ayres bowed over his walking stick. A Death who consorted with the living was very peculiar, quite a change from the habits of the old Death. But he supposed everyone, even young gods, was most fascinated by what they lacked. No wonder Death was drawn to life.

Death regarded him with interest, as if he were a talking dog or something equally improbable. "I believe I told you not to ring the bell without sufficient cause. Or are you so enamored of my father's—of *my*—realm that you wish to rush to the underworld?"

He is new. Ayres smiled. In his younger days, that

smile had been enough to send street toughs fleeing in terror for their souls. His vigor had been sapped by years of confinement and illness, but he was beginning to feel a bit of his old power and certitude return. "I have tasted death, my lord, and am content to push that plate away for now. No, I have information for you. But I wish to set the terms of our bargain. You said you would grant me a boon or two, and allow me into your good graces. I wonder if you might care to provide me with a more *formal* offer."

Death laughed. He sat on Booth's coffin again, turned to the lifeless mummy, and said, "Do you believe this? The lapdog tries to bargain! Everyone tries to bargain eventually. It's all part of the grieving process. But I don't do bargains."

"The average grieving man has little to offer. But I can tell you where to find Death's terrible sword."

Death twisted a ring on one of his fingers. The gem flashed with an inner emerald light. "Well. That would be worth a bit of parley. I suppose, if you did have such information, I might be willing to make an arrangement. What would you like? Jewels? Your youth? Some of those dark-haired young women I mentioned?"

"No, thank you, my lord. I wish only to be the greatest necromancer who has ever lived." It was true. Ayres had never wished for anything else.

Death yawned. "May as well wish to be the greatest dogcatcher that ever lived. The greatest garbageman. It's ambition, I suppose, but of a puny sort."

"I want direct power. I don't want to . . . mess about with all this." Ayres gestured at the chalk lines on the floor. "I want the ability granted to your servants in the underworld—to call the dead, and bind them, and raise corpses to do my bidding. I wish to wield this power directly. Without making sacrifices, without all the ritual."

"Ahhh," Death said. "Slightly more ambitious. If you can tell me where to find my lost family heirloom, I will agree to grant you this, on my honor."

Ayres nodded. He didn't ask for assurances. The gods could be treacherous, but they were also trustworthy in their way, and he did not doubt Death would do as he said. Fire burned, rain fell, wind blew, and gods honored their promises. It was ever thus. "Your sword is in the hands of Marla Mason, chief sorcerer of the city of Felport. The sword appears in the guise of a dagger, and has been passed from hand to hand over the generations, from one ruler of Felport to another."

"Truly?" The Walking Death rose. "In this very city? This is fate. Unless it's falsehood. It goes without saying, if this proves untrue, I will not just strip you of your powers, but of your flesh. Death will be a relief denied you. If you're even mistaken, with no intent to deceive, I will not be merciful, and will still hold you accountable for wasting my time."

"You have nothing but time, my lord," Ayres said. Death had promised him his reward, and Ayres no longer needed to bow and scrape. It was clear Death wanted the dagger more than he admitted. "I believe you would hold me accountable for sowing false *hope*." Death narrowed his eyes, and the dark aura around him blackened. Ayres bowed again, lower this time. No need to push it. "Of course, I understand the sword is a mere bauble of no real value, and that you only wish to acquire it for sentimental reasons. Nevertheless, I am pleased my information, meager as it may be, has some value to you. I'm sure you'll find it in Marla Mason's possession."

Death shook his head. "You've got steel in your back and fire in your belly, old man, I'll grant you that. Fine. You have your powers. If your information proves accurate, I'll even let you keep them. This Marla Mason. Would you say she's a reasonable woman? Willing to make a deal if it's in her best interests?"

"She's as stubborn as a constipated mule, actually. But I'm sure you can be very persuasive."

Death shrugged. "Mortals are grass. She'll bend or be mown down. Well? Are you going to raise this mummy or not?"

"Indeed." Ayres wasn't sure what to do—he didn't feel any rush of power, didn't feel any different at all.

"Simply speak the words, make your command," Death said. "The dead will answer you."

"Ah." Ayres cleared his throat. "Dead man, I bid you to rise."

The coffin began to shake. The withered mummy inside moved, its motions as alien and precise as those of a stick insect. It sat up, braced itself on the edges of the coffin, and climbed out, standing on unsteady, shriveled feet.

"Beautiful," Ayres murmured.

"Beautiful tyrant," the mummy said, voice a croak at first, but as it continued to speak, the tone became smoother, and took on a surprising resonance. "Fiend angelical. Dove-feathered raven." It—he—shook his head, and bits of dried substance flaked from his neck, settling into the folds of his old black suit. "Was there ever a book containing such fair matter, so vilely bound?"

Death grinned. "That's nice. 'Wake not a sleeping wolf. To wake a wolf is as bad as to smell a fox.'"

The mummy turned its head, slowly, and regarded the young god. "*Henry the Fourth,* Act one, Scene two," the mummy said.

Ayres felt his newfound certainty begin to shift. "Why does this thing speak?"

The mummy regarded him. "I am no thing, sir." The voice was still smooth, not emerging from the body's fleshless windpipe, but through magic. The accent was decidedly Southern. "I am John Wilkes Booth, a patriot and actor of some renown."

"What is this?" Ayres had caused the dead to speak before, but they always whispered, or shrieked; they did not speak as if they were alive, and this strange prodigy made him shudder.

Death laughed. "You asked to be the greatest necromancer who ever lived. I conferred those powers on you. They're more potent than the weak magic you once possessed. When you raise the dead now, if you're not careful, you'll jerk their spirits back into their bodies. As you did with this one. Farewell, Ayres. I'm sure we'll meet again."

"Wait—" Ayres said, but Death was gone, off into shadow. Ayres cursed and turned back to the spirit he'd unwittingly called up. "You. I've given you life so that you might serve me."

"I serve my country," Booth said, "and my family, and my art, and my God. I do not see why I should serve you."

"Would you rather return to . . . wherever you were before?"

"I have felt the worst of death's destroying wound," Booth said thoughtfully. "But the dread of something after death, the undiscovered country . . ." He shook his head. "I would not like to return there, no, sir."

"Stop quoting Shakespeare." Ayres was suddenly tired and more than a little cranky. "I don't even know much Shakespeare, and I can tell you're quoting it."

"The bard's words are silver and gold, sir," Booth said. "You may call me Mr. Booth, or John, if you prefer. How may I address you?"

"Ayres. Or Master."

"I call no man master, Ayres. But treat me as a gentleman, and I'll extend you the same courtesy."

"This is just *grand*." Ayres started to turn. He stopped. "You precede me from the room. I know what happens to people who put their backs to you."

"Only tyrants need fear me." Booth stepped past Ayres, toward the door, then paused. "I thank you for retrieving me from . . . that place. But my gratitude will allow your discourtesy only so much latitude, sir." He left the room.

Booth had never even glanced at the dead man in the chalk design, Ayres noticed. Being dead must alter one's priorities. *I must be more careful when I raise the next one.* Ayres wanted a servant, not a mummified roommate. Especially not a notorious racist assassin with delusions of grandeur and a tendency to spout Shakespeare without provocation. Still, a dead man with a proven willingness to shoot people in the back of the head could have his uses, Ayres supposed. He'd keep the mummy around for a while and see what opportunities presented themselves.

"I know I say you take the warrior ascetic thing too far sometimes, Marla," Rondeau said, strolling down the wide marble-floored hallway on their way out of the mansion. "But don't you think hiring a manservant is a bit of an overcompensation?"

"Shut up," Marla muttered, keenly aware of the valet walking behind her. She didn't like it when people walked behind her—years as a freelance mercenary made watching her back second nature—but Pelham wouldn't walk alongside like an equal. Marla could have ordered him to walk in front of them, she supposed, but while she was no stranger to telling people what to do, telling a *servant* what to do was a weirdly distasteful idea. "He's just coming along to help plan the Founders' Ball, then I'll send him back."

"Whatever you say, Lady Marla," Rondeau said. "But your kind will be first against the wall when the revolution comes."

Pelham smoothly swooped around them to open the front door, and when they exited onto the front steps, he hurried down to open the back door of the Bentley, bowing as he did.

"I ride up front, Pelham," Marla said. "You can have the back."

"I . . . if madam insists . . ." He sounded doubtful.

Marla sighed. "Don't call me 'madam.'"

"Yeah," Rondeau said. "A madam is somebody who runs a whorehouse. You have to watch out for the connotations."

Pelham blinked like a rabbit on his first trip out of the burrow. "Would you prefer . . . mistress?"

Rondeau snorted. Marla glared at him. "Connotations again," Rondeau said.

"Ah," Pelham said, clearly at a loss. "Then . . . ma'am?"

"How about just 'Ms. Mason,'" Marla said. She figured trying to get him to say "Marla" would be a lost cause.

"Of course." Pelham opened the passenger door for her.

"I can open my own car door." Pelham pretended convincingly not to hear her. She got in, and he closed the door, then climbed in back.

Rondeau got in the driver's seat, glanced in the rearview, and said, "Buckle up there, Pelly. If we get in a wreck and you go flying into the back of Marla's head, she'd never forgive me."

"Buckle?" Pelham said faintly. Marla turned around in her seat, frowning, and watched as he began fumbling with the seat belt straps, finally getting them latched. "I am secure," Pelham said formally.

"This is going to be fun," Rondeau said. "Is he going to sleep on a little cot next to your bed?"

"Shut up," Marla said again, though without much heat. Rondeau was going to give her hell about this, no matter what she did. She couldn't blame him. She'd do the same if their positions were reversed.

Apparently satisfied with the level of mockery for now, Rondeau started the car, and the stereo blared to life, rap music pounding out of the speakers. Marla liked this music better than the stuff Rondeau played at his nightclub, but only just. Pelham made a noise of horror from the backseat, and when Marla looked over her shoulder, he was pressing his palms against his ears. Rondeau must have noticed, because he turned the music down to a tolerable level. "Sorry about that, Pelly," he said. "That's just how we roll around here." He drove down the driveway and waited for the front gate to open. "So, this Founders' Ball, do I get invited to that?" Rondeau said.

"I guess, if you don't piss me off too much," Marla said.

"How about Pelly here? Will he go, to carry the train on your evening gown?"

"What did I just say about not pissing me off?"

"Comment retracted." Rondeau drove through the open gate. Glancing in his mirror, he frowned. "Hey, Marla," he said, voice low. "Pelly's back there all turned around in his seat. He's practically got his nose pressed against the back window, like a sad little kid in a movie."

"It's probably just sinking in that he has to work for me now." Maybe this wouldn't be so bad. Just think of him as an employee, not a valet or manservant, wash all that upper-class/lower-class crap out of her head—she had money, he needed money, he'd do some work for her. That was it. It was always nice to have another useful pair of hands. And she'd be able to quit worrying about the Founders' Ball, which was nice.

As they approached the bridge that spanned the Balsamo River, Pelham said, "I've seen that bridge from my window, but never crossed it. Thank you for this opportunity, Ms. Mason."

"What?" She turned around.

His eyes widened. "Apologies if I spoke out of turn. I noticed that you allowed your driver to take a familiar tone, and thought such a mode of address might please you, but I will be more respectful in the future."

"Her driver?" Rondeau said.

"No, I don't care that you talked," Marla said. "It's what you said. You've never crossed this bridge before? What, you only ever took the east bridge? This one's closer to the estate, though."

"I have never crossed any bridge, Ms. Mason," Pelham said apologetically. "I am not well traveled."

Marla closed her eyes for a moment. "Tell me, just how poorly traveled are you?"

"I have never left the grounds of the estate before, Ms. Mason. I never had cause to do so."

Marla faced forward, sank into her seat, and moaned.

"This is your first time outside the walls?" Rondeau said. "Oh, Pelly. What time does your shift end? You've got a lot of life's little pleasures to sample, my friend, and your tour guide's name is Rondeau."

"I do not yet know my schedule," Pelham said. "But I appreciate your willingness to allow me to join your society."

"Phone," Marla said, and Rondeau passed her his cell. She snapped off the rap music, then called the Chamberlain, and shouted sufficiently enough that she had to talk to only three underlings before the lady herself answered.

"Is there a problem, Marla?"

"This guy Pelham has never left your *house*!" Marla shouted. "What are you trying to do to me here? What, I'm supposed to teach him about public restrooms and how to use the bus and go to the grocery store?"

"He has left the house," the Chamberlain said calmly. "He's been all over the grounds. As for teaching him things, Pelham has an excellent theoretical grounding in all the tasks a valet might be expected to do. He knows how to deal with shopkeepers and tradesmen, fear not. I believe some of the household staff did training exercises with him, starting from the time he was very young."

"Is this a joke? This guy's been a prisoner?"

"Never that. Pelham's people have been servants of the founding families for generations. As you know, some years ago, the last scions of those families chose to leave the city to seek their fortunes elsewhere, much to the delight of myself and the ghosts I serve."

Marla grunted. Those spoiled rich brats had done nothing except party and dishonor their family names, and the Chamberlain had made life unpleasant for them. They all lived abroad on their trust funds now, and didn't even visit anymore. "Yeah, so?"

"They all took their personal servants with them. Pelham's family has . . . certain symbiotic tendencies. Through training and temperament and long tradition, they're only happy when they have someone to personally tend to. The relationships can grow quite close. But Pelham, poor Pelham, was the odd man out. He had too many brothers and sisters. When the heirs to the founding families chose their valets and lady's maids, Pelham was left unchosen. He's been at the house ever since, seeing no reason to leave, utterly unfulfilled, and I've been wondering for years how to settle him properly in an outside position. When I realized you had the makings of real aristocracy—the kind won by strength of arms and strategy, not accident of birth—I realized you'd be perfect."

"Me? Why not *you*? Gods, you've got dozens of servants already!"

"Nonsense. I *am* a servant, Marla. Head of the servants, yes, and often the public face of the founding families, which requires me to affect a certain regal bearing on their behalf, but I never forget my true position. Besides, Pelham is more than a hired man. His connection to the one he serves is profound. He's bonding to you even now. You'll never find a more loyal or trustworthy employee. And, yes, he may need to adjust to the realities of the world outside a bit, but he's been trained to cope with the unexpected, and he doesn't bat an eyelash at magic. I'm sure he'll work out fine."

"Look, you said we could break this arrangement anytime, and now you're telling me he's a parasite?"

"Symbiote," the Chamberlain said sternly. "And, yes, you could send him away, though it would tear him apart to be rejected, and I suspect he'd wind up utterly despondent, sleeping under a bridge somewhere. And he's certainly free to leave your service whenever he chooses; it's just highly unlikely he would ever so choose."

"Wonderful. I won't forget this."

"It *is* a boon, Marla, not a treacherous gift, I assure you. You'll see. Pelham will make your life easier in a thousand little ways. You'll have cause to thank me."

"Right. I'm sure." Marla flipped the phone closed and drummed her fingers on the dashboard.

"Hey, Marla," Rondeau said quietly. "The guy's back there crying."

Marla sank lower in her seat. She felt like shit, but she hadn't asked for this responsibility. Then again, she was no stranger to unwanted responsibility. She took a breath. The world was what it was. "Hey, Pelham. Sorry about all that . . . parasite business. I was just taken by surprise."

"You need never apologize to me, Ms. Mason."

She turned around in her seat again. "Hey. I don't apologize all that often. Just when I actually make mistakes, which Rondeau can tell you is pretty much never."

"To hear her tell it anyway," Rondeau said.

"If you're going to work for me, you can't be afraid to speak up. I'm not saying I won't smack you down occasionally, but don't let that discourage you. I realize there's a lot of stuff you don't know. But you can learn.

And there's plenty of stuff you do know that *I* need to learn. Like how to throw a party for a hundred or so of Felport's best and brightest and meanest and most dangerous. Think you can help me do that?"

"Of course," Pelham said. "I live to serve, Ms. Mason."

"Well, we'll see if we can find something better for you to live for, but I guess it's a start."

"Say," Rondeau said. "Do you know anything about the care and feeding of baby goats?"

Marla left Pelham and Rondeau at the club and went to take a walk. The goat was locked in the men's room eating a potted plant and drinking from the toilets. Pelham had been reluctant to leave her side, but she convinced him that Rondeau would teach him the ropes—answering phones, the ins-and-outs of Marla's rather free-form filing system, which people she was willing to take phone calls from, and which she'd just as soon avoid. She set off toward the esplanade, wanting to hit the center of Felport's tourism and get a sense of the summertime commerce, and as the Market Street Market wound down in the afternoon, the esplanade was the next best thing. Fiduciary magic wasn't her specialty—her consiglieri, Hamil, was the one who kept his finger on the pulse of the city's economics, with a little help from the chaos magician Nicolette—but she could get a crude sense of the health of a particular sector by quietly sitting and letting the city flow through her. She'd been chief sorcerer for nearly five years, and was finally beginning to develop what her predecessor Sauvage had called city sense, the ability to expand her consciousness until the city became almost part of her own body. With some effort, she could feel spikes in crime rates like sharp pains, taste pollution like morning breath, experience economic downturns like fatigue and bad traffic like clogged sinuses. Apparently the city sense became second nature after enough years, but Marla wanted to practice, and she found positioning herself with some physical analog of the quality she wanted to explore helped her focus.

The day was warm and lovely, and the esplanade was hopping. Most of the little shops had their doors open for the breeze, and people strolled in and out at a good pace. Marla sat down on a stone bench with a good view of the water and watched people in shorts and T-shirts stream by, kids clutching ice-cream cones, young women Rollerblading, lovers strolling arm in arm. Felport wasn't a real hub of tourism, but it was the biggest city in this part of the state, and so a lot of people from the sticks and suburbs came to see the occasional show, eat in good restaurants, take the kids to museums or the zoo or the little amusement park and boardwalk down by the bay. Marla closed her eyes and let the shape of the city coalesce in her mind, from Ernesto's vast junkyard in the south, then north to the green expanse of Fludd Park— gods, she hated that place, all bugs and dirt and ducks and trees—in the city's center and up to the rabble of student housing, on past the river to Adler College with its weird sculpture garden, and then east to the Heights where the Chamberlain lived, on to the old city with its cobblestoned narrow streets and historic buildings, over to the fancy houses with bay views, then down to the south side of the river again, to the clutch of skyscrapers and high-rises downtown, over toward the old industrial sector by the docks, down to the esplanade again, where Marla sat. The city felt whole and relatively safe, no pinpricks of interdimensional invaders, no waves of rage from some passing monster, most of the ordinaries going about their lives with the usual mixture of hope, anxiety, sadness, and joy, unaware of Marla or her kind looking out for them (and, admittedly, sometimes making a living off of them). Marla shivered with pleasure, a sensation like eating a perfect meal and being absolutely satisfied, neither under- nor overfull. Felport in early summer, before the intense heat and humidity really set in, was a wonderful place. So what if she had a party to plan? So what if she'd acquired a valet against her will? These were minor concerns. Her city was healthy. Life was good.

"Hello, Marla. I like your knife." The voice was right next to her, closer than should have been possible—she hadn't sensed anyone sitting next to her, and even immersed in her city sense, she shouldn't have been *that* lax.

"Do I know you?" Marla opened her eyes and gave the stranger a deep look. He was young, handsome, dirty-blond, with that just-out-of-bed messy hairstyle that probably took way more work than Marla's own ragged shag did. He was dressed in a nice dark suit and blue shirt, classy and not flashy, but he had on a gaudy array of rings, one on each finger, each with a different gleaming gemstone. He smelled like nothing at all, which was part of how he'd managed to sneak up on her.

"Not intimately," he said. "Not yet. But you know my work. I'm Death. You can call me *Mr.* Death."

"I used to know a goth kid back in Indiana who called himself Death," Marla said. "He got run over by a semi. That's what you'd call a self-fulfilling prophecy. You might want to reconsider your nickname."

"Mmm. Why don't you spare yourself grief and give me your pretty little knife?"

"Why don't you take a flying leap off a cliff? Piss off. You're crowding my space."

He put his hand on her wrist. Well, that was that. Touching her was a no-no. She grabbed his hand, intending to put him in a vicious twisting joint-lock that would have him on his knees before her, crying.

Instead, to her surprise, everything whooshed, and people yelled, and she was looking up at the sky, and she *hurt*. She sat up—pretty fast, all things considered, thanks to her old friend adrenaline—and realized she'd been *thrown* from the bench, and crashed into the low wall on the far side of the walkway. How had he thrown her? How had he gotten any leverage, sitting beside her? He was still lounging on the bench, cool as you please, and most of the passersby had taken off running, which was a reasonable response to sudden violence. *Guess he's a sorcerer.* Why couldn't new guys in town ever just introduce themselves? They all had something to prove. Marla stood up. "Bad move, out-of-towner," she said. "I turn people like you into compost." She launched herself toward him, spitting out a spell of deflection as she went, so if he cast another spell, it would bounce off her and back to him. He didn't move, and she leapt, ready to deliver a kick—with her magically reinforced steel-toed boots, no less—to his face.

He was up and out of the way faster than she could see, and before she even landed she reached into her pocket for the little vial of hummingbird blood she'd kept there. She crushed the vial, blood and glass stinging her hand, and all the light around her subtly blue-shifted as her metabolism and subjective time sense sped up a hundredfold. She couldn't spend too much time in this state—the crash after extended use made coming off crystal meth seem gentle—but for now, it should make her an unstoppable fighting machine, faster than any other primate alive. She spun, and Mr. Death was lounging by the low wall behind her. Fast, but she was certainly faster. She raced toward him, ready to deliver a punch that, at this speed, would probably cave in several of his ribs, but he moved out of the way, which really shouldn't have been possible. Marla nearly flew off the edge of the esplanade, which would've meant a long drop into the cold bay, but she corrected her course, landed in a crouch on the wall, and sprang back after him.

He swatted her out of the air nonchalantly, and she hit the ground hard enough to bounce. "This is silly." His voice wasn't the slowed-down drone it should have been; he'd somehow accelerated himself to match her. "Just give me the knife and I'll be on my way."

"You want the knife?" Marla drew her dagger of office and held it in a reverse grip, blade tucked up against her forearm. "You get the knife." Fighting an unarmed man with a knife wasn't sporting, but Marla was past the point of caring about sport. She wanted to kill this guy. If she needed to find out who he was later, maybe she'd bring Ayres out of retirement and get him to interrogate the guy's corpse. She came at him, ready to flick out her blade and finish this, but he moved, still faster than her eye could comprehend, twisted her wrist so hard she cried out and dropped the blade, and tossed her off to one side like an empty beer bottle. The dagger fell in slow motion at first, then clattered to the pavement as normal time reasserted itself. Marla groaned. She hadn't been tossed around like this in a while. She mumbled a little analgesic spell to numb the pain in her wrist, and watched while grinning Mr. Death bent down to pick up her dagger.

His scream, though not unexpected, was quite gratifying. His right hand was a spurting bloody mess, with most of his fingers dropping, severed, to the ground.

"My dagger," Marla said. "It doesn't like strangers." She whistled, two low notes, and the dagger skittered along the ground and flew into her hand, hilt-first. After giving the blade a shake to cast off the stranger's blood—every drop left the blade, which was part of the weapon's magic—she tucked it into the sheath at her waist. Mr. Death whimpered and cradled his devastated hand. Sirens wailed, approaching fast. Somebody had seen the fight and called the cops. Marla wasn't worried about the cops—she knew the mayor and the chief of police, and more important, they knew *her,* and what she really did for Felport—but she preferred to avoid the hassle. She considered trying again to kill him, now that he was wounded, but her time in the graveyard yesterday and the memories it prompted made her inclined to alternatives, like mercy. "You're a good fighter," she said. "That was a nice workout, and some of those tricks I've never seen before, but you better believe I'll learn them soon. This isn't the place to make a name for yourself, though. Leave town. If I hear you're still hanging around later, I'll make the loss of a few fingers seem like a pleasant morning."

He didn't answer, just stared at her and bled.

"You take care now." She walked away, leaving Mr. Death to gather up his fingers. A good magical surgeon could reattach them like new. Maybe he knew somebody who could do that back where he'd come from. Wherever the hell that was. She'd make some inquiries.

"I hope you'll forgive me for saying so," Booth drawled, "but this place has the distinct odor of age and staleness."

"The dead man complains to me of odors?" Ayres said from his folding chair by the window. "Make yourself useful by cleaning the place, then. I didn't bring you back to life so you could bitch and moan."

"Men of quality don't clean." Booth was looking at himself in a full-length mirror. He'd been doing that ever since Ayres cast a glamour to cover his hideousness. "This really isn't a very good likeness, Ayres. The tattoo on my hand is absent, for one, and I think my cheekbones should be higher."

Ayres had conjured Booth's illusory form from vague memories of the assassin's photograph in documentaries about Abraham Lincoln. He could make Booth look like anyone, but the assassin wanted to appear as he had in life. Vain bastard. "You're welcome to return to your prior state, and go around looking like an overdone piece of bacon, if you prefer."

Booth joined him at the window. "My apologies, sir. You've done a great kindness for me, and I won't forget that. May I ask, what are you looking for out that window?"

"Oh, I don't know. A plume of smoke. An earthquake. People running and screaming. Some sign of the titanic battle between Marla Mason and Death. Though I suppose it's likely to be a quieter affair."

"Mmm. If I'd known there was a duel in the offing, I would have offered my services as Death's second. Seems the least I can do, for his allowing me to leave . . . that place."

"I'm the one who brought you out of that place. And don't forget it."

"But you derive your power from his," Booth said, undeterred. "Much as a statesman derives his power from his constituents. Remove the goodwill of the people, and a politician is just a liar in a suit. Remove the goodwill of Death, and you're just . . . well, courtesy forbids elaboration."

"I can send you back to Hell," Ayres said.

"Not if I send you to Hell first," Death said, and Ayres rose as quickly as he could.

"My lord!" he cried. Death was spattered in blood, and his right hand was a crippled ruin.

Booth stepped forward and offered an illusory handkerchief, but Death waved him away. As Ayres watched, Death lifted his arm, making a fist with his remaining two fingers, and when he opened his hand, all his digits were back and whole.

"You might have mentioned that her dagger is enchanted." Death visibly seethed, dark energy crackling from his shoulders.

"I . . . my lord?" Ayres had never been more terrified.

"When I took the knife, it cut me," Death said. "Nothing cuts me."

"Due respect, my lord, but . . . I thought the whole point of that blade is its ability to cut anything."

Death grunted. "I didn't seize it by the blade. It turned in my hand and . . . bit me."

"I had heard rumors to that effect," Ayres said. "My apologies. I did not think any mere enchantment would hinder you, my lord."

Death seemed to consider that. "Indeed. It shouldn't have worked—mortal magic is no more than sparkles and light to me. Perhaps it's no mere enchantment, then. Perhaps it's a fundamental quality of the weapon, that it cannot be taken by force. My father would . . . would have known. The sword was lost before my time, and I don't know its whole nature."

"Some artifacts must be given willingly." Ayres took the risk of sitting back down. Death didn't seem offended. "They bind to their owners, and can only be given away willingly, or passed down through some other protocol. I know this dagger has passed from hand to hand for generations, from one chief sorcerer to another, since Felport's founding."

"So even killing Marla might not be sufficient," Death said. "It would just pass to her successor?"

"That is my understanding."

"Hmm. What if I became chief sorcerer? With the blade in my rightful possession, I could strip away all the enchantments that govern its conditions of ownership."

Ayres shook his head. "There is precedent that suggests only mortals can become protectors of Felport." He was thinking of Somerset's resurrection and attempt to regain control of the city. Somerset had been a heartless undead monster, and according to the stories, the dagger of office had burned his hand when he took it from Sauvage's corpse. After Marla killed Somerset, she took up the dagger, and with it the mantle of Felport's protector. Several of the other powerful sorcerers had supported her claim, and her position had held.

"I just want the blade," Death said petulantly, and Ayres thought, again, that he seemed very young. "How can I get it? I'm afraid peaceful negotiations are probably out of the question. Marla Mason and I . . . clashed."

Ayres mused. "I know little about her. She has a few loyal friends, but I suspect she might even let them die before bowing to you. She's stubborn. But perhaps . . ." Ayres hesitated.

"What?"

"I . . ." Should he say this? He loved Felport as much

as Marla did—it was perhaps the only thing they had in common. But the opportunity to cement himself in the new Death's good graces could mean great power for him. Cities rose and fell, but power was eternal. He made his choice. "Marla loves the city above all else. If Felport itself was at stake, she might be willing to make a deal. Remove her from power and take over the city yourself. You may not be able to rule as chief sorcerer, but you could become a sort of dictator."

Death smiled. "You may be on to something there, Ayres. Perhaps you're worth keeping around, after all. I'll go for her just before dawn, when she's tired and unprepared."

"Just let me know if my—" He almost said servant. "My associate Mr. Booth and I can be of service. He has some experience toppling heads of state, if I recall."

"*Sic semper tyrannis,*" Booth said agreeably.

4

"So who the hell was he?" Marla said, and Hamil shook his head, peering at his computer screen.

"There's nothing in the most recent edition of *Dee's Peerage*." Hamil scrolled through the digital database. The laptop was like a toy under his big hands. "The eight rings seem like a good unique variable, but no, I've found nothing." The great compendium of notable magic users didn't include every sorcerer in the world, but it damn sure should have mentioned someone capable of beating Marla in a fight, at least by an alias. Marla's own name had appeared there as soon as she found her magical cloak in a thrift store, though at first the description hadn't mentioned much *besides* her possession of the cloak. Her entry had grown considerably longer over the years. No one knew who updated *Dee's Peerage,* but new editions appeared mysteriously on every sorcerer's doorstep each year, once upon a time bound in paper that dissolved after twelve months, more recently on computer discs that decayed each year. Since the *Peerage* contained only widely known biographical information—no real secrets—no one was sufficiently motivated to track down its creator. It was also rather useful, usually, in cases like this.

"Crap." Marla leaned back in the leather chair. "Do you think . . . I mean, is there any chance . . . that he's really *Death*? Come to reclaim his property? We've all heard the stories, that my dagger's really a shard from Death's scythe, or that some sorcerer won the blade off Death in a card game, but I always figured they were bullshit. Could they be true?"

Hamil pushed his great bulk back from the computer. He had a specially designed high-end office chair that could have probably seated a polar bear comfortably. "The issue of the afterlife is a tricky one. There are plenty of stories of sorcerers going to the underworld—or places they believed to be the underworld. Ghosts exist, though most ghosts are just stuttering repetitive psychic stains, doing the same pointless things over and over. Persistence of personality after bodily death is also possible through magic—liches and the like. That proves there *is* something inside us, a soul or a spirit or a force of will, which can outlive the body's death. For those of us who don't become conscious ghosts . . . where does that spirit go? Some say to the afterlife, or to one of many afterlives, depending on the individual soul's beliefs and expectations. Most necromancers claim to know the truth about the afterlife, but their truths all contradict one another. Some theorize there's only a single underworld, a sort of malleable space that appears in whatever form the dead person—or, in rare cases, the living explorer—expects, consciously or subconsciously. If such a realm does exist, it's reasonable to assume it has a ruler, some ancient being or series of beings that is—or at least styles itself to be—Death personified."

"Thanks," Marla said. "That was nice and definite. Just what I needed."

Hamil shrugged. "It's not my area of expertise, I'm afraid." Hamil was a master of sympathetic magic, not corpses and ghosts. "You could ask the opinion of that necromancer who just got out of Blackwing. I know you have reservations about him, but he clearly wants to prove his usefulness. All necromancers interact with *something* that claims to live in the underworld."

"I'm not ready to eat my pride just yet," Marla said. "We'll see if Mr. Death decides to come back. With luck, the loss of a few fingers will give him pause. On to the other turd in the punch bowl of my day: I met with the Chamberlain. I guess it wasn't a total disaster."

"Good. I'm having a new tuxedo made for the ball."

"Oh, yeah? I didn't know there was enough fabric in the *world* to make a new tuxedo for you. Prices for cloth must be soaring all over the world, what with you sucking up all the supply. I should make some investments."

"A fat joke, Marla? Isn't that beneath you?"

She sighed. "Probably. Sorry. You just reminded me I have to find something to wear. I'm not looking forward to shopping for a dress. The Chamberlain was very specific about that. I gotta wear a dress. The ghosts of the founding families are particular about what women should wear. And if I send Rondeau to buy something for me, gods, can you imagine the slutwear he'd buy? I'd look like a stripper."

"I'm sure your new valet can help you find something suitable." Hamil gave the slightest of smiles.

Marla groaned. "Word travels fast."

"I won't mock you further. It's too easy."

"Thanks, Hamil. I'll make sure the caterers have plenty of those little shrimp puff things you like."

"Such benefits make life in your service worthwhile."

After Marla arrived at the club, cutting around the line that snaked outside and nodding to the bouncer on her way in, she headed straight for the back stairs that led up to Rondeau's apartment and her office, which once upon a time had been his spare bedroom. She wasn't much for dancing, and the horde of college students and hipsters in the club never failed to make her feel old.

Easing her way around the dance floor, she was first surprised and then annoyed to see Pelham tending the bar, moving with the precision of a Swiss clockwork figurine, pouring drinks and taking orders and eyeing the shouting customers with a combination of patience and concern. "Rondeau!" she shouted, and he was there, by her elbow, steering her toward a corner of the bar. He was dressed in a pin-striped suit that would have been tasteful if not for the giant fake orange flower dangling from his lapel, and the hideous polka-dotted bow tie. Once they were out of the press of the crowd, in the lee of one of the support pillars that dotted the floor, Marla snapped her fingers and said "Tace," causing a field of silence to wrap around Rondeau and herself, cutting out the pounding beat of the dance music and the dim roar of the merrymaking crowd. "Rondeau, why is my valet working in your nightclub?"

He winced. "I'm sorry! But one of my bartenders called in sick and the other one just flat no-showed. You know I'm useless behind the bar, and I was trying to find out if the bouncer knows how to mix drinks when Pelly just sort of appeared out of nowhere and cleared his throat and said that, being at liberty for the moment, he would be happy to serve. I knew you'd be pissed, but we were opening in five minutes, so I said sure." He glanced toward the bar. "And I have to give the guy his due. He knows the whole bartender's bible by heart! He may have never left the estate before, but he can mix a drink."

Marla sighed. "Call me next time you want to hijack my valet, would you? I mean, I don't *care,* but I'd like to be notified."

Rondeau grinned. "I thought you didn't even want the guy."

"I need somebody to hang crepe paper and to order the chocolate fountain and to sprinkle glitter on the swans, or whatever the hell rich people do to prepare for their parties. After that . . ."

"What, you're going to drive him to the edge of the woods and set him free?" Rondeau gestured. "Look at the guy. He practically begged me to put him to work! He's over there smiling, and it doesn't even look fake. He lives to serve. And you do need an assistant."

"I'm just not comfortable with the whole manservant thing."

"So pay him more than he deserves, if it makes you feel better. Give him lots of time off. Just as long as you pay me more, you know, on account of seniority."

"We'll see," Marla said. "I'm going upstairs. Holler if you need me."

"Sure you don't want to grab a drink? Pelly mixes a mean Manhattan."

"Maybe later." Marla went up the back stairs (which were invisible to casual observers, hidden under a look-away spell), and to her cluttered office. She switched on a brass lamp and dropped into the chair behind her desk, drawing her dagger of office from its sheath to set it on the desk before her. She idly spun the dagger on the blotter, and when it stopped twirling, the point was aimed at her chest. She grunted.

Marla owned two magical artifacts, which were two more than most people ever even *saw*. The first was her cloak. With the pale white side showing, it healed her, protecting her from taking physical damage. With a mental command she could reverse the cloak, making the bruise-purple side flip to the outside, and when she wore the purple, she became a monster, a pure killing machine. She'd discovered the cloak in a thrift store soon after she became an apprentice in Felport. The cloak shouldn't have been there—no one had sold it to the store, no employee had hung it on a rack, it was just *there*—and it had called to Marla, almost literally whispering to her. She paid the three dollars the clerk demanded, put on the cloak, and soon became something of a legend in the town, the ex-apprentice with an artifact, the stone-cold mercenary who would do almost any job, and who always demanded knowledge in payment instead of money—spells, tricks, secrets. At first, she'd been able to demand only a small lesson, but as she became more sought after and proficient in martial magics, she'd started acquiring tidbits of true power. Some people still grumbled that the *cloak* had the real power, not Marla, but if that was ever true, it wasn't anymore; she hardly wore the thing these days. It was simply too dangerous.

In her younger days, when she was bodyguarding and freelancing for a living, she'd used the cloak often, although it did horrible things to her mind. The cloak possessed a kind of malign alien intelligence, and whenever she put it on, that consciousness struggled to seize her body; even after she reversed the cloak, the alien mind lingered in her head for a few moments, calculating angles, plotting the death and destruction and subjugation of every other living thing on Earth. Over the years, the cloak's intelligence had grown stronger, and lasted for longer after each use, building up in her system like mercury poisoning. Marla had begun to fear she would lose her own mind entirely if she kept using it. These days she kept the cloak in a fortified wardrobe in her bedroom, a wooden monstrosity carved all over with dangerous runes and wrapped inside invisible spirals of binding. Mostly she kept the cloak locked up to prevent other people from getting it, but there were just as many wards to keep the cloak *in* as there were to keep intruders *out*, for in her darkest thoughts Marla sometimes wondered if the cloak was plotting its escape. She still occasionally brought it out of mothballs, in desperate situations, but she no longer depended on it, and even daydreamed about trying to destroy it, though most artifacts were as impervious to damage as they were mysterious in origin.

She thought about the cloak a lot . . . but she almost never thought about her dagger of office. It was her constant companion, but while she regarded the cloak as a half-tamed animal, a war-beast just barely under her control, she basically thought of the dagger as a fancy pocket knife. Was that a mistake? Was it something more than a useful tool? Something worth killing her over?

Maybe she should find out. She dialed Viscarro's number, and one of the subterranean sorcerer's lackeys answered, stammering that Viscarro was unavailable but would call back at his earliest convenience. "I don't care if it's convenient," Marla said. "Just get him to call soon."

She hung up, annoyed, and pulled down a few books from her shelf that referenced death and the afterlife and necromancy. Her library was a mishmash of inherited volumes—some from her predecessor Sauvage; some from her old mentor, Artie Mann—half of those had ancient bits of pornography tucked into the pages; some from the late sorceress Juliana, who'd owned the nightclub before giving it to Rondeau in her will. Marla wasn't much for books, having learned most of her magic in more practical ways, but she was interested in finding out what she could about capital-D Death, and sometimes sorcerous books had surprising insights. She began to read.

Hours later, Marla didn't have much more in the way of concrete facts, though she'd learned about the angel of death and his cloak of staring eyes and his venom-dripping sword, about death gods from Hades to Mictlantecuhtli to Hel to Eshu, and about realms of death from Annwfn to Sheol to Irkalla to the Ten Hells (including bee torture, the sixteen chambers of heart gouging, and the upside-down prison). Were they all just differing descriptions of the same being, the One True God of Death, and various cultural interpretations of a single actual afterlife, or were there dozens of squabbling death gods all wandering around down there (or up there, or over there), with their realms butting up against one another messily? Was there truly an afterlife at all?

Her head was swimming with visions of torments, caverns, scales, blades, crocodiles, rivers, murmurings, ice. She hadn't crammed like this since her days as an apprentice—and though none of the stories matched the description of Mr. Death precisely, there were stories of Deaths who walked the Earth, sometimes to harvest souls, sometimes to better understand what it was to be human, and there were arrogant Deaths who thought humans little more than flickering flies to be swatted away. There was no way to tell what stories were rooted in truths and which were utter fantasy, and none of them mentioned Death losing his dagger in a card game. But then, that was hardly the sort of story a death god would want spread around, was it?

She was opening a fresh volume, this one a collection of oral folktales from the Appalachians that was supposed to contain stories about outwitting Death, when a gentle knock came at the door. "Come in!" she called, and it opened to reveal Pelham, bearing a tray with three glasses. Rondeau entered after him. "Closed up for the night," he said. "Gods, I didn't know you had this many books! Where'd they all come from?"

Marla lifted a few stacked volumes from her desk and set them on the floor, making room for Pelham to set down the tray. "They've been here all along. You just don't notice books, unless they're about techniques for seducing women or cheating at cards."

"Please. Those are subjects I could *write* books on." Rondeau sat down in one of the chairs across from her. "Have a seat, Pelly."

"I really shouldn't," he murmured.

"No, sit." Marla gestured. "I mean, you brought a drink for yourself, so you might as well drink it."

"Rondeau insisted I prepare a cocktail for myself. I'm perfectly happy to drink it elsewhere."

Marla sighed. "Look, we're informal around here. I know that's not really your thing, but if you want to work for me, you have to do things the way we do them, right? So drink with us."

Pelham nodded and sat down, though he stayed on the edge of his chair, ready to leap into action at the least signal, it seemed. "What's the drink?" Marla sniffed her glass. She didn't drink much, preferring her faculties intact, but Rondeau had gotten her into the habit of a glass of wine or a cocktail to help unwind at the end of especially difficult days.

"Pelly invented it," Rondeau said. "He won't tell me what's in it!"

"My grandfather invented it," Pelham said modestly. "And it's a family secret, which I regret I cannot share."

Marla took a sip. It was faintly sweet—though not cloying—a mild fruity flavor that bloomed into pure spreading warmth as it went down her throat, hitting her belly like a belt of brandy. "That's a hell of a drink, Pelham. What's it called?"

"A Red Aloysius, after my grandfather," Pelham said. "Valet to Hollister Corbin, may his spirit persist."

Marla grunted. Hollister Corbin was one of the last late great badasses of the founding families, a mean son of a bitch and a war profiteer, she'd heard. His ghost was doubtless grumbling up in the Heights with his fellows.

"Hey," Marla said. "What did you end up doing with that goat, Rondeau?"

"Locked it in the special conference room with a tub of fresh water and a head of lettuce and some old carrots and stuff from my fridge. We'll get rid of it tomorrow. I'm sure somebody could use a goat."

"It'd better not crap all over my conference room," Marla said.

Rondeau grinned. "Well, you do have a manservant now, to clean up in that eventuality."

"I was never tasked to muck out stables," Pelham said. "Though, of course, if such services are required—"

"He's just taking the piss out of you, Pelham," Marla said. "Don't worry. Rondeau knows he's the only one I trust with cleaning up hypothetical goat shit."

"Good to know I'm useful." Rondeau slouched back in the chair, sipping his drink. "So Marla, I've been thinking."

"I already don't like where this is going."

"Oh, I was more just wondering, like, where do you see us in thirty or forty years?"

She snorted. "I'll probably be dead."

"Perish the thought," Pelham said.

"Yeah, maybe," Rondeau said. "Still, though, I mean, I've been thinking about goals. When I was a kid, my goal was to find enough to eat. Then my goal was to have a place to live, then to get a good job running with a crew like yours, then to have a business of my own . . ." He shrugged. "I got all that. Here I am, right-hand man to the chief sorcerer of Felport—"

"More like the little finger on my left hand," Marla said.

"—and proprietor of a nightclub that never goes out of style." It was true. There was a very minor come-hither spell on the club, just enough to tempt patrons into checking out the place, though Rondeau had to make sure the club was fun and inviting, or they'd all just walk right back out again. "But, I mean, what next? Should I meet a nice girl or boy or both and settle down? Try to become the world hot-dog-eating champion? Stop fucking around and apprentice myself to some sorcerer, try to learn some magic besides Cursing and a few knife tricks and how to open locks with spells?"

"I didn't realize you were so dissatisfied," Marla said. It would be a shame to lose Rondeau to some sorcerer. No one quite knew what Rondeau's magical capabilities were. He wasn't even really human, but an immortal parasitic psychic entity that had possessed the body of a homeless boy in Felport long ago. Rondeau didn't have any memories of his life before taking over that body, except for floating around in the air aimlessly, but he had some intrinsic magical ability, particularly the ability to Curse in a primal language that could literally change the world. Some thought Rondeau was mispronouncing the original Words that had created the universe, but Marla thought it was more likely he knew a few fragments of some basic programming language of magic, a fundamental language most sorcerers accessed indirectly through rites and incantations. There were certainly sorcerers who would be willing to teach Rondeau the mysteries in exchange for the chance to study him, but Rondeau had never seemed interested before.

"Eh, I'm not dissatisfied," he said, waving his hand. "And being an apprentice sounds like a lot of work and not much fun. Things are going pretty good. A new person in my bed every week, hanging out at the club every weekend, and there's never a dull moment with you when serious shit starts going down. But even though I'm no master of divination, I can kinda see the future when it comes to myself, and I think someday I might *get* dissatisfied, you know, and start to wonder, What's it all for?" He shrugged. "I blame Pelly's drink here. It's making me all philosophical. But you, you always seem so sure, so I just wondered . . ."

"I want to make Felport a great city," Marla said. "It's my home." She ran her finger around the rim of the half-empty glass. Maybe the booze was making her a little expansive, too. "Growing up, it was just me and my brother and my mom, and Mom's boyfriends—the less said about them the better. I never felt safe in my own place, not even in my bedroom, and I spent a lot of time pretty much running wild. I came here when I was a teenager, and Felport . . . took care of me. It was rough, sure, but I discovered magic here. I met people who challenged me, excited me, got me interested in something besides just working so hard I could sleep without dreaming. I love Felport more than I love myself. So as for what I want, I want this. The ongoing project. Using my magic to help the city prosper. Protecting it from those things that threaten it. I'll keep doing it for as long as I'm able."

"So we're not going to retire to the tropics and sit on some nice deck looking over the ocean in our old age?" Rondeau said.

Marla grinned. "Anything's possible."

"What about . . . family?" Pelham said, as if afraid to broach the subject.

"What about it?" Marla said. "Like I said, I don't have much family."

"Well, but you could marry, have children . . . I think family is very important."

"It's crossed my mind." Though her last lover had betrayed her and killed her friend Ted in this very room, not far from where Pelham sat now. "Let's just say I'm married to my job, and as for family, I've got Rondeau, and I've got Hamil, and a couple of other people you might meet someday, if you stick around long enough."

"Like who?" Rondeau said. "Since you're waxing all sentimental?"

Marla shifted in her seat, not quite squirming. "I don't know. People I can depend on. People who, if they called and said they needed me, I'd go help them, without any bargaining or bullshit, and who I know would do the same for me. Bradley, out in San Francisco. I guess Dr. Husch, though she's more like an older sister who pisses me off a lot." Marla took another sip of her drink and cleared her throat. All those relationships were relatively new—even Rondeau, her oldest friend, had been close with her for only seven or eight years, since before she became chief sorceress. She was used to fending entirely for herself, and she'd only gradually come to believe that having close allies could be as much an advantage as a liability. "I didn't draw a great hand when it came to natural family, so I'm a big supporter of making your own family where you find it."

Pelham sat with his mouth pursed, clearly disapproving of the notion of invented families, but then, he would be, wouldn't he? "How about you, Pelham? You want to meet a nice lady or gentleman and settle down?"

"Now that I have gainful employment, such a thing is a possibility, Ms. Mason. It would have been inappropriate in my previous circumstances. Though if you do not plan to have children, it is not imperative that I have children to further serve your line."

Marla shook her head. "So your whole ancestry is really intertwined with the founding families?"

He nodded. "They protected us. They brought us over from the old country and gave us a home. We have been with them ever since. Alas, the lines are sadly withered. I am pleased to be with you. The Chamberlain explained that you are the new aristocracy."

"When I hear the word 'aristocracy,' I reach for my knife," Marla said. "I'm a servant of the city, and the people who live here."

Pelham inclined his head. "It is a useful distinction, Ms. Mason. I, too, understand what it is to serve."

"He's got you there," Rondeau said. "Want to mix us a couple more drinks, Pelly?"

He glanced at Marla, who shook her head. "One's enough for me. You can go make a drink for Rondeau, but don't let him boss you around too much. Could you bring me up a pitcher of water, though? I've got some more reading to do. Rondeau, can you get him a cab over to my place? He can bed down in the apartment next to mine." Marla owned a former flophouse not far from the docks, and lived in one suite of the place.

"My place is with you, Ms. Mason," Pelham said. "I will remain here as long as you do, if it pleases you."

"Okay, I'll probably head home in a couple of hours. You'll be in bed by dawn. Just hang out downstairs with Rondeau or something. Play with the goat. I've got work to do, and these books aren't going to throw themselves across the room in frustration." She shooed them away and returned to her studies, barely even noticing when Pelham slipped in to leave a sweating pitcher of cold water. Distant sirens wailed through the window, cracked open against the summer heat, but that was just background music to Marla.

Her reverie was broken by the ringing phone. She picked up the receiver and grunted a hello, still reading.

"Marla, this is Hamil."

"Mmm. Did you know the Samoan afterlife for evildoers is called *O Le Nu'u-o-nonoa*?" she said. "And the whole land of the dead is called *Sa-le-fe'e*? That's kind of pretty."

"I did, and it is, though your pronunciation is atrocious. Marla—"

"And there's this story about a Zulu farmer named Uncama who chased a porcupine into its burrow and found himself in the land of the dead, where everybody talks backward and everything sucks. Supposedly a true story, not an ancient myth, passed down through the generations. Must have been a hell of a porcupine."

"It's good to see you studying up on the subject, Marla, but you should know—one of my spies saw a man who fit the description of Mr. Death a few minutes ago."

"Yeah?" She closed her book. "You sure it's him? He looked like an asshole who was missing some fingers?"

"The rings on every finger and the smirk were the real indications, actually, and it appears he found a healer to fix his hand. Marla, he was seen in the company of Ayres the necromancer, and an unidentified dark-haired man."

"Huh. So Ayres is mixed up in this. I knew that old bastard was going to be trouble. Where are they?"

"Downtown. A few blocks from the club. And coming your way."

5

"You don't have to come with me," Death said. "I understand your desire to bask in my glory, but really, it's unnecessary."

Ayres puffed a little to keep up with the striding god, and muttered a spell to make his knees stop creaking. His joints would ache terribly tomorrow in return for extra flexibility tonight, but magic was nothing but a series of uneven transactions, and Ayres was used to the trade-offs. "Marla is no friend of mine, lord, and if you don't object to my presence, I'd very much like to see the look on her face when you deliver your ultimatum."

"Oh, I don't care." Death strode purposefully along the dark sidewalk, toward the seedy part of downtown, where Marla's office was located. Ayres had expected him to teleport there or something, but apparently the Walking Death had earned his nickname, and preferred to travel on foot. John Wilkes Booth came along after them, hands clasped behind his back, gazing around at the tall buildings with awe. *He's like some ignorant hay-*

seed, Ayres thought. *The past is the functional equivalent of the middle of nowhere.*

"Nice rings," said a young man, stepping from a shadowy alley to block the sidewalk. He wore a baggy sweatshirt, and he lifted the hem to show the pistol in his waistband. "I wouldn't mind having me some rings like that."

Death didn't even break stride, just walked on as if the mugger wasn't even there. The man reached for his gun and tried to tug it out of his waistband, but it snagged on something, and Death just stepped right over him, kicking him almost incidentally as he passed, then stepping on his chest with his full weight when the man fell. The mugger started to sit up, cursing, and Ayres lashed out with his walking stick, cracking the boy in the side of his head. The lad groaned and lay still. Not dead, but no longer a threat. Death had nothing to fear from bullets, but Ayres was still mortal.

Booth paused, knelt, and took the pistol from the mugger's waistband, tucking it into his own belt.

"Do you even know how to use that?" Ayres said peevishly. "Guns have come a long way since your day. What did you shoot Lincoln with? A flintlock? A *musket*?"

"A .44 caliber single-shot Derringer," Booth said coolly. "A fine weapon, when held in a sure hand. Your buildings may be taller than those of my time, and your weapons more complex, but the essentials are the same, and I shall adjust accordingly."

"Maybe I don't want you to have a gun," Ayres said.

"I am happy to accompany you, and assist you in

your business, but do not presume to tell a gentleman whether or not he should carry a weapon, sir."

"That's it," Ayres said. "I'm sending you back to Hell."

Before Booth could speak, Death paused in his forward motion. "No, no. Keep him, Ayres. I like having him around. He reminds me of home, and I like the contours of his mind."

"My lord, I must insist. He is insolent, disrespectful, troublesome—"

"All words that could describe you, and the way you're addressing me." Death frowned, only slightly.

Ayres bowed his head. "Apologies, my lord." Inside, he seethed. Being dressed down, in front of Booth! The humiliation! He would raise another servant, a pliable servant, soon. If Death liked Booth's company so much, let them stay together, then. Ayres's nostrils suddenly filled with the unmistakable scent of decay, and his flesh began to itch, as if infested by beetles and maggots and grave-bugs. He squeezed his eyes shut and took shallow breaths, willing the hallucination away. His affliction returned to him in moments of stress and dismay, though he was always able to fight it back, thanks to his years of therapy. When the smell subsided, he opened his eyes, and Booth and Death were nearly a block ahead, side by side, talking. Ayres gritted his teeth and hurried to catch up.

"They're here." Rondeau sat with his back against one of the club's support pillars, a shotgun across his lap, barrel pointed vaguely toward the front door. He had a mild magical connection to the club, Marla knew, which allowed him to sense the ebb and flow of crowds, and it was sufficient to tell him when their visitors had arrived.

"Oh, good," Marla said. All the lights were on, and the club was bizarrely bright, looking far less spacious and cool with all its dirty corners and speckled floor tiles illuminated. Pelham was behind the bar, standing beside a row of mason jars containing live scorpions and mantids. They were sort of the magical equivalent of Molotov cocktails, already primed by Marla with long hours of enchanting, and they only needed to be thrown.

Marla gestured, and the doors flung themselves open, leaving Mr. Death and his associates squinting at the light. Well, the associates anyway. Mr. Death didn't appear to take any notice, nor did the doors flying open give him pause. He walked in, smiling and nodding. "Marla."

"I see you got your fingers stitched up. Want me to cut them off again? It could be, like, our thing."

Mr. Death held up his hand and examined it. "Flesh is a convenience for me, Marla. You can't hurt me. I'm a god. I'm Death."

"Oh, yeah? Which Death? Sammael? Ankou? The Morrigan? The Shinigami? Mot? Am I getting close? Or are you just some kind of generic Death? Crazy Pete's Discount Death God, like that?"

Ayres and the other man started to come in, and Rondeau said, "Ah, ah, hang back there, fellas. This gun's loaded with a lot worse than buckshot." They paused just behind the threshold.

"Those are old names, some of them," Mr. Death said. "I have answered to all of them. Everyone has a personal relationship with Death, Marla. Every culture sees me differently. Some as a savior. Some as a custodian. Some as a friend. Some as a monster." He spread his hands. "I encompass all those attributes, and have been know to appear in many guises."

"Really? All I've seen so far is 'smug' and 'overconfident.'" She nodded to Ayres. "So is he the real deal? You're a necromancer, so I figure you'd know. Is that why you're following him like a puppy?"

"He is what he says." Ayres was somber as always. "He is the Walking Death, the new god of the underworld."

Marla raised one eyebrow. Death looked annoyed. "New god? What, it's an elected office now? He got three-fifths of the cemetery vote?"

"Ah, the gods of death are, you might say, seasonal, or—"

"Shut up, old man," Death said wearily.

"Ohhh," Marla said. "The birth-death-rebirth thing? Like harvest gods and savior gods, shit like that? Out with the old and in with the new? The old god ages, and dies, and is replaced by new blood? So if I just wait long enough, you'll croak, and get replaced by a new Death, who isn't such an ass-wipe? So does the changing of the guard happen every winter or spring, or what?"

"The seasons are long for my kind, Marla," Death said. "Yet you still try my patience. I've come to ask you for the dagger."

"Oh, now you ask. How nice of you. Request denied.

Piss off back to Tartarus. Eat dust or take a dip in the lake of fire or whatever it is you do there."

"You, too, will die someday, Marla Mason," Death said. "You will enter my realm. Do you really want to be the sort of person I pay special attention to there?"

"I'll burn that bridge when I come to it. When I'm on your turf, we'll see how it goes. But right now, you're on my turf. And you're not welcome." She glanced at Pelham, who hefted one of the mason jars. "Neither are you, Ayres. Or you . . . who the hell are you anyway?"

The stranger bowed. "John Wilkes Booth, ma'am."

Marla frowned. "The guy who killed *Lincoln*?" She looked at Ayres. "Ayres, you brought John Wilkes Booth back from the dead? I mean, I figured you'd disobey me and raise some corpse, but you raised the corpse of a racist presidential assassin?" She shook her head. "That's fucked up, right there."

"Yes, well, there were circumstances," Ayres began, and Booth was harrumphing something about Marla impugning his honor and how Lincoln was never *his* president, but Death cut them both off.

"I came to offer you a deal, Marla. Give me the dagger peacefully, and I will leave your city."

"Because your daddy or granddaddy or whatever lost it in a card game with some sorcerer, is that why?" Marla said, drawing the dagger. "Because it used to belong to your family?" She held it up, letting the blade flash in the light, and watched Death focus on the weapon with all his attention. "That's the rumor I heard anyway."

"All you need to know is that I want it," Death said. "And that I am a god. Give it to me."

"You're stupid for a god," Rondeau said. "Can I shoot him?"

"Give me the dagger, Marla, or I will take your city from you," Death said.

Marla cocked her head. "You shouldn't make threats like that. You don't know what it does to me."

"I cannot take the dagger from you by force, but I have powers you cannot begin to comprehend. I can banish you. I can make this city my plaything, and make you irrelevant. The dagger—"

"Right," Marla said. "The dagger. See, the thing about this dagger is, it can cut through anything. Hell, we saw what it did to your fingers. That got me wondering. Flesh may be a convenience for you, maybe that body is just a costume you put on, but there's some essential *you* underneath . . . and I want to see if it bleeds." She leapt, dagger in her hand, and Rondeau fired his shotgun at Death just as Pelham hurled two mason jars full of chittering ensorcelled insects over the bar.

The shotgun was loaded with crystals that would freeze Death on contact and slow him down, so he couldn't move with that horrible inhuman speed, and the jars with their insects were venomous bombs that would poison and weaken him, screw up his magics and leave him dizzy and confused and, soon, dead. Of course, those attacks wouldn't work as well if he was *really* a god, which seemed more likely now than it had a few hours ago—at least, if Ayres could be believed. But Marla's dagger shouldn't care if he was a god or not.

Marla's dagger was a simple thing. It cut. Whatever touched the blade parted against it.

Time slowed. The shotgun pellets held still in the air. The mason jars hung, unexploded, in mid-arc. Marla, too, was suspended, paralyzed, but still aware. Death walked toward her, hands clasped behind his back. "Sad." He plucked a single hair from her head and twined it around his fingers, the wet follicle dangling. "Listen. I'm banishing you now. You will not be allowed into Felport until you agree to relinquish the dagger. I trust you'll come to your senses quickly." He tucked a little silver bell into her pocket. "When you're ready to make a deal, ring that, and I'll hear, and appear before you. But don't bother ringing it until you're ready to give in. I'll be most unhappy if you summon me under false pretenses. You don't want to make me unhappy. Do you know why? Because I'm a *god,* you stupid woman."

Marla couldn't strike, couldn't speak. He looked at the dagger in her hand longingly, sighed, and flicked his fingers. Everything went black, and the blackness moved around Marla with tremendous speed, and she was afraid.

"Oh, sweet unholy fuck." Rondeau stared at the spot where Marla had just been. He gestured at Death with the barrel of his apparently useless gun. "If you just disintegrated Marla, I'm going to break this gun off in your ass, pretty boy."

"Mind your tongue!" Ayres's voice quivered with

indignation or fear or some other emotion Rondeau couldn't be bothered to puzzle out.

Death chuckled. "Fear not, little man. I've just sent her to the time-out corner until she's ready to behave. Only banishment, not execution. In the meantime, I'll be running things here in Felport. I'm sure she'll come to her senses soon, but until then, I'll have to keep myself entertained somehow. First, of course, I'll need oaths of loyalty from Marla's former subjects. You may kneel before me here."

"How about you kneel," Rondeau said. "I've got something long and hard for you to suck while you're down there." He grinned and hefted the shotgun. "I mean this, of course. I run a family establishment."

"But then again," Death said, unruffled, "perhaps it would be better for you to swear fealty in a more regal setting. Where is Marla's throne room?"

"Throne room? Are you kidding? Do you believe this guy, Pelly?" Rondeau turned toward the bar, expecting to see the valet there, but Pelham was gone, or else hiding. Rondeau frowned. Pelly hadn't struck him as the cowering type, more a stiff-upper-lip-in-the-face-of-adversity kind of guy.

"Where did the other one go?" Death said. "The one behind the bar?"

"He vanished as well," Booth said. "I'll investigate."

Rondeau lifted the gun. "Hold up, Mr. History. This is my club. You don't want to go behind that bar without permission." Booth paused and glanced at Death.

"What's to stop me killing you now?" Death said.

Rondeau shrugged. "I'm not too worried."

Death approached, his movements somehow hypnotic, like watching a beautiful snake curl and uncurl. "Why is that?"

"You're the referee in a game I don't play," Rondeau said. He wasn't exactly *enjoying* this—he was worried about Marla, and about Pelham, but he wasn't worried about his own skin. "The whole death thing is something that happens to other people." Rondeau nodded. "Ayres knows what I'm talking about. All the sorcerers have heard about me. I'm famous."

The necromancer cleared his throat. "This man is . . . more than a man, my lord."

Death leaned close to Rondeau and sniffed. "Really? I smell flesh. Flesh is grass."

"If you think flesh smells like grass, you've been sniffing the wrong grass," Rondeau said. "And sure, the flesh is weak, but the spirit is badass. Kill this body, and my mind will just meander on over to Ayres there and hijack his stringy carcass, and when he dies of natural causes—which could happen any minute now, by the look of him—I'll just jump to another host." Rondeau's tone was jaunty, with more bravado than he felt. He didn't want to give up his young, strong, familiar body for Ayres's old one. The karmic and moral aspects of body-hijacking were troubling to him, too, but being an unkillable psychic parasite was the one strength he had here, and Marla had always taught him to play to his strengths.

"It's true, my lord," Ayres said. "Or so I've heard. Rondeau is a sort of . . . psychic squatter, riding in that body."

"So Booth there's a zombie, right?" Rondeau said. "And the nice slicked-back hair and such he's got, that's all illusion?" He pumped the shotgun and pointed it at Booth, who remained impassive. "In this bar, we shoot zombies in the head for free during happy hour."

Death yawned. "This is boring. Perhaps I can't kill you, but you certainly can't hurt me."

"Huh," Rondeau said. "This is what you call a Mexican standoff."

"But surely you care for something other than yourself? Perhaps if I put this bar to the torch you'll be more amenable to swearing loyalty?"

Rondeau shrugged. "This is Marla Mason's stronghold. Sure, burn it down, if you've got the mojo. It'd be tough to burn. But be prepared to reap the whirlwind when she gets back."

"You people are all very stupid," Death said peevishly. "I'm a god. I'm *Death*. Threatening me is ludicrous. It's like a snowball threatening the sun."

Rondeau shrugged. "They say there are only two certain things in the world: death and taxes. But I can't die, and I've never paid a dime in taxes, so I call bullshit on that. The only thing I believe in is Marla Mason."

Suddenly Death was beside him, wrenching the shotgun from Rondeau's hands and flinging it aside. Death had one hand on Rondeau's shoulder, the other on his thigh, and Rondeau had the feeling the guy could just flat rip him in half with the merest twitch of his muscle. He wanted to pee himself. Fucking treacherous body didn't have the courage of his mind's convictions. "Perhaps you can't die," Death purred. "But you can suffer, yes? Or would you rather pledge yourself to my service?"

"Yeah." Rondeau's throat was suddenly dry. "You make a compelling argument. Count me in. But, ah, I'm kind of embarrassed to do it in front of Ayres. Do you think, do you mind, would it be okay if I just like . . . whispered it in your ear?"

"Of course," Death said. "I am a reasonable master." He bowed his head.

Rondeau leaned forward. He put his lips so close to Death's ear that he could have kissed him. Rondeau opened his mouth.

Then he Cursed.

Ayres gaped as Death flew backward, as if thrown from a horse, and bounced off the wall. Rondeau—who, a moment before, had been at the god's mercy—wiped his mouth with the back of his hand, making a face like he'd tasted something awful. Booth rushed at him, pulling a knife he'd gotten from who knows where, and Rondeau made a terrible *noise,* something like a word, but this was a word that made the building's foundations—perhaps the very foundations of the Earth—groan in protest.

When Rondeau spoke, Booth's suit caught fire, which should have been impossible, since the clothing was illusory. A moment later, Ayres realized that Booth *himself* had caught fire, his mummified body burning like old dry wood, and the flames were merely emerging from the illusion. As Booth shrieked and rolled on the ground, Rondeau sauntered over, picked up his shotgun, and carefully took aim at Booth's head. The sound of the shot was shockingly loud, and Booth stopped moving, illusion wholly shattered now, and he was a just a headless corpse, half aflame, on the concrete floor, flecks of his mummified head scattered like chips of wood and dirty porcelain. Rondeau pumped the gun again and approached Ayres, grinning. "Hey there. You know, I told Marla she was being too hard on you. Let the old guy alone, I said. He's harmless, I said. Well, never let it be said I can't admit when I was wrong. If you like death so much, let's—"

Ayres didn't have much patience for speeches. He lashed out with his walking stick and knocked the gun out of Rondeau's hands. Rondeau's eyes went wide and his mouth opened, doubtless to voice another guttural incantation, so Ayres simply shoved his own fist into the man's gaping mouth and began whacking him upside the head with his stick. Rondeau tried to back away, but Ayres moved forward with him, and then Rondeau bit down on Ayres's hand, which hurt, but Ayres had believed his own body was a rotting corpse for over a decade; he could handle pain. Rondeau finally threw himself backward, and Ayres's fist came out of his mouth with a wet pop. Rondeau rolled away, then stood, swaying a little, clearly a bit groggy from the blows to the head. "You're a nasty old bastard," Rondeau said, perhaps with something like admiration.

Death moaned and started to move, and Rondeau was off like a shot, disappearing through a doorway at the back of the club that Ayres couldn't quite focus on—

the passage must have a look-away spell on it. Ayres was not quite up to giving pursuit, and besides, his god needed him. The old necromancer went to the groaning Death and knelt as much as his aching joints would allow. "Are you all right, my lord?"

"What—what—there was a darkness, a . . . a space of nothingness, I couldn't see, I couldn't think, I was not aware, but now I am aware of the lack of awareness if . . . if that . . ." He sat up, and the look on his face was something that, on a human, would have been existential terror.

"Have you never slept, my lord?" Ayres said. "Or been unconscious?"

Death looked up at him, then rose. "I do not remember the time before I came into existence. I was born—I came into being—with full awareness, and that awareness has been complete and uninterrupted, until . . . that. How did he do that?"

"Magic," Ayres said with a shrug. "A very old magic, to work on one such as you. Perhaps it was the language of Rondeau's true race."

"Unsettling," Death muttered. "But certainly an interesting new experience." He walked over to Booth and kicked the meat and ashes. "Rondeau did this, too?"

"Indeed."

"Hmm." Death made a vague gesture with his hand.

Suddenly Booth was whole again, his mummified form as solid as it had been yesterday, and he looked about him with the blank expression of a corpse. "Thank you, sir. The underworld appears much as I left it, and I am pleased to be back here."

"Yes, well, it seems I have need of allies." Strangely, the idea seemed to amuse him.

"This Rondeau," Booth said. "Can you banish him as you did Marla?"

Death shook his head. "I'd need to pluck a living hair from his head to make that work. And even then, the banishment would only apply to the body he has now. He could easily suicide and get a new body, and then we wouldn't even be able to recognize him."

"We shall simply be vigilant for his return, sir," Booth said. "If it's not too presumptuous, my lord . . ."

Death shrugged. "Speak."

"Why not simply kill Marla?" Booth asked. "I know the dagger would then pass to the next chief sorcerer of Felport, but if he proved unwilling to give you the blade, you could simply kill him. You wouldn't have to kill many before one of them agreed to give up the blade, I'm sure."

"Is assassination your only interest, Booth?" Death picked up a fallen chair, placed it upright, and sat down, crossing one leg over the other. "My nature is bringing death. Does your . . . your *postman* sort mail for enjoyment? Why would I kill for fun?"

"Fun, my lord?" Ayres said, feeling he'd lost the thread of the conversation before it was even well under way.

"Booth wants to know why I don't kill chief sorcerers until one of them gives me the dagger. Because it's clumsy, obvious, and boring. It's the difference between swatting a fly or pulling off its wings and watching it crawl around injured until it dies. The latter is more entertaining. I'm going to live for a significant percentage of eternity, gentlemen. Boredom is very dangerous for my kind. Marla Mason is arrogant. It will amuse me to break her. Let her wander in the wilderness for a while, wondering what I'm doing here, with her city."

"That is the way to lay the city flat," Booth said, voice resonant with relish. "To bring the roof to the foundation, and bury all, in heaps and piles of ruin."

"Well, that's one way to go," Death said. "I could rain devastation on this place, let Marla watch the smoke rise in the distance, etc. But don't you think it would bother her more if her city *didn't* fall apart without her? If it turned out she wasn't needed here at all?" He grinned, and his smile was not at all like that of a skull. It was much worse.

"Ingenious, my lord," Ayres said, relieved. He still loved Felport, and had no desire to see it razed. Fortunately, Death's principle trait seemed to be a sort of whimsical cruelty.

"We could kill a few people, though, just to make the point," Booth said.

"We'll see. Death is a wonderful stick to threaten people with. The most basic form of coercive power. But once they're dead, they just go to my realm, to a hell of their own devising—or of my devising, if I take a special interest. But it's more fun to watch them squirm up here."

"Rondeau might still make trouble," Booth said. He ran a hand through his illusory hair, as if remembering his recently shattered skull.

"I disagree. Rondeau is likely lost without Marla,"

Ayres said. "He is her lackey and little more, despite his show of pique just now. I imagine he'll hide and wait for his mistress to return. You will not find most of your opponents even that formidable. Rondeau has certain qualities that make him uniquely suited to opposing you, but if you don't let him whisper in your ear again, his magic shouldn't trouble you."

"How did you stop him?" Booth's tone was caught half between annoyance and appreciation.

"I am a very old man, as you have both observed. I have learned a great many things in my life, including how to deal with people like Rondeau." In truth, he'd just been lucky, but why not make himself seem more impressive in the eyes of Death?

"You're actually older than I am," Death said. "In years only, of course. In essence I am as old as the first living thing that ever died on Earth. But perhaps I underestimated your usefulness." He sighed. "I'd like to take over Marla's city, bring her people to my side, humble her, prove my strength. Where should I begin?"

"Not with Rondeau. With . . . some of the more reasonable sorcerers. Those who will understand which way the wind is blowing." He thought of Viscarro, but Viscarro would probably seal his vaults at the first whisper of trouble, and while Death could surely circumvent Viscarro's security, Ayres thought it wise to give his master an easier win to start his conquest. "There's a sorcerer named Granger who rules Fludd Park, and is intimately familiar with nature magics." He was also essentially a half-wit, hereditary heir to a little minifiefdom of green space within the city. His ancestors had been great sorcerers, but Granger was a good-natured fool with inherited power and a famous name. He would give in to Death's demands easily, Ayres suspected, and once one of the city's leading sorcerers joined them, it would be easier to win over the others.

"Yes, fine," Death said. "We'll take a walk in the park." He paused. "I still can't believe Marla doesn't have a throne room. No one has standards anymore."

Rondeau knew what to do. There were procedures. Marla had considered the possibility of a hostile invasion by overwhelming forces—hell, it had almost happened not long ago, when those things that called themselves faeries came pouring out of Fludd Park—though Rondeau had never expected to be the one spearheading counterinvasion operations. Marla was supposed to be here, taking charge, rallying the troops, fucking shit up. But the situation was what it was. Rondeau used an untraceable enchanted cell phone to call Marla, and when he got nothing, not even a ring, he called Hamil and Ernesto, Marla's closest allies among the city's sorcerers. He gave them the coded phrase that meant hard-core shit was most assuredly going down. Half an hour after he knocked out Death with a well-placed Curse, Rondeau paced around in what had once been a bomb shelter, underneath the old Savings and Loan building, waiting. He tried to distract himself by browsing the yellowing old paperbacks—1950s potboiler bestsellers—stacked among the crates of dusty rations and bottled water, but though Rondeau usually found distraction easier than concentration, he couldn't stop thinking about how bad the situation was.

Hamil arrived first. "What's happened?"

"The god of *death* happened," Rondeau said.

Hamil nodded. "He came to the club?"

"He came, and he banished Marla." Rondeau related the story, not even embellishing his own exploits as he normally would. Hamil listened gravely, and when Rondeau was finished he clapped him on the shoulder.

"You did well. We need to get in touch with Marla. I tried calling her on the way over, but . . ." He shook his head. "No answer. I'm more disturbed by the fact that she hasn't gotten in touch. If Death is truly what he says—and if he brushed aside Marla's magics as easily as you say—then she could be anywhere."

"How the hell can he banish her?" Rondeau said. "She's the chief sorcerer of Felport! She is the city, right? So how can he keep her out of herself?"

"He has the power of a god. He can do most anything he wishes. But you're right, Marla is the city. Even if Death tries to rule properly, Felport will suffer in Marla's absence, stutter and shudder like a poorly maintained engine, but it will be a long time before the results become catastrophic. Death may attempt to take her place, but he's inhuman. He can't be chief sorcerer, can't truly take her place—but he *can* become a tyrant, an occupier. We can only hope he doesn't decide to burn the city down or kill all the inhabitants to make his point."

"We'll fight him, right? Until Marla gets back?"

"I will fight," Hamil said. "In my own way. And you will do your part, I'm sure. But the other sorcerers . . .

you know them, Rondeau, at least well enough. They're intensely self-interested. Nicolette is a chaos magician, and Death taking over Felport will only cause more chaos and increase her power. She won't mind. Granger moves where the wind blows. Viscarro will just hide underground until he has no other choice, then he will ally himself with whichever side seems strongest. The Bay Witch may not even come out of the water—honestly, she might not even notice if the city changes hands. The Chamberlain works for a consortium of ghosts, and who knows how those ghosts will feel about Death? As for Ernesto . . . if he were here, I would be more confident. But he seems to be dawdling, which worries me. He likes Marla, but I'm not sure how much deeper his loyalty goes. The fact is, Death is more powerful than Marla. If he wants to take over Felport, he can. I'm not sure what Marla can do about it."

Rondeau sputtered. "Are you kidding? This is *Marla*. She's a force of nature!"

"No, she's not. You know I think as highly of her as you do, but Death . . . Death is *literally* a force of nature. An irresistible force. Irresistible to everyone except you, of course. You might be the only man in the city who can openly stand against Death, because he knows he can't just end your life if you become too boring or inconvenient."

"Fat lot of good it does me," Rondeau said.

"Oh, it might do a lot of good." Ernesto emerged from the shadows of some secret entry to the bomb shelter, axle grease shining on the lapel of his ragged tuxedo. "Sorry I didn't get here sooner, but I have a bug in this room, so I heard everything." He tapped his ear. "I'm hurt, Hamil. I'm a loyal Marlista through and through. There's already some shit going down out there, and it's not even dawn—Granger has sided with Death, and they're visiting Nicolette now."

"That was fast," Hamil said. "They'll be knocking on our doors soon."

"Yep," Ernesto said. "And I think we'd better be there to answer them, and we'd better play nice, too. Oh, we shouldn't roll over *too* quick, but we shouldn't be so much trouble he kills us."

"You're just going to let this guy take over?" Rondeau rose, clenching his fists. "Let him destroy everything Marla's built here?"

"Now, now," Ernesto said. "Settle down, kid. We can keep him from fucking up stuff too bad if we pretend to work with him, maybe. But *you* don't have to play nice. I doubt you'll be able to get close enough to him again for your Curses to work—he'll be on the lookout for that—but there are other options. Since you're the one guy old Skull and Bones can't kill, you're the perfect candidate to wage a little asymmetrical warfare."

"What?" Rondeau said, bewildered.

"He means you should lead the resistance," Hamil said, nodding. "And I think it's an excellent idea."

"Me?" Rondeau said. "Look, guys, I hate to put it like this, but I'm Marla's sidekick, not Che fucking Guevara."

"I should hope not," Hamil said. "Che Guevara lost. You have to win."

"*Viva la revolución,*" Ernesto said.

6

Marla sat up, sneezing in a cloud of pollen and shredded flowers. She'd landed on her back—though where she'd fallen from, she wasn't sure—in a patch of wildflowers beside a two-lane blacktop road. The quarter moon was high, crickets were chirping, and she felt like she'd been shoved into a burlap sack and rolled down a rocky hill while people ran alongside and hit her with sticks. "Death, you fuck," she said, and sneezed again. She activated her night-eyes so she could see in the darkness around her, but there wasn't much to see. Suddenly panicked, she looked around for her dagger, and found it in the blue and white flowers at her side. She snatched it up and sheathed it at her belt, then stood up, wincing as her knees popped. There were flowers on the shoulder on both sides of the road, and pine woods beyond. The only other item in the landscape was a battered metal sign ten feet in front of her that said "Welcome to Felport."

Death had picked her up and dumped her on the

outskirts of town, on some road she didn't recognize. She wasn't even sure if she was north or east of the city; there were lots of woods on the outskirts in both those directions. Dumped in the middle of the night, in the middle of nowhere. Death would pay for that. She gritted her teeth and started to walk toward the sign, when someone grunted and moaned across the road.

"Pelham?" She hurried across, to find her valet sprawled half in a drainage ditch, his neatly pressed jacket smeared with dirt and rucked up, revealing his pale soft belly. "Are you all right?"

"I am . . . battered but whole, Ms. Mason." She helped him to his feet, where he futilely tried to brush grass and weeds off his coat. "Ready to aid you however I can."

"What are you even doing here? Did Death toss you, too?"

"I am linked to you, Ms. Mason." He bowed slightly, then climbed out of the ditch. "I suppose when he . . . sent you here . . . he sent me as well."

"Okay, I'm going to call Hamil and get us a car." She opened her cell phone and dialed, but it only hissed and crackled static in her ear, and she cursed in frustration. "Damn it, no reception." Yet the phone's display showed a clear, strong signal. That was troubling. "We'll have to go on foot until the phone starts working."

"Of course." Pelham took a tentative step. He would have fallen straight into the ditch again if she hadn't grabbed his arm.

"You can't see, can you? Damn it, you should've mentioned."

"I'm sorry. Of course you're right. My apologies."

Marla sighed. "I just meant . . . here. *Fiat lux*." He gasped as her spell increased the effectiveness of his vision, allowing his eyes to slurp up stray moonlight and dim reflections so he could see almost as well as in daylight. "Let's march." She started down the road at a fast clip.

Her pace slowed considerably when she passed the edge of the "Welcome to Felport" sign, fell to her knees, and began vomiting. Pelham hurried to help her, but he started puking, too, though he still tried to crawl toward her. Marla attempted to move forward, but with every inch she moved into Felport, her convulsions became more severe. It was hard to think about anything while noisily voiding her stomach contents, but she had little doubt this was Death's doing—he'd banished her, after all, and he'd apparently chosen a very visceral way to keep her out of the city. Cursing—not magical Curses like Rondeau's, but mundane, if vociferous, ones—as she heaved, she lurched and dragged herself back beyond the perimeter of Felport, followed by Pelham. The nausea and pain stopped immediately, but the aftereffects lingered. They both lay shuddering on the shoulder for a while, and finally Pelham spoke up. "That was most unpleasant."

"Yeah." Marla wiped her mouth with a handful of pulled grass. She didn't even have any water to wash her mouth out. "I guess you are linked to me, the way you were hurling there. Death probably didn't realize you'd get dragged along, but if I get banished, you get banished." She sat up. "Let's inventory. No phone. Can't get into the city. Boots and nothing to kick. A knife and nothing to cut. I've got this bell Death gave me, and maybe Hamil could do something nasty with it, but I don't have his expertise with sympathetic and contagious magic." She considered ringing it and trying to attack Death again when he appeared, but one definition of insanity was doing the same thing over and over and expecting to get a different result, and Marla may have had her issues, but she wasn't insane. "Altogether? Not so good."

"Just let me know what I can do to help."

She laughed. "I'm at a bit of a loss myself. Maybe if a car comes by we can hop in and ride into Felport, but I think we'd just hurt worse the farther in we got. I've got a few talents, Pelham, but kicking ass while puking my guts out isn't one of them. Whatever this magic is, I doubt I can beat it. Death must really be a god. Such powers are . . . resistant to intervention. I think the only reason he couldn't just take my dagger is because one of his ancestors, or incarnations, or whatever, made the thing, and lost it fairly. The gods have to keep their promises and follow certain rules, the same way you and I have to breathe and eat and sleep, and there might be a way to beat Death if I can figure out what rules govern his actions. But gods don't like telling you what those rules are, unfortunately. Have you ever played the card game Mao, where the other players don't tell you the rules, and you have to figure them out as you go along? I hate that game."

"I see," Pelham said, not very helpfully.

"Sitting still bugs me." She stood up, wrapping her

grass-stained cloak around her body. She wished, fleetingly, that she'd been wearing her lethal purple-and-white cloak when Death barged in on her. She would have kicked the asshole up one side of the world and down the other if she'd been wearing the artifact, though using it again might have driven her permanently insane. *Small price to pay to be spared this embarrassment,* she thought sourly. "Can you walk, Pelham?"

"Yes, Ms. Mason." He rose, too.

"Don't you want to know where we're walking to?"

"I will follow wherever you go, of course."

She sighed. "I don't know where we're going."

"Do you have any allies outside the city?" Pelham asked. "Who might be able to get a message back to your associates?"

"I had the same thought. Dr. Leda Husch, head of the Blackwing Institute. She can help. Blackwing's like an hour drive outside of the city, it'll take forever on foot. But I don't even know where exactly we are, so I'm not sure which way to start the forced march." It was frustrating. In the city she always knew her location, but out here . . . she was in the wilderness.

"We're on Asleid Road, on the north side of the city, Ms. Mason," Pelham said.

Marla blinked. "How do you know that?"

"I have examined all the maps, Ms. Mason."

"Yeah, but I mean, maps don't show, what, trees? What's your landmark?"

"There are very fine satellite maps that contain a great deal of detail. And my sense of direction is very good." He pointed. "That sign indicates sharp curves for the next eight miles, which is consistent only with Asleid Road. I can lead us to the Blackwing Institute—though, as you've said, it is approximately fifty miles away, which is, hmm, about twelve hours of walking time?"

"We can make it in ten," she said. "It's—gods, it's almost four in the morning, and I haven't slept and neither have you. Well. I've got spells that can keep you going even when you think you're going to collapse. We'll have to eat like pigs when we get to Blackwing to recover the calories. It's mostly hospital food, but it'll do. And maybe we'll get cell coverage on the way." Marla doubted the last, assuming Death had somehow put the kibosh on her phone, but figured voicing some optimism wouldn't hurt Pelham's morale. Not that his morale seemed even slightly dented. He was proving pretty stalwart so far.

"If I may lead, then?" he said, and she nodded, and fell into step behind him.

After a few miles, the sun began to touch the edge of the sky, and Marla *finally* got her sense of direction decently oriented. They'd seen a couple of cars, but none were going the right direction; all were headed toward Felport, not away from it. Marla considered a carjacking, but she didn't think she'd fallen quite that far yet. They were sure to hit a little gas station or something soon, and maybe she'd have more luck with a pay phone than her cell.

"Look, a motorist in distress," Pelham said, and up ahead there was indeed a little sedan with its hood up and the flashers on, a guy sitting on the back, smoking a cigarette and looking at them with interest. "Do you need assistance?" Pelham shouted.

The man was young and tired-looking, dressed in a T-shirt that said "Allison Wonderland" over a stylized picture of a guitar. He tossed his cigarette onto the pavement. "You look like *you* need assistance, guys," he said. "Like you slept in a field last night. I've just got a broken-down car." He looked Marla up and down. "Cool cloak. Do you work at a Renaissance fair or something?"

"Or something. So is help on the way?"

He nodded glumly. "Called for a tow truck twenty minutes ago. They weren't sure when they'd get somebody out here. I'm at Adler, taking summer classes, trying to graduate, and I got an early start today to go see my parents for the weekend. I thought my car would make it one more round-trip, but no such luck."

"Bad luck," Marla said. "Hey, can I borrow your phone?"

He passed over his cell, and Marla tried to call Hamil, but she got squeals and pops and static again. "No answer," she said, shrugging, and gave the phone back. Damn it. Death was thorough.

"Tell you what," Marla said. "We'll get you on your way and save you the cost of a tow truck, if you're willing to give us a ride to Annemberg."

"Annemberg? Isn't that, like, one stoplight and some cows?"

"Yeah," Marla said. It was also the home of the Blackwing Institute. "I've got a friend there."

"Oookay," the guy said. "It's sort of on my way. If you can fix my car, sure. I don't know what's wrong with it, other than it's old. I don't really have tools, though. Maybe, like, a wrench. I mean, don't get your hopes up."

"Don't worry," Marla said, clapping Pelham on the back. "My man Pelly here is a wizard with automobiles, isn't that right?"

"I do have some small facility," Pelham said.

The college boy lifted an eyebrow. He'd be cute, Marla thought, if he hadn't been born when she was, oh, fifteen. "He's a mechanic? No offense, guy, but you look like a hobo butler."

"He gets that a lot," Marla said. "Let's check under the hood, shall we, Pelly?"

They went around to the front of the car and bent over, Pelham poking at wires and cables and whistling absentmindedly through his teeth. "Oh, dear, oh, dear," Pelham said. "This vehicle hasn't been maintained at all. The Chamberlain would fire any driver in her fleet who treated her automobiles so shabbily."

"Wait, you can actually fix cars?" Marla said.

Pelham frowned. "Of course."

Marla laughed. "You never cease to amaze, Pelly. But don't worry about it." She put her hands on the engine block, meditated for a moment, and spoke a phrase Ernesto, the scrapyard sorcerer, had taught her. Her nostrils filled with the scent of burning oil, and she felt her heart—the engine of her body—stutter once or twice before finding its rhythm again. She exhaled, and a thin plume of car exhaust emerged from her mouth, making Pelham cough. She stood up. "Try to get it to start," she said, and the college boy obligingly climbed in and turned the key. The engine purred beautifully, and the driver gave a cheer. "Just a little magic to give any old beater an extra few months of operation," Marla said.

"I wonder how long it'll take before this guy realizes the car doesn't even use up gas anymore?"

She let the hood drop, grinning, and went around to the passenger side, crushing fast-food bags and disposable coffee cups underfoot. Pelham got in the back.

"I'm Roddy," the driver said, sticking out his hand.

"I'm Marla," she said. "That's Pelly. Pelham, I mean."

"Pelly is fine," her valet said, with his accustomed dignity, and, perhaps, a hint of pleasure. Maybe all Pelham had needed to help him loosen up was a nickname to call his own. Marla could hope.

"Let's hit the road, Roddy," Marla said, and he pulled off the shoulder and drove.

"What was wrong with it?" he said. "It hasn't sounded this good in years!"

"Loose cables," Marla said promptly. "Pelly spotted it right away. Nothing big."

"I don't know shit about cars," Roddy said. "I'm a philosophy major." He glanced Marla's way. "Not very practical, I know."

"Hey, philosophy teaches you how to think," Marla said. "Thinking's the most versatile tool in the world."

"So, if you don't mind me asking," Roddy said, "what are you two doing wandering the back roads outside Felport? I come this way because I like the scenic route, but it's a long walk to Annemberg."

Marla considered, then said, "We were banished from Felport by the incarnation of Death, and we're headed to Annemberg so I can meet up with some allies and set up my government-in-exile."

"Ooookay," Roddy said.

"Nah, I'm just screwing with you," Marla said. "We were hitchhiking, but the redneck who was giving us a ride got pissed when I wouldn't give him a little nookie in a gas station bathroom, and he chucked us out by the side of the road."

"That sucks," Roddy said amiably. "Hitching's dangerous, though. What if the guy hadn't taken no for an answer?"

"Aw, hell, Pelly's a master of ninjitsu."

"No, only judo," he said, alarmed.

Roddy laughed, and switched on the radio, and they made the rest of the trip to the tunes of Willie Nelson and Merle Haggard.

Marla sort of wished they'd kept on talking, shooting the shit. With nothing but music and the hum of the road and the passage of fields and cows and trees out the windows, she had way too much time to fret over her desperate situation.

About ten miles from Annemberg, she finally had the bright idea to try calling Leda. Maybe she was only prevented from getting in touch with people in the city. She asked to borrow Roddy's phone again—if she used hers, he would have wondered why she'd borrowed his earlier, and he already thought she was odd—and dialed Husch's private line, one of only half a dozen numbers she knew by heart.

Dr. Husch answered promptly. "You have the wrong number." Marla imagined that was how she answered every call to that line that came from an unknown number.

"It's me, Marla."

"*Marla,*" Leda said. "Good heavens. Hamil called me an hour ago. He was afraid you were dead, or stuck on the moon or in the caldera of a volcano."

"No, I'm alive and . . . well, alive anyway. Look, I'm about ten miles from your place; I found a nice kid to give us a ride. Just wanted you to know I was on the way."

"Ah, you can't speak freely," Leda said. "Of course. But I take your visit to mean you can't get back into the city?"

"True enough."

"And . . . you have a plan to rectify this?"

"Always. I'll fill you in when I get there."

"I'll have an extra breakfast sent up to my rooms for you."

"Make it two. Pelham's with me."

"Who's Pelham?"

"All will be revealed." Marla flipped the phone shut and passed it back to Roddy. Leda's number wouldn't be stored in the phone's memory—neither people nor computers could remember that number without Leda's permission—so she didn't have to "accidentally" drop his phone out the window to keep him from having embargoed contact information.

"Here's fine," she said, and he slowed the car at the crossroads.

"Here? There's no here here! It's a stoplight in the middle of nothing."

"I know where we're going," Marla said. "Thanks, Roddy. Good luck with the philosophizing."

"Good luck with the, ah, incarnation of death." Marla thanked him, sincerely, and hopped out of the car, Pelham following. They waved as Roddy drove off, then Marla set off across a field that wasn't much different from any other field. Once she'd gone a few yards, the illusory camouflage shimmered, the Blackwing Institute's long tree-lined driveway was revealed, and the mammoth bulk of the hospital appeared in the distance. A golf cart was approaching them at a good speed, doubtless piloted by one of the many cheerful, mindlessly obedient homunculi who served as cooks, orderlies, and general assistants at the Institute. Dr. Husch was the only person on staff with a mind of her own, but that was okay. She had only about a dozen patients—fewer, now that Ayres was out—and some of them didn't even require therapy, only containment, like Elsie Jarrow, the insane chaos magician, or Norma Nilson, the nihilomancer, who had an aura of despair so palpable it could make rattlesnakes commit suicide.

The golf cart pulled up alongside them, and Marla and Pelham hopped on. The scrub-clad homunculus driving turned the cart around and drove them to the house, without a word.

Dr. Husch was waiting on the steps for them, wearing a severe black dress that somehow only made her seem sexier, in an untouchable vintage blond movie star sort of way. She kissed Marla's cheek, which was an overwhelming display of affection for her; she must be really worried about all this. She stepped back and regarded Marla and Pelham. "You're both bedraggled. Come in. There's coffee."

Marla followed her through the imposing front doors, into a marble-floored foyer, and up a grand staircase. "This is the hospital?" Pelham said, looking around. "It rivals the Chamberlain's house in splendor."

"It's a nuthatch, yeah," Marla said. "But it used to be a mansion, built by Mr. Annemann, an old-school sorcerer. He was a master of creating artificial life—homunculi. There's a whole army of his homunculi here, dressed like orderlies. They work at whatever you dress them as, and they eat lavender seeds and earthworms. It's messed up."

"With the kind of money Marla provides to fund the facility, I can only afford staff who don't need to be paid." Dr. Husch paused in her ascent of the stairs to scowl down.

"What happened to Mr. Annemann? His name sounds familiar," Pelham said.

"Oh, he's still around," Marla said. "He's in a hospital bed, in a coma. Dr. Husch takes good care of him." She glanced up. Leda was walking stiffly, but she usually did, so it was hard to tell if she was made nervous by the line of Marla's conversation. Probably not. Leda knew Marla well enough to know she would be discreet. "She was his apprentice, and after he went to Comaville, she kindly offered her services as a therapist and jailer and zookeeper for sorcerers who go cuckoo and become a danger to themselves and others and me."

That was mostly the truth. Annemann *was* in a coma, though Leda was the one who'd put him there, shooting him in the head with a little pistol years ago. Though she looked like a normal human woman, Leda was actually one of Annemann's homunculi, an imitation of humanity created to be a sex toy—dolled up properly, she'd look like a nineteen-year-old sex kitten, which was why she affected more severe dress these days, trying to hide her light under a tight librarian's bun and business suits. Annemann had made her too well, though, and unlike his other creations, she'd had a mind and motives of her own, and despite her creator's aloofness and occasional cruelty, she grew to care for him deeply.

Naturally, she assumed he'd secretly cast a love spell on her.

Over time, she came to resent the spell, the way it made her feel, the way he treated her like an object, and so she shot him, hoping to kill him and break the spell. Marla imagined that she'd wept when she pulled the trigger. The bullet had ravaged Mr. Annemann's brain, and any spell he'd cast would have dissolved when his consciousness did . . . but Leda had gone on loving him, which suggested he'd never cast a spell on her at all. She'd been laid low by grief and guilt, and as a result, she'd chosen to dedicate her life to helping sorcerers who'd lost their minds. Lots of sorcerers called themselves "Dr. This-and-that," but Leda was rare in that she actually had a couple of doctorates, having gone to grad school with false papers. She was good at her job, and

Marla admired her toughness, though they got on each other's nerves if they spent too much time together.

Leda showed them into her modest apartments, which were perfectly homey aside from the wall of high-tech surveillance equipment that allowed her to monitor her patients twenty-four hours a day. Leda didn't sleep. Some of her patients didn't, either. A homunculus in a lab coat watched the screens, wearing a pair of oversized headphones, and he paid them no attention at all, focused on his charges.

"Sit and eat." Leda pointed them to a small dining table set with silver trays.

Marla dropped into a chair at the head of the table and leaned forward, inhaling the welcome smell of coffee, bacon, eggs, toast, hash browns, and silver-dollar pancakes. "My compliments to the homunculus you stuck a chef's hat on," Marla said, and dug in. Pelham made a more formal thank-you and began eating, too.

"So," Dr. Husch said. "Your plan is . . . ?"

"Government in exile, for now." Marla snapped a piece of bacon in half. "This is too crispy. Bring me a phone, we'll call Hamil and tell him how to arrange things. Damned if I'm going to let some uppity death god try to call the shots in my city. We'll make life so unpleasant for him that he'll beg to leave."

"You haven't called him yet?" Leda snapped her fingers, signaling an orderly. "I just assumed . . ."

"My phone didn't work," Marla said. "Neither did the phone I tried to borrow. I think Mr. Death put some bad mojo on me, made it so I can't contact my troops. Pelham can't call them, either, because magically speaking, he's indistinguishable from me—it's a long story. What do you know about how things stand in the city? Is Rondeau okay?" She wasn't too worried—Rondeau was a survivor, but there was a difference between just surviving and being okay.

"He's in hiding, according to Hamil. He gave Death an earful of Cursing and escaped in the chaos."

"Nice." It was good to hear Mr. Death could be harmed, not just by her dagger, but by Curses, too. Those weaknesses gave her hope there might be others. "Look, since I can't contact them directly, do you mind passing messages for me?"

"I don't have much choice." An orderly appeared with a tray holding an old-fashioned rotary phone on a long cord. He set it on the table, and Leda dialed with quick precision. "Hamil," she said, after a moment. "Marla apple camera scowl." She frowned. "What do you mean you don't understand? I *said,* 'Marla sandal scissors glass!' "

"Shit," Marla said softly. "You're talking gibberish, Leda. Give me the phone."

Frowning, confused, Leda handed over the phone, but before Marla even got it to her ear she heard the squeal and crack of static and feedback. "Damn it," she said, and gave back the phone. "Tell him . . . tell him what the weather's like."

"Hamil, the weather here is clear and a little cool, but I suspect it will get hotter as the day goes on."

"Now tell him what I'm eating," Marla said.

"Marla panda swamp toilet casket—damn it, stop interrupting!" she said, annoyed.

"It's weaponized aphasia," Marla said. She shoved her plate away, her appetite gone. "Tell Hamil you'll call him back."

"I . . . we'll talk again soon." Leda hung up. "Aphasia? I wasn't saying the words I thought I was saying?"

"No. Whenever you tried to say something about me, it just turned to gibberish and nonsense." She sighed. "I guess we should stay hopeful. Got something to write with?"

Leda called for a notepad and a pen.

"Okay, try to take dictation. 'Hamil, I need you to get rid of Ayres, because right now he's the only one providing Death with intelligence about our operations.' Okay, read that back."

"Hamil, emu candle tonal hepatitis," Dr. Husch said miserably. "The words looked right when I *wrote* them, but now . . ." She shook her head.

Marla snapped her fingers and gestured, then took the pen and notepad and tried to write her own note. When she lifted pen from paper, there was nothing but gibberish written there, all the wrong words. Death was mucking with their minds, tweaking the language-using centers of their brains and making it impossible for Marla to convey a message to her associates in the city. "Maybe if Hamil came here," she said thoughtfully. "But then, he probably couldn't carry messages or orders back, either. Information can get out, to reach me—I'm sure Death wants me to know what's happening in Felport, that he's in control—but I can't send any information in. Death is smarter than I thought."

"If he's truly a god, Marla, then the universe . . .

contorts itself to suit him." Leda shook her head. "I don't know what you can do to stop him. This is more than the magic mortals do. Have you considered giving in to his request? Just handing over the dagger?"

Marla grunted. "Things aren't that bad yet, Leda."

The doctor raised one perfect eyebrow. "You've been banished from your city. You can't get back in, and you can't give orders to your lieutenants. Your home is occupied by an ancient and formidable power. How could it be worse?"

"The difference between you and me is, I've got a lot more imagination," Marla said. "I need to grab a shower. I think best in the shower. You mind?"

"Of course not. You know where the bathroom is."

"Thanks." Marla tossed her napkin onto her plate and left the room, trying not to show how tired and dirty and beaten-down she felt.

Standing under the steady pounding stream of hot water, Marla tried to relax her bunched-up muscles, but her body was just as tense as her mind. She closed her eyes and stood in steam and wetness, poking and prodding at her problem with all her strategic and tactical know-how, but every stratagem struck one unavoidable problem: she couldn't get into the city. How could she wage a battle when the battleground was so far away? She wasn't just defeated, she was irrelevant. Death was in her home. It wasn't enough for him to rule the underworld—oh, no, he had to go walking in the world at large and take over her city, to leave behind his land of the dead and fuck with her city of the living . . .

She opened her eyes. She had an idea. It was a big idea. Possibly a stupid idea. But it was certainly the last thing in the world Death would expect her to do.

Marla got out of the shower, toweled off, and put on one of Leda's oversized terry-cloth robes. By the time she went into the living room, where Pelham and Dr. Husch were comparing techniques for polishing silverware, Marla was grinning.

"Hey, Leda," she said. "Let me borrow your phone again."

"Who can you possibly call?"

"Just a friend of mine who can help me with my new plan."

"And what plan is that?"

"I'm going to invade the underworld," Marla said.

7

By noon the day after Marla's banishment, Rondeau had a base of operations in the Wolf Bay Café, a funky little place by the beach with a kitschy Native American theme, decorated with airbrushed posters of translucent wolves superimposed over the moon and befeathered dream-catchers dangling from the roof beams like outré spiderwebs. The café was frequented mostly by ordinaries, but the owner was a minor sorcerer and a Marla Mason loyalist, so she gave Rondeau use of the back room, which appeared to be a storage space for extra tables and chairs. Still, he was in no position to be picky. At least he had a place to rest his weary ass, and a protocol for secretly contacting Hamil and Ernesto, his agents on the inside. What he didn't have was any earthly idea at all what he should be doing.

Rondeau sat at a table, sipping a large strong coffee, pondering his options. The apprentices in the city were abuzz, and Rondeau was good at picking out bits of choice information, though most of what he heard was doubtful or just outright wrong—Marla was dead, Marla had abdicated, Marla's closest advisors had sold her out; the Walking Death was the angel Lucifer, he was the secret leader of the Slow Assassins, he was Marla's brother; Rondeau had mortally wounded Death, he had taken a bullet meant for Marla, he was hiding in the sewer wearing Marla's cloak. Ha. He wished.

He wasn't sure how to lead a resistance in a city where only one in a thousand people even knew there was a hostile occupation going on. It wasn't like he could bomb Death's offices, or poison the food of the god's troops, or try to rally the citizens in a popular uprising. Marla's was a shadow government, a secret empire of magic and criminality. Marla and her kind protected the city from interdimensional invasions and hostile spirits and evil wizards, and in exchange, the mayor and police chief cheerfully let them have illegal gambling operations, run unregulated import-export businesses, and make unhindered real estate deals. It was symbiosis. But now Death had taken Marla's place, and the civilian government wouldn't care, as long as he kept the werewolves from the door. And while other sorcerers would surely chafe at being under the thumb of a god, they wouldn't necessarily struggle too much as long as their business and studies could continue. Rondeau began to wish he'd asked for a giant slug of whiskey in his coffee, just to make his uselessness more bearable for himself.

"Rondeau? I'm here to help you however I can."

Rondeau looked up from his cup. An Asian man with round rimless glasses and a damp-looking complexion stood before him. "You're Mr. Beadle," Rondeau said. He was good with names and faces, which was one reason Marla liked having him around. "You work for Hamil, right?" Beadle bowed. Rondeau tried to remember his specialty. "You're, like the opposite of a chaos magician, right?"

"I prefer order to entropy, yes," Beadle said. "I was distressed when this Walking Death character appeared. The city was finally approaching a stable equilibrium, and now, well . . ." He twisted his mouth in distaste. "May I sit?"

"Sure, sure," Rondeau said. "So. You're my resistance, huh?"

"Oh, there are others. Langford, of course, is eager to join us, though he'll expect to be paid—Hamil will take care of that. And Ernesto is lending us the use of Partridge."

"Now we're cooking." Langford was an independent contractor, and a biomancer—a sort of cross between a sorcerer and a scientist. He'd done a lot of work for Marla, and was knowledgeable and capable of cool shit. As for Partridge . . . well, Partridge just burned things. Sometimes burning things was what you needed. "I think we can scare up some help from the Honeyed Knots and the Four Tree Gang if we need more hands, too," Rondeau said. The gangs were made up of disgraced apprentices, alley-wizards, and minor magicians who lacked the discipline or inclination to become real sorcerers, but they could be useful—most knew just enough to be dangerous.

"Yes, we have personnel," Beadle said. "And I can

help with the logistics of any operations. But, if I may ask . . . what are we doing, precisely? My instructions were brief and somewhat cryptic."

"We're the resistance." Rondeau shrugged. "We're supposed to get Death to leave Felport."

"And how do we do that?"

"We make sure he doesn't have any fun. We make his life *miserable*. This isn't like some political occupation, you know? Death could have just killed Marla, but he wants to play at being king up here where the breathing people hang out. So we'll make sure it sucks for him. I get the feeling he's not used to a lot of backtalk where he's from. The dead are probably easy subjects to lord over. Let's show him how living people resist."

"Thank you," Beadle said, apparently with real sincerity. "That's exactly what I was hoping for. A mission statement. A vision. I'm no good at those, you see—setting policy isn't my gift."

"So what is your gift?"

"Implementing policy," Beadle said. "Tell me: how do you feel about bombs?"

"I feel pretty good about them."

"This will do." The Walking Death looked down from the windows of the penthouse on the sunny summertime glory of Felport's gleaming financial district and, in the distance, the bay. He held a fine cigar he'd found in the apartment.

"It's a lovely place, sir." Ayres joined him on the balcony. "This was the sorcerer Sauvage's apartment, and before him, it belonged to Somerset. Both great men, though the latter was greater than the former. Marla inherited this place when she took over as chief sorcerer, but . . ." He shook his head. "She chose to preserve it as a memorial to Sauvage, and to go on living in some horrible fleapit of a place near the docks. I can't understand her at all."

"She does seem a bit inscrutable." Death leaned on the balcony. "I love the air and the view here, Ayres. The air and the view in my realm? Not so pleasant, I assure you." He took a drag on his cigar, then blew a few smoke rings into the wind. "You living people certainly know how to live. Where's Booth?"

"Tracking down the last of your appointments, my lord."

"Mmm. I have to talk to more of them, do I?"

"It's best, my lord." Death had gone around and visited a few of the city's leading sorcerers—Granger, and Nicolette, and Ernesto, and Hamil—who had all reacted as Ayres had predicted. Their misgivings were ultimately irrelevant, of course. Once Death proved his power by neutralizing their sad attempts to attack and fight him, they all bowed their heads. Death hadn't forced any of them to swear loyalty in circles of binding, however, which meant they could betray him. Ayres had asked why he took no precautions against treachery, and Death laughed. "Any feeble attempts at resistance will be more amusing than annoying, I'm sure. Besides, I'm a god, and we always keep our promises, which is why we make so few of them. Any circle of binding requires a certain degree of reciprocity, you see, for the magic to balance—I'd be forced to promise something in exchange for their promises, and I'd just as soon avoid the bother. If you knew you were going to exist for as long as *I* am, you'd be less promiscuous with your own promises."

Death still needed to see the other sorcerers, though, so Nicolette and Booth had gone to fetch them. The apartment door opened, and Booth came in, scowling, followed by the Chamberlain, who was as elegant as always.

"The black bitch is here," Booth said, and Ayres quickly crossed the room and struck him across the face, hard enough to rock his illusory head back on his illusory shoulders.

"Do not insult your betters," Ayres said. "Or I will make your bones lie down again."

"She's no better of mine." Booth rubbed his cheek, expression strangely thoughtful. "She's pretty for a colored, I'll grant you, but she's uppity."

"You'll have to forgive Booth." Death strolled in from the balcony. "He's the product of another era, and he was rather unreconstructed even then. Still, for as long as he's been dead, you'd think he'd realize you're all the same color underneath."

"I have other people to track down for you, sir." Booth bowed to Death.

"Yes, shoo," Death said, and Booth left, without glancing at either Ayres or the Chamberlain.

For her part, the Chamberlain only looked at Death. "Should I judge you by the company you keep?"

"I don't care how you judge me. Booth hates black

people, and also Yankees, and uppity women, and it's all very tedious. I don't know how he musters the enthusiasm, honestly. I don't care enough to hate any of you."

"You only exist because of us," the Chamberlain said. "You are defined by us, by our cessation. When the last human dies, you will die with her."

"Oh, no, no. I'm the death of all living things, from cockroaches to whales to kudzu to yogurt. Humans are just the most entertaining, because you worry about death so much, and think so hard about the aftermath. There is no afterlife for a field of corn, you know, when it's mown down. But you humans, you just have to go somewhere, and you all come to me."

"And yet, here you are, come to us. Are you going to offer me a seat?"

"Common courtesy is for those who care," Death said. "Listen, swear your loyalty to me, would you? I'd like to sample some of the scotch in that cabinet."

The Chamberlain crossed her arms. "I am willing to accept your rule in this city, for now, but you should know—the Founders' Ball is this weekend, and if you rule the city, you must host the party."

"Do not give the lord of death an ultimatum," Ayres said. "How dare you?"

The Chamberlain ignored him, as she always, always had when she'd met him in the past, and it made Ayres's blood boil for the hundredth time.

"A ball, hmm? For whom?" Death seemed mildly curious.

"The ghosts of the founding families of Felport demand tribute every five years. An elaborate party, honoring their efforts to create this city. If the party is not held . . ." She shook her head. "They'll destroy it all. You won't have a city to run by morning."

Death laughed. "You think I'm afraid of ghosts? They're just refugees from my realm! If they fuss, I'll toss them into the deepest Hell I have. They won't dare bother me."

The Chamberlain stiffened and gained an inch in height, which was impressive, given how tall she already held herself. "The ghosts of the founding families deserve more—"

"Settle down," Death said. "It's fine. I love a good party. We never have parties in my realm. How about this: we'll have a grand masque. Everyone will come in costume. I'll drag up some of the greatest musicians in my realm for the night, I'll use all my glamours to make the ballroom into a pleasure palace to rival Xanadu, and I'll pull subjective time like warm taffy and make the night seem to go on for days. Will that be acceptable? I bet it will outclass whatever *Marla* had planned."

The Chamberlain curtsied formally. "Indeed, my lord."

Death waved her away, and she swiftly departed. "Who's next?"

"Only Viscarro and the Bay Witch," Ayres said. He wondered if Viscarro would come out of his hole, or if they'd have to go into the vaults after him. Death and Ayres returned to the balcony, this time with drinks in hand, and took in the view for a few moments, until the doorbell sounded.

"I've got the Bay Witch," Nicolette said, barging in,

white overalls spattered with paint, charms dangling from her dreadlocks. She was a chaos magician, a relatively new addition to the top of Felport's magical hierarchy, and had never liked Marla much anyway. She'd become an eager ally of Death. "Come on in, hon."

"I don't like it this far above sea level." The Bay Witch entered tentatively, looking past them to the window and the glimmer of the bay's waters beyond. She was, Ayres thought, the oddest of Felport's sorcerers—she looked like a blond surfer-girl in a blue wetsuit, dripped seawater wherever she went, and was happy only when she was in the waters of the bay. Ayres wasn't sure what she did down there—talked to fish, cleaned up pollution, just swam around? As far as he knew, she had no business interests, no apprentices, no enemies. Technically she also oversaw some of the small islands in the bay, but by all accounts she preferred to stay under the waves. She was barely part of the ruling party of Felport at all, but she'd been friendly with Marla, who always included her in their councils, so here she was.

"Oh, my," Death said. "Aren't you briny?"

The Bay Witch looked at him quizzically. "You're the new boss? Different from the old boss?"

"I am the Walking Death. This is my city now. Will you be loyal to me?"

"Are you the death of everything, or only people things?"

Death blinked. Not even he was sure how to deal with her, it seemed. "All living things."

The Bay Witch nodded. "I need you to kill all the quagga."

"Quagga?" Death said. "Is that some kind of . . . slang term? An ethnicity? Are you asking for a genocide?"

"They're clams," Nicolette said. "The whole way over, she's been bitching about clams."

"Quagga. And zebra mussels." The Bay Witch crossed her arms. "Invasive species, taking over the bay. They're thick on the sea floor, I can't kill them all. You can kill them all?"

"I . . . yes, I could," Death. "But why should I?"

The Bay Witch shrugged. "Marla would have, if she could have, which she couldn't, I guess."

"Is this . . . a condition of your loyalty?" Death said.

"What? The quagga, I said. They're killing the bay." She spoke slowly, as if talking to an idiot. "Kill them, or all the native species will be crowded out. Will you do it?"

"Ah. I suppose. I can't see why not." He went to the balcony and looked toward the water. "All right," he said after a moment. "They're dead."

"Good," the Bay Witch said. "I owe you a favor, then, okay? Let me know when you want it." And then she left, almost running from the apartment, but not as if she were running from something; instead, like she was running toward her favorite thing.

"Crazy witch," Nicolette said. "But that's as close to a loyalty oath as you're going to get out of her, probably. She takes owing favors seriously. I think because barter is the most sophisticated economic model she can comprehend. I'm going to look for Viscarro."

"You people certainly do ask for a lot of things," Death said.

"Such is the plight of the leader," Ayres said. "Your subjects in the underworld never ask you for things?"

"Oh, yes, a cessation of pain, freedom, etc. But that's like asking for the sun to stop shining. They rail against the fundamentals of their conditions. They don't ask me for *favors*."

"Here, you may rule with honey or the whip or both," Ayres said.

"I just want Marla to give me what's mine. I thought she'd roll over quicker than this, I must admit, but it seems she wants to be stubborn. She'll learn the extent of her limitations soon enough, I'm sure, and surrender. In the meantime, I want to be entertained, and prove I can do her job standing on my head."

"Being a leader does have advantages," Ayres said. "What would you like?"

"I'm new to the flesh," Death said. "I like cigars. And I like scotch. What else do you recommend?"

"Ah. I can think of . . . a few things. But I haven't spent time in the city in a few years. I'll have to make some inquiries."

"Do." Death poured himself another drink.

"Perhaps I should prepare a room for *you*," Dr. Husch said over lunch. "I think you could use some therapy."

Marla yawned. After announcing her plan, she'd crashed in the spare bedroom, sleeping peacefully because, at last, she knew what to do. She wasn't completely awake now, though the plate of spicy sausage and peppers was doing wonders for restoring her energy. "I'm not crazy, Leda. I'm just bold."

"Mmm," Dr. Husch turned to regard Pelham, who ate with great delicacy and precision, chewing every bite thoroughly. "Mr. Pelham, do you think Marla is insane?"

Pelham dabbed at his mouth before answering. "It would be inappropriate for me to . . ."

"Oh, be honest," Marla said.

Pelham cleared his throat. "Your plan, in its bare outlines, does seem a trifle incautious, Ms. Mason."

Marla shrugged. "I don't see why. If Death is in my city, that means his city—or realm, or whatever—is lacking leadership. I'll go down there, kick the living shit, if you'll excuse the expression, out of whoever stands in my way, and take control. Then we'll see if he's amenable to a little exchange of hostages. I'll be back in Felport in no time, and he'll know I'm not somebody to fuck with."

"How do you know he won't just kill you?" Leda said.

Marla grinned. "After he sees what I can do, the last place in the world he'll want me is in his underworld."

Leda sighed. "Your self-regard is formidable as always. Fine, then, a more practical question—how do you plan to get to the underworld? It's not a place living people are supposed to go. There's debate on whether or not it even exists."

"Oh, it exists," Marla said. "I believe the guy in my city is the incarnation of Death—how else could he be that badass?—and if he's real, that tells me his realm is real, too. As for how I'll get there, don't worry about it. I know a guy. What time is it on the West Coast?"

Leda checked her watch. "Around noon."

"Even movie stars should be out of bed by now," Marla said, and went to the phone, which still sat on the dining table. She dialed rapidly, and after a few rings, a familiar voice answered.

"Bradley Bowman, as I live and breathe," Marla said. "How the hell are you?"

"Marla?" B sounded surprised to hear from her, reasonably enough; Marla wasn't much for chatting, and as far as she was concerned, phones were an intermittently necessary evil. "I'm . . . well, it's complicated, but not too bad. How are you? How's Rondeau?"

"I'm bad. And Rondeau's probably in deep shit, too."

"What can I do to help?" he said, and there was a little warm blossom of happiness in Marla's heart. B was one of the few people in the world she would help out with no questions asked—well, not many questions anyway—and it was gratifying to know he felt the same way about her.

"When I was in San Francisco, you told me about a train you saw once. Do you remember?"

He paused. "Shit. Marla, do you have a butler now?"

She frowned. "Um . . . he's a valet, but yeah, I can see how you'd make that mistake. Why?"

"I had one of *those* dreams last night." B was a seer—he was more than that, too, but prophetic dreams were one of his more obvious gifts. "There was a man in a black suit; he looked like a butler, I thought, carrying a great big suitcase monogrammed with the initials 'MM,' the letters intertwined. He was running like hell along a platform, chasing a train. I knew the dream meant something, but I didn't recognize the guy, and I haven't had time to find an oracle to interpret it for me. I didn't think about it, but the initials, 'MM,' that could be you." He sighed. "So, yes, I remember telling you about that train. But Marla, whatever you're trying to do . . . Hell. Who do I think I'm talking to? If you've decided, you've decided."

"I'm always willing to hear your counsel," Marla said. She'd met B during her trip to San Francisco the winter before. He was a former movie actor who'd lost his promising career when he began having visions and prophecies, his behavior becoming increasingly erratic and his psyche ever more fragile. Marla had helped him come to terms with his gifts, and had even found him a powerful teacher to help train him as a sorcerer.

"This train, if you take it to bring someone back . . . it doesn't work out the way you'd hope. Trust me. I know."

"I'm not going in after anyone, B," Marla said. "I've got other reasons for wanting to get down there. Can you help me?"

"I can take you to the place where I saw the train," B said. "Based on that dream I had, if it's really about you and your . . . valet? . . . then there's a good chance the train will come."

"Good man," Marla said. "I'll call you once I get a flight figured out. Tell your boss man I'm coming, would you?"

"Sure," B said, and he sounded suddenly weary. "I'll let him know as soon as he wakes up."

"Cole is still sleeping?" Marla said. "It's late there. He always struck me as the up-with-the-dawn type."

"He's . . . sleeping a lot lately," B said. "I'll tell you about it when you get here."

Marla hung up. "That's that," she said. "We've got a ride. Pelham, I don't guess I can convince you to hang out here with Dr. Husch?"

"I should go where you go, Ms. Mason," Pelham said. "I'm sure I can be of assistance."

"Pelham, I'm going to *Hell*," Marla said. "Literally. Some kind of underworld anyway, though I don't know if there'll be fire and pitchforks. You're used to fancy mansions. Really, I'll understand."

He frowned. "I would prefer to accompany you, ma'am."

Marla held up her hands. "Okay. Just making it clear this is your own free will here; I'm not forcing you." She turned to Dr. Husch and smiled her biggest, sunniest smile, which used muscles she almost never utilized. "So, Leda, my friend . . . can you loan Pelham and me some cash so we can buy plane tickets? And arrange a ride to an airport for us? Um, an airport that isn't Felport International, since I'm guessing I can't get to that one without puking my guts up?"

Dr. Husch narrowed her eyes. "You want *me* to loan *you* money?"

"Come on," Marla said. "I got you all that fancy surveillance equipment."

"Only after someone escaped from the hospital and

nearly destroyed your city," Dr. Husch said, frowning. "Do you know how much it costs to heat this place? You do realize I'm feeding you peppers from my garden, and the cheapest sausages known to mankind? Things here are run on a shoestring, as you know."

"Leda, this is important," Marla said. "When I'm back in Felport, you know I'll pay you back with interest—"

"If your ridiculous plan doesn't end in tragedy, you mean, killing you and your innocent manservant," Dr. Husch interrupted. "Which is by no means a certainty. I don't know how I can in good conscience—"

"We both know you're going to give me the cash," Marla said, annoyed. "Can we quit wasting time here?"

"Your tone is not—"

"If I may," Pelham said politely. "I believe we can pay for plane tickets, Ms. Mason. I know several of your company credit card numbers by heart, which should be sufficient to purchase tickets via the phone or the Internet."

They both looked at Pelham, and he blinked, apparently embarrassed by the scrutiny. "Company cards?" Marla said. "I have those?"

"Rondeau showed them to me."

"What company?" Marla said.

"Cloak and Dagger Property Management," Pelham said.

Marla chewed her thumbnail. "That sounds kind of familiar," she said at last. "Rondeau thought the name was funny. We own a lot of property in the city, do a lot of rentals. I guess it makes sense to have company cards, but Hamil handles all that stuff, I mean the money details. I just go down and scare the drug dealers away from the buildings if they get out of hand, you know?"

"At any rate," Dr. Husch said, "it seems I won't have to violate my personal policy against loaning money to friends. I find it only puts a strain on the relationship."

"I'll strain our relationship," Marla said. "We still need some walking-around money for cabs and shit."

"As for incidental expenses, I have several hundred dollars drawn from petty cash, which Rondeau encouraged me to carry," Pelham said. "He told me you seldom carry funds, so I took the liberty of preparing for contingencies. I left a receipt, of course."

Marla grunted. "Well, okay, then."

"If you have a computer, Dr. Husch?" Pelham said, and Leda directed him toward her office.

Marla and Dr. Husch sat together at the table in silence for a moment, then Dr. Husch said, "He seems quite competent."

"He's doing pretty good for his first time out of the house. But I think a descent into the depths of Hades might be a little too much for him. I'm hoping I can convince him to stay with my friends in San Francisco."

Dr. Husch reached over and covered Marla's hand with her own. "You'll be careful, won't you? You're the greatest friend this hospital has ever had."

Marla raised her eyebrow. "As much as you bitch and moan about not getting enough funding?"

"Sauvage and Somerset were even worse. But just because you're better doesn't mean it's enough." She paused. "I'm . . . sorry about Ayres. For the trouble he's caused. I know he's mixed up in this somehow."

Marla nodded. "I don't know if he's the reason Death came to town, or if Ayres was just happy to serve him when he did show up. I mean, he's a necromancer—I'm not surprised he picked Death over me. I didn't give him much reason to be loyal to me, honestly."

"Still, if I'd kept him confined here . . ."

"No, no. You did right. As far as I can tell, he doesn't believe he's a stinking corpse anymore, which means you did your job, cured him. He wasn't confined here for being an opportunistic backstabbing power-hungry asshole. Ayres had a hand in fucking me over, I'm sure, but he was sane when he did it. Don't blame yourself."

Pelham came back into the room. "I had to pay dearly, but I found a flight from Magnus County Regional Airport to Chicago, and from there to San Francisco, leaving tonight."

"Cow country airport," Marla said. "It's only a few hours away, but we should get there early to be safe. Thank gods I've got a couple of legit-looking IDs on me. Do you have papers, Pelham? They're draconian at airports nowadays, and you won't get by on your good looks."

"I have my passport, ma'am."

"You've got a passport? But you never even left your yard before yesterday!"

"Still, one must always be prepared," Pelham said reasonably. "I also have a valid driver's license, classed to allow me to drive ordinary vehicles, motorcycles, hazardous-waste tanker trucks, and school buses. The Chamberlain had an instructor come up to the estate to give me the test."

"You didn't even know how to fasten your seat belt yesterday!"

"I never rode in the backseat before that," he said reasonably.

"Well, good. I'm glad you can drive. I hate driving. We can skip the school bus for now, though." She rose. "Speaking of which, Leda, can you spare an orderly to give us a lift?"

"Of course. I wish I could drive you myself. But Norma Nilson has been banging against the walls of her cell all morning, and I need to keep her under observation."

"Fair enough," Marla said, and after a moment's hesitation, she embraced Dr. Husch, a bit awkwardly, and the doctor hugged her almost as stiffly in return.

"Have safe travels," Dr. Husch said. "Come back alive and well. I doubt Death will be a very generous supporter of the mentally ill."

"I'll miss you, too." Marla went to put her boots on.

8

Pelham did surprisingly well on the airplane, after Marla finally got him to settle down and stop asking for things—apparently all the Chamberlain's lessons in air travel had started from the assumption that Pelham and his boss would be traveling in first class, possibly sometime in the 1950s, when people still wore formal wear to fly. He had a little trouble coping with the tiny seats in cattle class, though the flight wasn't crowded, and Marla was pleased they'd gotten a whole three-seat row to themselves. Pelham finally subsided into pensive silence once he realized the "stewardesses" wouldn't be bringing champagne and lobster thermidor, and that, yes, those thin little blankets and sad little pillows were the best they could offer, and no, there really wasn't any way to move the seats in front of them up a bit to provide more legroom. He sat in the aisle seat, so he didn't look out the window, which might have freaked him out, Marla thought—he'd never flown before, of course, and knowing about flight in theory was different from looking down and seeing tiny cities below.

"This isn't very glamorous, is it?" Pelham said about half an hour into the flight, and Marla grunted. She was reading one of those SkyMall catalogs and marveling, as always, at the fundamental idiocy of the human condition; people bought *stuff* to try to make themselves happy, when everyone with any sense knew you became happy by doing things, not having things.

"There's not so much glamour in our business, Pelham. Well, there is in the sense of illusion, but not so much fanciness."

"The Founders' Ball would have been glamorous, I think."

Marla closed her magazine and swore. "I forgot all about the ball. There were more pressing issues. Crap. It's this weekend? Damn it. Last time the ghosts didn't get their party, the Great Fire of Felport was the result. I'm hoping to wrap this business up soon, but hell, I don't really know what we're getting into. Maybe the Chamberlain will make some kind of other arrangements to keep the ghosts satisfied, if she's not busy fighting with the incarnation of Death, but assuming we get back in a few days and the party hasn't been worked on at all, how long will it take you to arrange something?"

"That varies a bit, Ms. Mason. The three-sided triangle of commerce applies—of fast, good, and cheap, you may choose any two. I could create a sad specimen of a party quickly and for relatively little money, though to create something more impressive for a modest outlay would take more time than we will have, I imagine—"

"Don't worry about the money. Money, we got. So you could do something fast if we threw enough cash at it?"

"Of course," Pelham said. "From your conversation with Dr. Husch, I assumed . . . never mind. It's not my place."

"What? You thought I was broke because Leda complains I don't give her enough money? Listen, Pelham, the budget for the Blackwing Institute every year would easily fund a real hospital—the kind with hundreds of patients—with money left over to buy all the doctors gold rims for their car tires. Leda just wants *more* because when she has extra money, she pours it into research projects, paying shamanistic healers and biomancers and aura-manipulators to come work on her craziest, most dangerous inmates. She thinks she can rehabilitate Elsie Jarrow given enough time." Marla shook her head. "I admire Leda's dedication, don't get me wrong, but giving her money is like chucking cash into a black hole, and I could beggar myself and tax the other sorcerers until they were ready to overthrow me, all without making her happy. So we make sure she has enough for basic operations, and a bit more for her research projects, and that's it. But, no, we're okay financially."

"Ah," Pelham said. "I misunderstood. Your office is in Rondeau's apartment, and I understand your home is rather . . . unprepossessing, so I assumed you were under a financial strain."

"I don't live as extravagantly as the Chamberlain does, it's true, but that's just not the kind of life I come from, you know? I wouldn't know what to do with myself in a big old mansion. I don't look at the money stuff too closely, but being chief sorcerer of Felport is a sweet gig. It's like being a crime boss and a feudal lord all rolled into one."

At the "feudal lord" bit, Pelham's eyes lit up, and Marla sighed and went back to her magazine.

Eventually they landed in Chicago, and that's when Pelham started getting twitchy.

"Damn it, Pelly, *run*!" Marla said. They had a tight connection, and their flight was all the way across the airport, naturally. Chicago O'Hare was a huge complex of misery, absolutely thronged with people, and Pelham was trying to walk with care and dignity, apologizing to everyone he jostled.

"Surely they'll hold the plane for us," Pelham said, and then apologized to a fat businessman who ran over Pelham's foot with a giant rolling suitcase.

"Surely they *won't*!"

"Oh, dear. But . . . forgive me, I need to take a personal moment, ah . . ."

Marla stopped by the departures screen, glancing at their flight, which was on time, and, godsdamn it, already boarding. "What are you on about?"

Pelham blushed scarlet. "I need to adjourn to the gentlemen's facilities, Ms. Mason."

"Why didn't you piss on the plane!" She shouted loud enough to make people edge out of her way.

"I—I did not realize there were facilities available, and—"

"Just go, then!" Marla started physically shoving him toward the nearby men's room.

"I beg your pardon?" Pelham said. "I don't mean to slow us down, but I'm unsure—"

"There! Where all those guys are going! With the little sign with a picture of a little guy on it! Go in there and piss, would you?"

"A public restroom?" he said, the way someone else might say, "A dead body?"

"Yes, damn it! What, you think they have special slow-ass valet bathrooms? Go! We need to run!"

Pelham gingerly stepped into the steady line of men going to the bathroom, and Marla tapped her foot, waiting. And waiting. And waiting.

Finally she couldn't wait anymore, and she barged into the bathroom, where Pelham was muttering to himself and scrubbing his hands at the sink.

"Whoa, it must be ladies' night!" a grungy guy with a giant backpack said. "The line for the girls' room too long?" Men at the urinals glanced at her and made various rude or scandalized remarks. Pelham didn't appear to notice.

"What the hell are you doing?" She grabbed his shoulder and spun him around. His eyes were wide and wild, his thin hair mussed, his lips twitching.

"He's been washing his hands for, like, ever," said the guy with the backpack. "He's got that obsessive-compulsive disorder, I bet."

"It's so . . . filthy," Pelham whispered. "A man urinated on the floor. I had to relieve myself into a basin fixed to the wall, and it flushed with a horrible loud sound as soon as I turned away."

"Yeah, it's a motion sensor," backpack guy volunteered.

"And then the sink would not give sufficient water," Pelham said. "There are no knobs, and it seems to spray forth capriciously, with no rhyme or reason—"

"Dude, the sinks have motion sensors, too," backpack guy said, and Marla whirled on him, snarled, and he left with great speed. Marla reined in her anger and patted Pelham gently on the shoulder.

"Come on, Pelly. Stiff upper lip. We must carry on. Okay? We've got a plane to catch. Can you hurry for me?"

"But . . . my hands . . . the conditions here, so unhygienic, I fear—"

"It'll be okay." Marla leaned in close. "I'll sterilize your hands with magic, okay? Whisper a little death word to kill every microbe. Okay?"

Pelham looked at her like a starving man at a doughnut. "Yes, Ms. Mason."

Just then a security guard came in. "Lady, you have to—"

"We're leaving," she said, and started to go.

The guard stepped into her way, and Marla checked her desire to fling him against the wall. That would not help them catch their plane. "Look, miss, really—"

"This is my mentally challenged cousin," Marla said. "Ask any of those idiots snickering by the urinals— he was in here freaking out over germs, and I just came to get him."

"It's true," someone volunteered. "Dude was trippin'."

"You really want to give this place a reputation for hassling retarded guys?" Marla said, and the guard frowned and stepped aside. "Thank you." Marla pulled Pelham out after her.

Pelham didn't speak, but he did sprint, so Marla was content. They got to the gate just as the attendant was closing the doors. "Two passengers here!" Marla bellowed.

The attendant turned on her with a frozen smile and shook her head. "Too late. I'm sorry," she began, and Marla stepped up to her and grabbed her hands.

"Please," Marla said, and threw her mind at the attendant's, an overriding plea, a request that didn't appeal to the conscious mind at all but to some deeper, fundamentally human part.

"Ah, of course," the attendant said, and made a call, and opened the gate.

Marla leaned on Pelham a little as they went down the jetway. "Shit," she muttered. "Blunt-force mind control is a bitch." She just barely made it to their seats. They had two together, miraculously, on a very full flight, and the overhead bins were all full, so it was a good thing they had no baggage besides her rolled-up cloak—she didn't want to call attention to herself in an airport, and a woman in a black-and-silver cloak got noticed. She balled up the cloak into a makeshift pillow, strapped herself in, and passed out. She woke up three hours later with a pounding headache, to darkness outside the plane's windows. She slurred "Water." Pelham had gotten a bottle of water from somewhere, and he passed it to her. She chugged it noisily and moaned. "That sucked. I usually carry some little stones enchanted with one-shot compulsions—they don't hit me so hard. But I don't have any charms with me, and doing it direct mind-to-mind like that, oof, I don't recommend it."

"Ms. Mason, I can't apologize enough," Pelham said. "I lost control, and forced you to strain yourself. I am humiliated."

"Well, yeah," Marla said. "What happened to you back there?"

"Too many people," Pelham said, shaking his head. "In the nightclub, it wasn't so overwhelming. I had something to do, serving drinks, and I hardly stopped to notice the crowds, the sheer number of people—and when I did, I told myself it wasn't many more than had attended the last Founders' Ball, though it was, really. In the airport, surrounded by all those strangers, the press of people . . ." He shuddered. "I'd never seen so many people together all at once, going about their own business. I think, somehow, I didn't realize there were so many people in the world. Oh, I know, there are six billion people on Earth, but that is only a number, and this . . . this was fact, and flesh."

"Wow," Marla said. "So you get anxiety attacks when there are too many people around. Kind of makes sense. No offense, Pelly, but you've led kind of a sheltered life. And you've had a bit of upheaval lately. Yesterday you were in the place you'd lived all your life, and today you've been banished from the whole city. No wonder you freaked a little. It's okay. I hate crowds, too. I don't ever like to be in a group that's bigger than I can incapacitate single-handedly if they get possessed by a malign intelligence. You know. Contingencies."

Pelham almost smiled. "Thank you, Ms. Mason, for being understanding."

"Hell, I'm glad to know you have a weakness. You were getting a little spookily omnicompetent there for a while."

"I try to give satisfaction." He definitely smiled that time.

"What's the movie?" Marla said, glancing at the pretty people on the tiny screen over their seat.

"Something about someone falling in love with someone, but they are currently angry at each other over a simple misunderstanding that could be solved with the briefest of explanations. I . . . do not watch many films. I fail to see the appeal here."

"Wake me when we land," Marla said, and went back to sleep.

"Death is at a brothel," Beadle said, entering the back room of the Wolf Bay Café.

Rondeau whistled. "One of the Chamberlain's fancy houses, or . . . ?"

Beadle shook his head. "One of Ernesto's clubs, not far from the old air force base."

"Rough trade," Rondeau said thoughtfully, and began flipping his butterfly knife open and closed and open again, thinking. "He's secured the loyalty, however temporary, of every major sorcerer in the city, and now he's off having *sex*?"

"For free," Beadle said. "Naturally, as he is king of the sorcerers now. The girls don't know who they work for, but they understand the meaning of 'VIP.' "

"He's probably the kind of guy who leaves dead hookers by the side of the road," Rondeau said.

"I doubt that," Langford said, looking up from his clipboard, which bulged with papers of various sizes. He was thin, bookish, intense, wearing a disturbingly stained white lab coat. "He was probably a virgin not long ago. I suspect he is only recently incarnated. Gods don't normally wear flesh, you see, though sometimes the human mind chooses to see them in human forms, as comprehending their true nature is difficult. But if Death bled from Marla's knife, it seems reasonable to assume he's in a physical body, albeit a magically augmented one. There is some mythological precedent for Death coming to Earth in human form. I suspect that, having a body for the first time, he is attempting to explore the *joys* of that body. Pleasures of the flesh may divert him for a while."

"Hmm," Rondeau said. "So if he's in a body, could we . . . blow him up?"

"Oh, yeah," Partridge said from his table in the far corner. He kept to the shadows—he was scarred all over, and sensitive about it—burning matches and snuffing them between his calloused fingertips, until the whole back room smelled of sulfur. "Let's blow something up."

"He could conceivably be damaged, if caught by

surprise, though he would simply repair his body," Langford said.

"I know we can't kill him, but if he goes someplace expecting a super awesome time and he gets exploded instead, that'll put some piss in his peaches and cream, won't it?" Rondeau said. "Nobody likes pain, and people who've basically never felt pain before *especially* hate it. So let's say he heard there was a powerful sex magician around, maybe Mary Madeline Monroe, eager to show her devotion to the new boss. . . . I know for a fact she's in Thailand right now, but that's not common knowledge, so . . ."

"A decent-enough plan," Beadle said. "I can put it into operation, send certain messages through certain untraceable channels. Death is vain, and an appeal to his vanity may work. I'll try to set up a meeting for tomorrow, in a place we can . . . damage extensively . . . without harming any ordinaries in the process. But it would be more efficient if we can combine this with some other objective. After all, if we know where Death will be, we will have freer access to places where he *won't* be."

"Well," Rondeau said. "I had this idea. Kind of crazy, but, well . . . You know Marla's cloak. Maybe we could get that. And I could put it on."

"Now *that's* a way to do some damage," Partridge said, in his smoke-shattered voice.

"I don't like her cloak," Langford said. "She allowed me to study it once. It . . . resists analysis. There is a certain logic to most magic, however hidden, but the cloak defies understanding."

"It would be a great asset," Beadle mused. "I

calculate that its advantage to our cause would outweigh the dangers inherent in its use. It would give us the potential to strike directly at Death, and allow us to do more than merely annoy him."

"The thing is, it's in her apartment, in a heavily fortified wardrobe."

"Hmm," Beadle said. "There is an order to binding spells. Given time, I could undo them."

"How much time?"

Beadle shrugged. "A couple of days, at a guess, though I'd have to see the spells to be sure."

"So we grab the wardrobe and take it someplace secure," Rondeau said. "And you crack it open. With luck, Mr. Death won't even know something's missing."

Beadle nodded. "Shall I implement this plan?"

"Oh, yeah," Rondeau said, thinking: *Being a leader is pretty sweet. You just say "Do this," and motherfuckers do it.*

Beadle got Langford and Partridge together and talked to them about building bombs, the more magically potent the better—like fragmentation weapons filled with charmed shrapnel, shit like that. Between Partridge's skill for destruction and Langford's technical know-how, Rondeau had hope they'd put together something good. He sat back, grinning. He had a good crew. They had a plan. This was going to work.

"That was fun. Now I'd like to see where Marla lives," Death said, emerging from a shoddy room in Ernesto's brothel. "I can't believe she doesn't have a throne somewhere." Ayres sat out front with the madam. They'd been discussing the good old days when Felport was still an industrial juggernaut and there was a thriving air force base bringing in lots of business for the girls. Booth was pacing out front in the evening air, frustrated that he couldn't have sex, that he didn't even want to have sex, though he'd been quite the ladies' man in life—he had an illusory human form, but underneath, he was all mummy.

"Of course," Ayres said, stifling a yawn. Death didn't sleep. "It's near the waterfront. Though I doubt she has a throne, my lord."

"Ah, well," Death said, cheerful, his assignation having put him in a good mood. "Too bad. Maybe she has *something* good, though."

B was waiting for them at the airport, standing beside a vintage roadster parked in the white zone. He looked scruffily handsome, as always, but a lot less tired than the last time Marla had seen him. Marla embraced him, and he hugged her hard.

Stepping back, she said, "B, this is Pelham; Pelham, this is Bradley Bowman." She looked his car over. "Nice wheels."

"It belongs to Cole," B said. "I can't believe it still runs, but that's magic for you." He glanced around. "Listen, we should probably get out of here and haul ass for the East Bay, okay? Susan Wellstone won't be happy if she finds out you're here."

Marla snorted. Susan had been her biggest rival in

Felport, before she came out west to take control of San Francisco. "My visit doesn't have shit to do with her. Thinks the world revolves around her."

"Yeah, well, nevertheless," B said. "I know you like looking for trouble, but I get the feeling you must have trouble enough already, yeah?"

"I guess I'm pretty well stocked trouble-wise just now. Let's ride." Marla hopped in the passenger seat, and Pelham squeezed into the backseat, which was just about big enough for him.

"I'm gonna head south," B said. "Then cut back across to the East Bay. It's a longer trip, but it gets us out of the city faster."

"San Francisco is hostile territory?" Pelham said. "Oh, dear."

"Susan doesn't have a compelling reason to assassinate me anymore," Marla said, "but I imagine she might give it a try for old times' sake. So, are we going straight to the train? I need to get moving."

"We won't make it tonight," B said, driving away from the airport, past a vast dark expanse of water, onto a freeway with only sparse traffic.

"What the hell? You've got a timetable for the mystery train?"

"It came a little after midnight last time," B said, shrugging. "After the train station was closed. I've got a feeling it'll come at the same time tonight."

"Local time is a bit after 12 A.M.," Pelham said, and yawned, as if realizing how late it was made him tired.

"And we're a long way out from the train station we need," B said. "I mean, maybe any train station will work, maybe it's about *who's* waiting, and not where, but I figure our best shot is to replicate my last experience, right?"

"Right," Marla said, leaning back. "Damn it. Twenty-four hours lost? I can't afford that kind of time."

"I kind of wanted to talk to you about Cole anyway," B said. "And about me, for that matter."

"Problems with Cole?" B's teacher, Sanford Cole, was a legendary sorcerer who'd been present for the founding of San Francisco and served as court magician for the Emperor Norton in the late 1800s. He'd put himself into a state of suspended animation, vowing to return to consciousness only when San Francisco was threatened. Last year, when Marla was in town on unrelated business, San Francisco had very nearly been destroyed, and Cole had awakened and come to her for help in saving his city. He'd decided to stay awake afterward in order to teach B how to use his powers, and help him become a full-fledged sorcerer, instead of just a guy who had prophetic dreams and waking nightmares.

"Yeah. Cole's spending a lot of time asleep. Like, days. And he's pretty much narcoleptic. Right in the middle of a lesson, he'll just drop. He's a tough old guy, Marla, but whatever spell he cast on himself to sleep the decades away, I think it's too strong for him to shake off as easily as he'd expected. It's trying to pull him back under."

"That's rough. He's only been teaching you a few months."

"I've learned a lot, but mostly I've learned how much I have left to learn. And one of these days, Cole is going to fall asleep and just not wake up again—at least, not in my lifetime. I need to figure out what I'm going to do with myself then. Susan Wellstone won't let me be part of her organization in San Francisco because I'm friends with you. Not that I'd want to join up with her, but she's really the only game in town. There's not much of a magical presence in Oakland—the big honcho there is a sex magician named Delanie, and once she realized I wasn't into girls, she lost all interest in me. She doesn't care if I hang around, but she won't teach me or give me work. The sorcerers in Marin are all either snooty or hippies, and neither one appeals to me. The South Bay is all half-crazy technomancers living in gutted buildings that used to be dot-com headquarters before the crash. Not my scene." He shook his head. "I considered Hollywood—I still know some people down there, but they're all ordinaries, and as for the SoCal sorcerers, those guys are nuts. As Cole's apprentice, I have some status, and some options—he still carries a lot of weight around here—but when he's gone, I'll be an outsider again." He sounded frustrated, and Marla's heart went out to him. When she'd found him, he'd known there were monsters in the world, but he hadn't known there were also people like Marla, devoted to *fighting* monsters. She'd shown him a whole subculture, and helped him find a place in it. Now that place was in danger. Marla could sympathize.

"I'll do whatever I can to help, B," she said.

"Great. Because I was hoping I could come out to Felport and be *your* apprentice."

Marla closed her eyes. Taking on an apprentice was

an enormous responsibility, and she already had so many responsibilities that she sometimes felt them as a physical weight. She thought of all she had to do already, every day, and an image of that Rodin statue *Caryatid Who Has Fallen under Her Stone* appeared to her—a woman crushed beneath the weight of the stone she held. But this was B. . . . "Let me talk to Cole," she said at last. "He'd damn well better wake up for me. I have ways of getting a guy's attention that you don't." She paused, expecting Rondeau to make a dirty joke, but of course, Rondeau wasn't here, and she had no idea how he was doing. She was suddenly very tired. "And we'll see if I can even get back to Felport again. Things are bad, B. Really bad."

"Marla—" he began.

"I can't answer you yet. Please. I will, just as soon as I'm able, okay? I promise."

"Understood."

They crossed a long bridge, and Marla felt a stirring of longing for the much smaller bridges that spanned the Balsamo River in Felport. They rode into the East Bay, the hills a darker shade of night in the distance, over and under a tangle of freeway overpasses, down through a grimy downtown that reminded Marla painfully of her own city. B kept driving, finally going up into the hills, on dark and foggy roads, up and up, past redwoods and quiet dark houses, finally cresting a high ridge that gave a clear unobstructed view of the bay and San Francisco beyond. He parked the car on a little strip of gravel. "Cole doesn't like Susan," B explained, "so he didn't want to stay in San Francisco. She kept bugging him constantly, even when he fled to Marin, sending him gifts, trying to get him to 'advise' her, which really meant telling her how great she was. He decided to come here to Oakland, but he wanted a spot with a good view of the city, and it took forever, because most of the hills are so built up. We finally got this place. Susan never bothers us now. People in San Francisco look down on Oakland. Did you know, during the 1906 earthquake and fire, when refugees had to leave San Francisco and come to the East Bay, some of them made signs that said 'Eat, drink, and be merry, for tomorrow we go to Oakland'? Bastards. I like it over here."

"Where's the house?" Marla said.

"Oh, that's the roof there." B pointed at what Marla had assumed was some kind of observation deck. "There are stairs leading down. The house kind of clings to the side of the hill."

"Gods," Marla said. "Tempting fate much? This is earthquake country. Mudslide territory! What if the house falls off?"

B laughed. "Come on, Marla, Sanford Cole lives here. This house isn't going anywhere as long as he's in it."

"All right. I guess he can make it safe. But the idiots who built this house need to be committed for their own safety."

"Earthquakes?" Pelham said nervously. "Mudslides?"

"Also wildfires," Marla said.

"There hasn't been a serious wildfire here in the hills for years," B said. "Though it is wildfire season now. So watch where you toss your matches." He got out of the car, and they followed him down the stairs and into the house. The living room was big, lit by antique lamps that reflected warmly from the gleaming hardwood floors, and sliding doors in the floor-to-ceiling windows gave access to a redwood deck cantilevered out over the hillside, providing an even better view of the lights of the city across the bay.

Sanford Cole, white-whiskered and small, sat in a wooden rocking chair facing the view, head back, snoring.

"He's been like that for two days," B said. "I blew an air horn at him and it didn't wake him."

"I'll make some tea." Pelham bustled off toward the kitchen.

B watched him go, then turned to Marla. "What's the story with him?"

"A long one," Marla said. "But he's a good guy, if a little shaky just now. Look, go ask him to fill you in on why I'm here, okay? Tell him to tell you about the Walking Death. I'm sick of even thinking about it, and I'd rather let Pelham bring you up to speed."

"What are you going to do?"

"Wake up Cole."

"How are you going to do that?"

She chewed her lip for a moment. "You don't really want to know."

B nodded. He knew her well enough not to press that particular line of inquiry any further.

Marla went over to Cole. She leaned forward, putting her face close to his. "Hey, old man, I need a hand." She jostled his arm, and pinched his nostrils shut, and slapped his cheeks, and none of it had any impact. He'd slept in some barrow somewhere for decades at a time, and a few pokes from a visiting witch wasn't likely to rouse him. She sighed. "You're giving me no choice here, Cole." Leaning even closer, she put her lips to his ear. "I'm going to destroy San Francisco," she said. She thought about all her losses, her banishment, her misery, her worry, her fear, and she fed those thoughts into a flickering flame of hate, hate casting around for a target, and it settled on Susan Wellstone, her old nemesis—the last person who'd made her feel as helpless as Death was making her feel now. It wasn't hard to get that hate burning fiercely again. Marla had spent her entire adult life trying to make sure that she was never powerless, and now she'd been pushed into this position of helplessness again, her only hope a mad scheme to invade the underworld, a plan that was less a plan and more a desperate sort of flailing. And Susan had made her feel the same way, out of her depth, desperate. Marla had been forced to make peace with Susan, to come to a compromise, to let her leave Felport and become the queen of San Francisco, and that never sat right with Marla, that such a cowardly scheming conniver should be *rewarded* for her treachery, for her plan to kill Marla. Gods, Susan deserved nothing but pain, and what better way to hurt her than to destroy San Francisco, to summon earthquake, wildfire, mudslide, tsunami, economic downfall, infrastructure collapse, riots, *annihilation*. It would hurt Susan, and it would help Marla let off a little steam, make her feel strong, make her feel potent, make her feel *anything* but helpless. Marla thought about destroying San Francisco. She thought about it seriously. She thought about it seriously *even harder*.

Sanford Cole sat upright and gripped Marla by the throat, choking her with phenomenal strength, and Marla went to one knee, gasping, barely able to break his hold, even though his attack was hardly sophisticated. Cole lunged up out of his chair, looking terrified and suddenly very old. He said, "Marla?" in a voice of infinite bewilderment.

"Sorry, Cole," she said, rubbing her throat, her voice a croak. "You wouldn't wake up. I knew you could never sleep through San Francisco being threatened, so . . ." She shrugged and got to her feet. "I psyched myself out."

"You . . . didn't really mean it."

"Oh, I meant it," Marla said. "Right then, at that moment, destroying San Francisco was my one and only goal. But I don't mean it *anymore*. I just needed you to wake up."

"That's clever." Cole sat down again. "Nasty, mean, rather unconscionable . . . but clever."

"Pelham, make some coffee, too!" Marla shouted. She knelt before Cole. "Good to see you again, old fella. I hear you're having some trouble staying awake."

He sighed, and looked stricken. "It's hard to remain conscious. I want to train Bradley, I promised you I would, but after sleeping for so long, wakefulness is hard, when my city isn't being threatened." He looked longingly toward San Francisco. "And it's changed so much, it saddens me. Susan Wellstone is a perfectly adequate leader, don't misunderstand me, but . . . she's self-righteous. Smug. Elitist. When San Francisco began, it was a jostling boomtown, high and low culture mingled. Oh, there was always a world of difference between Nob Hill and the Barbary Coast, but the divisions didn't seem quite so unbridgeable back then. Or perhaps I'm only a sentimental old fool, viewing the present through a lens of nostalgia."

"B asked me if he could be my apprentice if you went back to sleep," Marla said.

Cole's eyes widened. "He's a *seer*, Marla. A wizard of perception, of finding oracles and magic, of looking-in. You are . . . a different sort of sorcerer."

"I know," Marla said. "You study things, and I kick them. I'd teach him in your tradition as best I can, but some of my flavor is bound to rub off on him. Still . . ."

"A somewhat incompatible teacher is better than no teacher at all," Cole said.

Marla nodded.

"I wish . . . I think . . ." He winced. "I think that might be best. If you took over as his teacher."

"Okay," Marla said, and it was decided. Sanford Cole was one of the wisest and most powerful sorcerers on Earth, and if he said it was for the best, Marla would go along with it, however inconvenient it might prove to be.

Pelham entered bearing a silver tray, a pot each of coffee and tea, and several cups. "I didn't even know we had a full tea service," B said. "Where did you find that?" He noticed his conscious master. "Cole! So good to see you! Has Marla told you why she's here?"

Cole frowned. "I assumed you called her because you were concerned about me."

B shook his head. "No. I mean, I did mention you were having trouble staying awake, but that's not why she's here. It's . . . quite a story." He glanced at Marla. "May I?"

She nodded, and B told Cole about Death's demands, and Marla's banishment, succinctly and accurately enough that Marla only felt compelled to butt in and clarify half a dozen points. When B was done, Cole frowned. "I see. Well. That certainly doesn't sound like the Death *I* know."

"You know Death?" Marla said.

"I should," Cole said. "I'm the man who won the dagger from him."

9

You won Death's dagger?" Marla waved away the cup of coffee Pelham brought to her side.

"Yes, in a Senet game in Egypt, just before I came to America in the early 1700s." Cole accepted a cup of tea, and his eyes took on a faraway look. "I gave it to one of my apprentices, a man named Malkin, before he went off to seek his fortune."

"Everett Malkin?" Marla said. "He was the first chief sorcerer of Felport, back when it was barely just a city!"

"Yes," Cole said, nodding. "He did well for himself."

Marla was stunned. "Why did you never tell me one of your guys founded my city?"

"You must understand, he was only one of countless apprentices I brought with me to the New World," Cole said. "Many of the early chief sorcerers were my men, in New York, Chicago, Pittsburgh, Norfolk, Savannah, Detroit. . . . All dead now, of course, or immortal and mad."

Marla nodded. Cole was partly legendary for his involvement in helping European sorcerers get a foothold in America during the early settlements, sometimes clashing with the local totemic and shamanistic magic in the process. "So you won the knife off Death, and just gave it away?"

Cole shrugged. "In human hands, though useful, it is essentially a weapon, and weapons are not my forte. Malkin was the most accomplished martial magician under my tutelage—indeed, I was a poor fit for him as a teacher." He glanced at B, and then at Marla, but didn't comment further. "I thought he could use it more effectively than I could. I was building a nation in those days, you see, and I tried to make sure everyone had tools to suit them. Felport was a haunted place in those days—'the fel port' the first settlers called it, and an early attempt to make a permanent home there ended with all the inhabitants vanished or dead. Even the natives shunned that place by the bay. Malkin cleaned up the bad element, drove away the dark spirits that dwelt there, and the knife helped him do it. He worked a great magic to make sure the blade would stay forever in that city." Cole shook his head. "But Death would not return for his weapon, not after losing it fairly. He was an honorable god."

"I think that particular Death retired," Marla said. "There's a new god, calling himself the Walking Death."

"Heavens," Cole said. "I'd heard tell of such things, that long ago there was a different Death . . . it makes a certain amount of sense. Death is tied to life, and birth, and rebirth, to the harvest and the tides and the seasons and cyclical things. So the old Death is gone." Cole bowed his head. "He was no crueler than he needed to be, that one, and he was a gracious loser. I'm sorry his son, or heir, or new incarnation, is such a sad replacement."

"What on earth did you wager against his dagger?"

"It was not a dagger then, but a sword," Cole said. "Death's terrible sword. It can cut through anything. Dreams. Hopes. Memories. Ideas. Certainties. In human hands, its powers are greatly diminished. Imagine a child trying to lift a two-handed broadsword—it never could. But a small knife, yes. We mortals are as children to the gods, in strength, at least, and I could not wield the sword, and so it transformed into a dagger when the hilt touched my hand, and a dagger it has remained."

"Interesting," Marla said. "But, again, what did you *bet*?"

"A gemstone, mined from the depths of Hades, according to legend, reportedly the most beautiful jewel in Hell. Death wanted it very much, and I agreed to play a game of chance with him." He shook his head. "I don't have the jewel anymore. I gave it to another of my protégés, to help him found a settlement in the Pacific Northwest. I was so bold in those days, Marla. Nearly as bold as you are now. Invading the underworld." He chuckled. "Good show."

"Do you think it's possible?" Marla said.

"Possible, yes. Possible for *you*? I don't know. The journey will be perilous, even if Bradley can find an entry point for you. How exactly it will prove perilous, I don't know. I've never been to the underworld. But from the hints Death dropped during our long game, I understand it is a mutable place, shaping itself to fit the unconscious expectations of the soul that enters. As malleable as the medicine lands. What do *you* think Hell will be like, Marla?"

"I don't know," she said honestly. "When I was a kid I was generic Protestant, but once I got old enough to think about it I became an atheist. Nowadays I know there are gods, or things so much more powerful than people that we might as well call them gods, but I don't especially worship them—most of them are just as fucked up as people, with no more moral or ethical sense than a jackal."

"They have morals and ethics," Cole said. "Very strict codes, in fact. Just not human ones. There's no telling what Hell will look like for you. But when you get there, fight your way forward, always forward. The direction doesn't matter—direction is a convenience there, a conceit. Just don't backtrack. Eventually, after who knows how long, you should reach the center of that realm, and there you will find a throne. It seems that throne is likely to be empty now, as its rightful ruler is playing house in Felport. All you have to do is sit on the throne, and Hell will be yours to command."

Marla grunted. "That's all it takes? Then why doesn't some dead guy sit on the throne?"

"The dead may not. They cannot sit on that throne any more than you could sit on a throne of water or smoke. And as for the demons and administrators and tormentors who staff Hell, they would never dare. They are merely the fingernail cuttings and stray hairs of

Death, and he can dispel them with a glance, with a thought. Death himself could kill you, of course, and then you would be in his realm, at his mercy. He would have killed you already, I'm sure, but the dagger would just pass to your successor, so your death does him little good. Assuming you survive long enough to sit on his chair, however, you will become like a god, too—and, I suspect, the knife will change to a sword in your hand." He paused. "You will have great power then. Promise me you will only use that power to make Death return your city to you, and trouble you no longer."

"Cole, all I want—"

"*Promise.*" His eyes were suddenly fiery. "You are a human. You should not have the power of a god. You are not bound by the rules they are bound by, and to have such power without such rules would be disastrous."

Marla swallowed. "Okay. Whatever you say. I don't want to rule Hell, Cole. I want Felport back."

"Then I wish you well," Cole said. "Be careful in the underworld, Marla. I've heard stories. The dead . . . they can be dangerous to the living. They may not be rational, reasonable. Some may even be mad."

"You're telling me that dying makes you go bat-shit crazy?"

"Dead people aren't insane," Cole said. "Ghosts are, often, because they are lost, confused fragments stuck in the wrong place. But the dead, when they're in the underworld, are no madder than you or I. However, when faced with a living person, the dead can *become* insane, as the touch of water can send a hydrophobe into a rage. Others may become delusional, lost in time and space, forgetful of whether they're alive or dead. And that confusion can be contagious. Be on your guard. The dead may not be able to kill you—I've heard conflicting reports—but they can confuse you, enchant you, wrap you in illusions that prey on your insecurity and guilt, leave you lost and wandering." Cole yawned enormously. "Forgive me. I think I need a nap." He leaned his head back, and just like that, he was asleep.

"That was more informative than I'd expected." Marla went to sit with B and Pelham on the deck, leaving Cole to his sleep, not that their conversation was likely to disturb him. "That old guy just settled what are, as far as I can tell, millennia-old questions about the nature of death gods and the afterlife. I mean, assuming he's right."

B rolled his eyes. "Cole is always right. It's annoying."

"I'm always right, too." Marla took the cup that Pelham patiently proffered. "Do you find me annoying?"

B said, "I keep asking how old he is, and he won't tell me. I made a joke that I thought he was actually Merlin, and he said Merlin wasn't all he was cracked up to be. I couldn't tell if he was kidding. And now he can't even stay awake."

"He's had a long life. It's no surprise he's tired," Pelham said, and Marla looked at him quizzically. Pelham came out with the funniest things sometimes, things that hinted at depths Marla couldn't imagine. Literally couldn't imagine—how much wisdom or experience or insight could Pelly have possibly developed as a ward of the Chamberlain's estate?

They looked out at the city. Marla was unwinding, almost against her will, as she sipped from her cup. Twenty-three hours before she could make her rush for the underworld. She'd have to spend the time preparing herself . . . somehow. Cole probably had quite a magical library. Maybe she'd study up. Cole had talked about how Death's dagger had formidable powers in the right hands, and she was curious about that, but she doubted he would wake up anytime soon. Maybe his journals would have the answer, if they weren't enciphered.

"So," B said after a while, "did you two decide my fate?"

"Oh," Marla said. "Sure. You can come back with me, assuming we return from the underworld in one piece."

"Marla, that's amazing," B said. "I can't thank you enough. I'll miss the West Coast, but it'll be good to spend time with you and Rondeau."

"I'm going to bust your ass, Bowman. And not in a good way. It's going to be hard work, being my apprentice. Lots of on-the-job training, if you know what I mean. Starting tomorrow. You've been to the underworld before, so I'll need your help."

"About that," B said.

"You've been to the afterlife?" Pelham said, awed. "Truly?"

B squirmed a little, and even in the darkness he looked uncomfortable. "Before I really knew about magic, I had these dreams, and sometimes spirits talked to me, or monsters. Once I realized I wasn't going crazy—or at least that the source of my craziness was external, not internal—I started trying to help the people I dreamed about. One guy wanted me to help him find the underworld, so he could bring back his girlfriend, who'd died from a bee sting."

"Did it work?" Pelham asked.

B shook his head. "I don't know. I never saw him again."

"What was it like down there?" Marla said. "You never told me."

"For me, there were monitor lizards, and trees made of stone, and a cavern so big it had its own night sky, and a woman who had a beehive in her chest. So, basically, it was like one of my prophetic dreams. I think Cole's probably right—it's an individual experience."

"We'll see how it looks tomorrow night, then," she said.

"Marla, I can't go," B said. "The driver of the train was very specific about that. It's a one-time trip—at least, while you're alive. Next time I take that train, I won't be breathing."

Marla frowned. "I could use your help, B. You have a way of communing with the spirits that could be very helpful in a place that's full of them. How about you just get on the train with us, and see what happens?"

"I can't. It's not that I don't want to. I *can't*."

"Why, because of the rules? Screw the rules. Rules are for other people."

B shook his head, clearly uncomfortable with disagreeing with her, which was a reaction Marla supported. "It's not a rule like 'don't step on the grass,' it's a rule like 'every action has an equal and opposite reaction.' A rule of nature."

"Magic is all about breaking the rules of nature. Bending them anyway."

"Marla, the train isn't really a train," B said, exasperated. "It's an event, a trauma, a transposition. It's a magic so big and delicate that it turns your brain inside out and shows you images drawn from your dreams just so you can cope with it, so you can comprehend it. It's mystery with a capital 'M.' Do you remember the oracle we consulted, the Possible Witch, how otherworldly she was, how alien? Or your purple-and-white cloak, the way you feel its mind poking at your brain with tiny little wiry fingers? These are things from outside the Earth, they were around before people were, they'll be around when people are gone. Just because they look like witches or cloaks or trains doesn't mean that's what they are, it's a disguise they wear, it's your brain doing you a favor and draping the transcendent in something opaque, because looking at it directly would burn out your mind and your soul and your humanity." He was almost shouting by the end, his voice loud and booming, a well-trained actor's voice, though he wasn't pretending, just projecting.

"Huh," Marla said. "I guess Cole has been training you well. Okay, you can't go; I understand. I'm just pissed about it, is all. I really could use your help."

B laughed, a little nervous, a little relieved.

"I will join you, Ms. Mason," Pelham said.

Marla patted his shoulder. "I know you will, Pelham. I'm counting on you, too." In truth, she wondered how

Pelham would cope. He'd freaked out in a crowded airport terminal. How would he react in the throng of the dead who surely inhabited the underworld? Then again, maybe Hell was an empty place. She could imagine it both ways.

"Guess I'd better get some sleep," B said. "Big night tomorrow, huh?"

"Can you point me toward Cole's books?" Marla said. "I think I should do some reading. I slept on the plane."

"What shall I do, Ms. Mason?" Pelham said.

"You'll have to entertain yourself, Pelham. I'm all out of projects for the moment." He was a needy little valet. He'd been helpful, too, sure, but he was not so much out of his depth as utterly out of his element. Taking him to the underworld . . . gods. She only hoped she could bring him back alive. "I'll see you in the morning," she said, and followed B to the library downstairs.

"It's a squalid, fetid pit," Death said, kicking aside an old footstool in Marla's living room. He'd gotten past her formidable defenses by simply pushing open her door—all the runes hacked around the door frame had glowed blue and then sparked and gone dark, shorted out by his godhood.

"There's aluminum foil on the rabbit ears of the television," Ayres said, half-awed, half-disgusted. Both Death and Booth looked at him with bewilderment. Neither one of them understood how old and chintzy and ridiculous that was, and Ayres knew if he tried to explain, they'd look at him like he was doddering and irrelevant. "Perhaps her bedroom will be more interesting." Ayres led the way, pushing her bedroom door open with his walking stick in case there were booby traps. There were none.

The room was messy, the bed unmade, the closet door open and spilling mounded clothes. While Death examined the closet, Booth went to her bedside table and picked up a book, then laughed. "Look at this," he said. "It says it's an 'alternate history' of the Civil War, with the South triumphant." He put it in his jacket pocket. "I'll enjoy that."

"I rather doubt it will put the slave-owners in a good light, Booth," Ayres said. "You'll be disappointed."

"It may not be Shakespeare, but I'm sure it will be diverting, all the same." Booth picked up another object from the table. "What's this?" he said. "Some kind of woman's hygiene implement?"

Ayres came closer to look, then made a face of disgust. The object was long, cylindrical, vaguely phallic, and bright purple. "It's—"

The thing began buzzing in Booth's hand, and he swore and dropped it. "It's full of bees!" he shouted, and Ayres laughed.

"Simpleton," he said. "It's made for—"

"What is *this*," Death said, voice oddly flat and menacing. Ayres turned to him, pausing only to switch off the noisily buzzy vibrator, and wiped his hand on Marla's bedspread.

"Ah, that is something," Ayres said. A large wooden wardrobe stood in the corner, covered in hanging bits of clothing, but there were runes and markings and spirals of binding drawn all over it, copper nails driven into the wood, bits of crystal and leather and feathers and insect chitin dangling from wires wrapped around the nail heads. "That's a vault, sir. Doubtless where Marla keeps her most prized possessions."

"It's not a throne, but it will do." Death reached for the doors. He whistled. "Well. Those are some impressive spells of protection. *I* even feel a little tingling in my fingertips, when most mortal magic touches me not at all." He wrapped his hands around the knobs on the wardrobe doors and tugged them open.

Suddenly Death staggered back, gagging, and fell over the bed, landing on Marla's vibrator and jostling it into the "On" position again. He scrambled across the bed and crouched on the far side, beside Booth, who looked at Ayres in confusion; a look Ayres gave him in return. Ayres peered into the wardrobe, where Marla's greatest artifact hung. It was pure white, so white it hurt the eyes to look upon, and the lining was the purple of crushed flowers and certain bruises. A silver pin in the shape of a stag beetle held it together at the throat, and it hung on a hanger carved of some deep dark wood, also marked all over with fiercely glowing runes. "It's only her cloak, sir," Ayres said.

Death laughed, but the laugh was half a gag. "A cloak. It looks like a cloak to you. I have never before wished for the blindness of a mortal. To be spared this vision. That . . . *thing* . . . I can't . . . it's alive, but not from this world, not within my power. . . . Close the doors. Close them!"

"Sir, by the look of those runes, if either Booth or I touch the wardrobe, we will be killed instantly. That is, I would be killed, and he would likely burn, again."

"I should prefer not to burn again," Booth said.

"Give me your stick," Death said, and Ayres handed over his walking stick. Without rising from his crouch behind the bed, never taking his eyes from the thing inside the wardrobe—and what *did* that cloak look like to a god's eyes?—Death smacked the wardrobe doors with the walking stick, and they swung shut, clicking closed with a sound like bones clacking together. The stick smoldered, and crumbled to dust, scattering the bed with ashes. Ayres sighed. That was a good stick. It had inertial enchantments that helped him to swing it with far more force than his muscles could generate on their own. He'd have to get a new one now.

Death turned his head away from Booth and noisily vomited. Wearing a body clearly had its disadvantages.

"The smell . . . how can you bear the smell?" he said.

"I smell nothing, sir," Ayres said, and Booth concurred.

"Stupid useless humans," Death said. He fled the room.

"A craven and a villain else," Booth murmured.

"He sees things we cannot," Ayres said. "The cloak is old and powerful. Perhaps more than anyone suspected."

"Still, to run from a woman's garment," Booth said. "Well, he's very young, for a god."

Ayres felt a fleeting moment of fellowship, then he

remembered that Booth was a racist egomaniac, and a disobedient servant as well. "Come, let's attend to him," Ayres said, and Booth followed.

Death seemed a bit more in control now, sitting in the living room on Marla's futon, a drink in his hand from her bar; there were bits of broken glass and spilled alcohol all over the place. "I won't have that thing in my city," he said.

"The cloak, sir? Ah, what is it, exactly—"

"Don't question me!" Death roared, and he crackled with that dark aura again, skeins of night unspooling from his body and darkening the air. "Damn you both for a pair of nattering old women! Just obey!"

"What shall we do with it, sir?" Ayres said. Locking it in one of Viscarro's vaults might be an option—that was in the city, true, but very secure. Unfortunately, Viscarro had so far refused to answer any summons sent by Death's "loyal" followers, and Death had been more interested in having sex in his new body than in kicking in the doors of the subterranean sorcerer's fortress.

"That woman who dripped," Death said. "The one who asked me to kill all those shellfish and said she owed me a favor. Bring her here."

Ayres took out his cell phone, but it was dead. He wasn't in the habit of keeping the things charged—any device invented in the last few decades of his life tended to slip from his mind when he wasn't forcibly reminded. "Booth, go fetch Hamil, or find one of his little urchins to send a message."

"I believe I have asked you not to give me orders, sir," Booth said. "I am a patient man, but—"

"Shut up!" Ayres shouted. "You are an undead slave, a thing I brought back to life to serve me, and by all the gods, you will carry me on your back as if you were a horse if that is my desire, else I shall rip your spirit from your body and operate your mummified carcass as a puppet! I grow tired of your endless bitching and moaning, you mad vain monster! Now go! Or would you test me?"

"I will go," Booth said, surprisingly calm, and left the room.

"She doesn't exactly have a cell phone," Hamil said, while Death paced and seethed. "I've sent out all the appropriate messages, and she'll come when she comes, but the only timetable she follows is the tides." Hamil was dressed in an enormous robe and silk pajamas, and he yawned behind his hand. Booth had dragged him out of bed and brought him over in a gypsy cab, and now the assassin lounged by a window, watching the conversation with a look of distant boredom. Hamil cleared his throat and said, "May I ask what this is regarding? The Bay Witch is formidable in her way, but perhaps I could be of more immediate assistance, as I'm already here?"

Death punched a wall, and it cratered, leaving a hole twice the size of his fist. He stared into the hole for a while, took a deep breath, and said, "Ayres, I'm going to distract myself with drugs and fucking. Here." He tossed a bell to Ayres, and the old man managed to catch it without fumbling. "Ring this when the drippy witch arrives. In the meantime, stay here, and just . . . be watchful." He stormed out and away.

Hamil sighed and looked Ayres up and down. "You've certainly hitched your wagon to a star, haven't you? We'll all remember your part in this, Ayres. Death will get bored eventually, and when he leaves you behind, well . . . As I said, we'll remember."

"You allow a colored man to talk to you that way?" Booth said. Hamil turned slowly toward the dead man, fixing him with a look of deep concentration. Booth returned the glare frankly for a moment, but then he started to shift and squirm a bit under Hamil's unblinking stare, finally turning aside and muttering something about manners and civilization and everything his fellow Southerners had fought and died for. Ayres started laughing, and Booth hunched his shoulders and retreated into the bedroom.

"He's a reprehensible thing," Ayres said. "I only wanted his body, you know, to fetch and carry things for me. Pulling his mind out of the underworld was a mistake I think more and more about rectifying."

"You are a fool, Ayres," Hamil said quietly. "You've brought Death himself up into the world, into our midst, into our city. Do you not realize the damage he could do?"

"Your mistress, Marla, gave me no choice," Ayres said. "If she'd just let me work, let me ply my trade, I could have been an asset. I could have advised her, even, as I advised Sauvage and Somerset before her—"

Now Hamil laughed. "You advised them? I knew them both, Ayres, intimately, and they did not consider you a confidante. Sauvage found you strange and off-putting, but useful enough to keep on hand until you went mad. And Somerset . . . if he thought of you at all, he thought of you the way a mechanic thinks of a wrench. As a tool to use when the job calls for it, and utterly unconsidered at all other times."

"You do not know of our secret counsels." Ayres's voice trembled, from anger, he told himself, only from anger.

"Oh, yes," Hamil said. "I'm sure they were very meaningful. But you think Death considers you an advisor, too, don't you? A confidante?" Hamil smiled broadly. "Why, I thought this was pure tragedy, but there is comedy in it as well. Ayres, poor Ayres—Death considers you a slave, exactly the sort of slave you meant the mummy of John Wilkes Booth to be, only Death was far more successful. If you died tomorrow, Death might frown for an instant, but then he would find someone else to fetch and carry for him, and forget you forever."

"You're wrong," Ayres said. "I am the greatest necromancer who ever lived. I am—"

"Tedious," Hamil said, and took his leave.

Booth emerged from the bedroom. "He is a big buck, isn't he? With a mean look in his eye. Still, you shouldn't let him speak to you as if you were—"

"Silence." Ayres rounded on him. "Go now and fetch me a new walking stick. Stout dark wood. I don't care where you get it, if you have to go into the woods outside the city and cut it from a tree with your teeth, *fetch* it."

"You should not—"

"Go." Ayres lifted his hands, and Booth's body

jerked about like a marionette on strings—capering around the apartment, jerking and stumbling and banging into the bar, stepping in broken glass from Death's tantrum, tripping over the futon, continuing to dance even as it fell.

I am the greatest necromancer who ever lived. The dead could not disobey him. Ayres had been so awed by Death's presence, had been bewildered by Booth's capability for speech and thought, he'd allowed himself to be distracted. But he had power now, power that did not depend on the regard of more powerful men, power of his own, a boon from the god of death, not a loan. "Go of your own will, or I will march you like this!" Ayres shouted. "You liked slavery, didn't you? Killed a president because you were so sad to see slavery go? Well, I can accommodate you, then, Mr. Booth—you are *my* slave. Step. Fetch. Go." He slammed Booth against the closed door, then released his control when Booth bounced off. "Do you understand?"

The mummy, in his human glamour, crouched for a moment, then rose. "I understand," he said, and departed.

That was good, Ayres thought. But it was only the beginning. He had power. He was the new lord of Felport's right hand. He would do great things.

The Bay Witch arrived, dripping on the carpet, before Booth came back. Ayres greeted her warmly, offered her a drink—she declined—and then rang the silver bell.

Death emerged from the bathroom, zipping up his

pants. "My dear Bay Witch," he said, all smooth urbanity. "That favor we talked about. I need to call it in."

"So soon?" She cocked her head. "What is it?"

"There is a box in that bedroom," Death said. "I'm going to have it wrapped in chains. Heavy chains, magical chains, enchanted chains of binding. And then I want you to take it to the deepest part of your watery domain, and sink it."

"It must be something you want to lose," the Bay Witch said.

"It just needs to be deep, where no one else will ever be able to find it."

"All right," the Bay Witch said.

Ayres frowned. "Aren't you even curious? About what we want buried?"

She shrugged. "Land things. I don't care about land things. I have millions of dead mussels and clams to clean up."

"You're welcome for that." Death smiled. "Say, when all this is done, would you care to have a drink with me? Get to know each other?"

"I drink brine," the Bay Witch said. "Have your man bring the box in all its chains to pier 14. I'll be waiting there."

"You're a very beautiful woman," Death said.

"Yes. I know." The Bay Witch said it as if admitting to an embarrassing medical condition, and then she went away, leaving a puddle where she'd been.

"Humans," Death commented. "Subset, women. Very bewildering."

"Mmm," Ayres said.

"Well, go fetch the chains, and so on," Death said. "I left a whore in mid-thrust, and should be getting back."

Ayres nodded. "Booth should return soon, and I'll see that he—"

"Not Booth, not later. You, now."

Ayres flushed, mortified, glad Booth wasn't here to see this.

"By the time I come back, I want that . . . *thing* . . . in there to be falling into the sea. I've neutralized the spells sufficiently that you can move the wardrobe, but don't even think, for a moment, about *opening* it."

"Sir, I am old, I fear I cannot move—" Ayres said.

"I gave you power over the dead," Death said. "Must I hold your hand and wipe your ass and show you which way the sun rises? Get the dead to help you, if you must, if you are too weak and infirm to shift a box. This is a city of millions of souls. Some of them are out there in alleys and bar fights and hospitals. Call to them. Bring them here. I've known carrion beetles who were smarter than you. When you've disposed of the wardrobe, don't come back to this place. The stink of that *thing* is everywhere in this apartment, and it's clinging to you already." With that, Death left the apartment, slamming the door after him.

Ayres closed his eyes. That had been unpleasant. But it was a good reminder. He did have power. It was time he used it. He went to the window, looked down on the humid summer night streets of Felport, and whistled for the dead.

10

Rondeau spent the night sleeping in one of Hamil's secret safe houses, in a storage shed in a rooftop garden. He'd never been to the garden before, though he'd heard of it, a green oasis in the middle of the financial district, on the roof of an insurance building. Some rich old coot of a businessman had built the place decades before and left a big chunk of money behind in his will to keep it going. The garden was open during daylight hours to anyone who cared to visit, and sometimes there was live music on weekends. Lots of local office drones came up to have lunch beneath the fruit trees and sit by the ornamental fountains. But Rondeau had it all to himself at night, and he liked it that way, sitting on a stone bench and watching koi swim in a pond, though he felt a little disloyal for enjoying the place—Marla would have found it unpleasant, a perfectly good rooftop ruined with out-of-place nature. Gods, he missed her.

When morning came, he descended to street level

and took subterranean tunnels directly to the back room of the Wolf Bay Café. The owner brought him a strong coffee and a change of clothes—shorts and an oversized T-shirt with a picture of a smiling anthropomorphic doughnut on the front.

At the stroke of nine, Beadle strolled in, newspaper under his arm. "The hook is set." He sat down across from Rondeau. "I loosed a rumor in the brothel Death visited yesterday evening that Mary Madeline Monroe was eager to test her sex magic by copulating with a god. Monroe's own reputation as a lover of unparalleled skill and enthusiasm did the rest—I didn't even have to embellish. I've heard from sources that Death returned to the brothel very early this morning, in the wee hours, and word of the rumor reached his ears. He was intrigued. We'll send him a note from her this morning, asking if he'll meet her at moonrise tonight, at a warehouse near the old rail yard."

"Nice," Rondeau said. "And it's even a waxing moon. That's good, for sex magic. You know"—he made a vague gesture in the vicinity of his lap—"symbolism."

"Mmm," Beadle said. "Langford and Partridge are at the warehouse now, wiring the place. We'll cast a keep-away spell around the perimeter to keep any ordinaries from getting hurt in the explosion. The note will say there's a spell to ensure their privacy, which should keep Death from wondering."

"Pretty clever plan we've got, huh?"

"Actually, it's base and transparent," Beadle said. "The sort of plan anyone could make, and almost anyone could see through. But we're counting on Death's arrogance, vanity, and absolute unfamiliarity with the concept of armed resistance. There are no revolutions in the underworld. How can the dead rebel against death? It would be like a fish rebelling against water. If we're lucky, this will work, but we'll have to be a lot more clever next time. I imagine the god learns quickly."

"Ah, but next time we won't have to be smart, because we'll be strong. We'll have Marla's cloak."

"We'll go to her apartment, you and I, while Partridge and Langford make sure things with our dictator go smoothly."

"It's a plan," Rondeau said. "So any word from Hamil or Ernesto?"

"No." Beadle shook his head. "I heard Death roused Hamil in the middle of the night, but I didn't get any details, and we shouldn't expect to hear from Hamil immediately. His position is delicate, and he doesn't want to tip his hand. At this point, Death doesn't even know there *is* a resistance, and Hamil doesn't want to do anything suspicious."

"Great," Rondeau said. "So . . . we've got all day before we move. What are you going to do?"

"I'm going to run through the plan a few thousand more times. It's just my way."

"I think I'll go meet with the Four Tree Gang," Rondeau said. "I bet they'll join our cause. They're a bunch of sneak thieves and second-story men, could be good for recon and intel. Do you know where they're hanging out these days?"

Beadle checked his notes and scribbled the current address of the Four Tree Gang's ever-changing headquarters, an old frat house near the college. The frat had been disbanded after a scandal involving various prostitutes of assorted genders and rather inventive hazing rituals, made public when some videos were leaked to the Internet and went viral. "Meet back here at 7 P.M., and I'll let you know if everything is going as scheduled."

Rondeau went out the back way, down the stairs to the secret tunnel, whistling. Maybe there were still some kegs at the old frat house. The Four Tree Gang knew how to party, and what was a revolution without a little fun?

"Come on," B insisted. "There must be some things you like doing. Where you're going . . . not to be a downer, but sometimes there's no coming back from there. This could literally be your last day on Earth. You should have some fun. You can't do anything else until after midnight."

"I want to punch Death in the face," Marla said. They sat in the early-morning sunlight of Cole's deck, and Pelham was in the kitchen smoking some kippers, or whatever valets did when it was time to make breakfast. Cole snored from the living room, steady as the breaking of ocean waves. "I want to be sitting in my office looking for messages from my spies in the classified section of the newspaper."

"You still use newspapers? That's old-school. Susan

switched over to using 'missed connections' ads on Craigslist to pass messages."

"Susan Wellstone can bite my—"

"Breakfast." Pelham came out bearing a tray. They moved over to the picnic table and tucked in, Pelham joining them at Marla's insistence—she'd break him of his deference eventually. She didn't mind respect, or even total obedience, she just wanted them for the right reasons—because she was scary, not because she was rich.

"How about you, Pelly? Marla's no fun, so what do you want to do? You're in California now. Think big. Though we should probably avoid going into San Francisco."

"Ah," Pelham said, blinking. "I don't . . . ah . . . Hmm." He retreated into his bacon and eggs.

B sighed. "You two. It's going to be a laugh-a-minute romp when I get back to Felport, isn't it?"

"You'll have Rondeau to keep you entertained, in the rare moments when I'm not working you like a dog," Marla said. "Hell. Okay. This is your town. Show us the sights, then."

"That's an idea. I know a place in Oakland's Chinatown that sells knives and swords and all sorts of lethal-edged instruments."

"That's promising," she said.

"And when was the last time you went to see a movie?" B said.

Marla frowned. "It's been a while. But I can see a movie anywhere."

"Ah," B said, "but at this movie theater, there are beat-up old couches, and pizza, and beer. On *tap*. And there's all this decaying flaking faux-Egyptian decoration all over the walls."

"Okay," Marla said. "I can tentatively admit that might be interesting."

"And after that," B said, "I'm going to take you to a café that's also a capoeira studio. You can drink yerba maté and watch capoeistas jump around."

"I know capoeira," Marla said. It wasn't her favorite martial art, but it had some nice elements, and it tended to attract beautiful practitioners. She wasn't averse to taking in some eye candy.

"They might let you do a demo," B said.

"You sound like you've been planning this," Marla said, suddenly suspicious. "Why'd you even ask me what I wanted to do, if you had all these ideas?"

"Politeness. I knew you wouldn't want to do anything. And then we're going to the zoo."

Marla grunted. "Do they have deadly predators there?"

"Loads," B said, grinning.

"Mmm. I grudgingly consent." She drank her coffee, gave B a brief smile, and thought about all the things a person might like to do if they were about to descend into a land from which few ever returned, and from which no one returned unchanged. Spending time with one of your only friends in the world probably wasn't a bad choice.

"Ah, Booth, how nice of you to return," Ayres said. The assassin stood in the doorway of the penthouse, holding a decent-looking walking stick, looking about with obvious dismay at the half a dozen animated corpses that were dusting, straightening, and generally making Sauvage's old apartments suitable for habitation again.

"I looked for you at Marla's, but—"

"You eventually had the wit to seek me here. Aren't you bright." Ayres snapped his fingers, and one of the fresher-looking corpses—you might have mistaken her for merely ill, in dim light—hurried to fetch him a drink. Ayres didn't even need to speak. He didn't even need to snap his fingers, really; that was just theater, for Booth's benefit. These corpses were not animated as Booth was. They were essentially appendages of Ayres's own body, and he needed only think to move them. "Meet your new brothers and sisters!"

"These are no kin of mine." Booth threw the stick at Ayres's feet. "Your staff."

"I think I'd like it if you called me *lord*," Ayres said. "As I call Death lord. It's a title fitting for a god, and I am your god."

"I will never call you that. You overstep yourself."

"But don't I have the power of life and death over you, Booth?" Ayres reached out his hand, curled his fingers, and clawed through the air. Booth gasped, fell to his knees, and slid a couple of feet along the carpet. "Try it. 'Lord.' Go ahead."

"Never," Booth said, and Ayres tugged a little harder, hooking his ethereal fingernails into Booth's spirit and dragging it out of his mummified body. Booth moaned. Ayres let the spirit go, and it snapped back into the assassin, sending him sprawling on the ground.

"Now," Ayres leaned forward, "choose your next words carefully, Booth."

"My . . . lord," Booth said.

"There we go. Death will be pleased I've finally housebroken you."

Booth struggled to his feet and straightened his illusory clothing with great dignity. "Where is Death?" A beat. "Lord."

"I'm here." The god of death appeared, as he so often did, from a room he hadn't previously inhabited, and crossed to Sauvage's bar. "I've worn out every whore in that brothel, and they're grumbling they must be paid, or else they'll starve. I told them you'd take care of it, Ayres. Surely Marla has coffers that are rightly mine now?"

"I'll see to it, my lord," Ayres said.

Death appeared to notice the walking corpses for the first time. "Oh, my, Ayres, you've finally decided to find some help. Good, good. I like having a few dead ones around."

"Does it remind you of home, my lord?" Booth inquired politely.

"Not at all. Where I come from, we have the spirits, but not the bodies. *These* are bodies, stripped of their spirits. All fall under my authority, of course, flesh and spirit both, but no, rotting meat-husks don't remind me of home. You are the only one here who reminds me of home."

Booth practically preened, and Ayres gritted his teeth.

"My lord," Booth said, in his smooth, urbane voice,

"perhaps you could see fit to put me directly under your authority, so that I might better serve you. I spend so much time helping Ayres now, I fear—"

"Cease your prattle." Death tossed back a whiskey. "I've just listened to five whores complain endlessly about hunger and exhaustion, and I'm in no mood to listen to you. I gave Ayres dominion over the dead, and you're dead, so do as he says. I told him not to banish you. Be grateful."

Ayres grinned at Booth viciously, victoriously. "My lord. Among mortals, titles are important. The other sorcerers might accept my authority as your spokesperson more readily if you called me, say, consiglieri, or prime minister—or, perhaps, vizier?"

Death belched. "Call yourself King High Shit of Excrement Hall, for all I care, Ayres. Tell me, have you heard of a woman called Mary Madeline Monroe? I'm told she wants to fuck me."

"Ah," Ayres said. "Yes, she is a famed sexual magician. I imagine she would leap at the chance to pleasure a god." She'd reportedly fucked an incubus, a succubus, a rakosh, something radiant that claimed to be an angel, a djinn, and various lycanthropes, and increased her magic tenfold with every conquest.

"Yes, but is she worth a lay?"

"I have never experienced her intimate company, my lord, but her beauty is supernatural, and her skills are reportedly unparalleled."

"Right, then. I'm fucking her this evening. Is there any pressing business I should attend to before I visit this casino Nicolette has been telling me about?"

"There is the matter of Viscarro, sir," Ayres said. "He is the only sorcerer of note who hasn't sworn fealty to you. He refuses to emerge from his spider hole."

"All right, fine, I'll go kick down his door tomorrow. That all?"

"The Chamberlain called to remind you that the Founders' Ball is rapidly approaching, and she hopes you will have sufficient time to prepare."

"Those ghosts have her whipped, don't they? Remind the Chamberlain that I'm a *god,* and that I'll make sure the party is the greatest this city has ever seen." He started to go, then paused. "That thing I told you to take care of."

"Chained, bound, passed on to the Bay Witch, sunk to the depths."

"Good man." Death actually slapped Ayres on the shoulder on his way out the door.

Ayres took a deep breath. He made all the zombies stop, turn, and stare at Booth, who lounged against the wall. "Oh, Booth," Ayres said. "I need you to run a message over to the Chamberlain for me."

Booth straightened, sputtering, "That uppity colored—"

"Shh," Ayres said, pressing a finger to his lips. "I've told you, don't bad-mouth your betters."

A lock of dark hair fell into Booth's eyes, and he brushed it away, his eyes damp, his expression partway to madness. "You could contact her over your telephone," Booth said, carefully pronouncing the last word. "That would be faster than sending me afoot."

"Mmm, but sending you takes so much less effort

than dialing a phone. Get a move on, and tell her the Walking Death has the matter of the Founders' Ball well in hand. Be polite, Booth. Obey the Chamberlain as you would obey me."

The assassin slunk away, and Ayres leaned back in the chair, closing his eyes. Only mid-morning, true, but he needed a nap. Being the greatest necromancer in the world was tiring work.

Beadle had a magic mirror slaved to a pair of spectacles Langford was wearing, so he and Rondeau could watch Death head for his date with high explosives. The two hid out in an alley two blocks from Marla's apartment, huddled around the hand mirror like schoolkids sneaking a portable TV into math class to watch a ball game. Langford was on a rooftop across the street from the target location, looking down on the likeliest approaches to the warehouse.

"I think that's him," Rondeau whispered, as if Death might hear him. The tiny image on the screen sharpened as Langford adjusted the glasses, and the god jumped into clear focus, strutting along the deserted street as if he owned the place—which, increasingly, he did.

Death rapped on the warehouse's side door, opened it, and stepped inside.

"Here we go," Beadle said.

There was no sound from the mirror, but they heard the explosion distantly anyway—it was only a couple of miles away. Langford ducked out of the way, but smoke and dust wafted down around him, and Rondeau and

Beadle cheered. The image jerked as Langford moved across the roof, probably crouching and scuttling, but then he paused, focusing on something on the rooftop. "What's that?" Rondeau squinted.

The image came closer, and Rondeau gasped. "Shit. That's Death's *hand*." The hand was blackened, torn off about an inch below the wrist, and missing its pinky finger, but it was unmistakable—there were still rings on all the fingers that remained. Langford's own hands, clothed in white surgical gloves, entered the frame, reaching for the severed hand.

"No, no," Beadle murmured, and Rondeau sucked air through his teeth. Langford was curious. He was a scientist. The idea of having the hand of a god to study would be irresistible to him, even if the hand was just the equivalent of a glove for a being of such power. But before Langford could pick up the hand, it rolled over, stood up on its fingers like something out of a bad horror movie, and scurried away across the roof, presumably to reunite with the other fragments of the god. Langford held up his hand in an A-OK sign and the image on the mirror went dark.

"We'd better get to Marla's before he puts himself back together again," Beadle said.

"I know we didn't do any permanent damage," Rondeau said, breaking into a wide smile, "but doesn't it make you happy, knowing we just pissed off that fucker *bad*?"

* * *

Death slammed into the penthouse, startling Ayres and Booth, who sat in gloating and tense silence, respectively, watching the flickering images of a black-and-white movie on the enormous television. "Someone will die for this," the god growled, and Ayres and Booth exchanged glances.

"What's wrong, my lord?" Ayres struggled to his feet, using for leverage the stick Booth had fetched him. It was a good stick, though he hadn't cast any enchantments on it yet.

Death glanced at the television, and the channel switched to a breaking news report, a glossy brunette at a news desk speaking seriously about an explosion in a warehouse down by the old train yard, no injuries, fire contained, officials investigating, possible gas leak. "That," Death said, "was the site of my rendezvous. Someone tried to blow me up." He stalked through the room, toward the bar, stepping on the glass-topped coffee table as he went, not even noticing when it shattered beneath his boot. He poured a glass of vodka and sucked it down. "That hurt. I lost most of my old body, and had to make a new one. It was inconvenient. I have to get the flesh from somewhere, you know. Fortunately there were lots of rats killed in the explosion, so I just harvested their cells." He held up his hand and stared at it. "I thought the knife cutting off my fingers was bad. This was . . . fire. Sharp things. Heat. My flesh melting, fusing to my bones, bits of me falling from the sky and thumping down . . ." He shuddered. "I'll never forget that. I want to make someone *else* feel that. That bitch tricked me."

Ayres opened his phone and called Hamil. "Mary Madeline Monroe tried to kill Death. She must be brought to justice."

"Mary Madeline Monroe is in Thailand studying the sexual culture of ladyboys," Hamil said. "I rather doubt she's even aware of the Walking Death's existence."

Ayres closed the phone. "Sir. My lord. The sex magician is not in the country. You were betrayed. Some conspiracy."

"Fools," Booth said. "They should know you cannot be assassinated. You are *Death*. Death does not die."

"No, they can't kill me," the god said. "But I can kill them. Better, I can make them wish for death, and then withhold it. Who was it, Ayres? Who could have done it?"

Rondeau? Ayres wondered. Could he have arranged something like this? Rondeau struck Ayres as basically a spear-carrier—capable of improvising, of course, but to plan something like this? Before Ayres could speculate aloud, however, Death answered his own question.

"Viscarro. The one sorcerer of note who hasn't pledged himself to me, who thinks he can hide from me. It was him."

Ayres wasn't so sure, but he nodded anyway. "He does despise change, and he has many apprentices to help him plot such a scheme. It could have been him, my lord." Viscarro was also somewhat protected from Death, since his life was hidden away in a stone somewhere in his vaults. Ayres wanted to tell the god that Viscarro was an undead thing, but he couldn't—he'd sworn secrecy in a circle of binding, and to speak now would be the death of Ayres himself.

"We'll deal with him, then," Death said.

"Now, my lord?"

"Let him think I'm dead, or driven off," Death said. "Let's see if he comes out of his hole, see if he makes contact with any other conspirators. We'll go see him, either way, at first light tomorrow. In the meantime, Ayres, take your slaves here to the nearest cemetery and start opening graves. Set every corpse you dig up with the task of digging up another corpse, and animate those. I want a little army of corpses at my back. I can't be everywhere at once—not without giving up these bodily delights I've come to enjoy—and it's time this city respected me. I've been too kind to them, but if they want to fight me . . . well, we can fight."

"The ordinaries might notice hordes of skeletons on the street, my lord," Ayres said.

"So drape them in illusions," Death said, waving his hand. "Give them the semblance of life."

"My skills at illusion are not so powerful, I fear." Ayres hated to admit any weakness in front of Booth. "I could not disguise so many."

Death made a frustrated sound. "I have to do everything? Fine, you have my proxy. My realm is a realm of illusions, and you may use some of my power to make my army look like living souls. Fetch shovels and dig! This whole building is empty. Let's fill it with warriors." Death cracked his knuckles. "If Viscarro is the rotten tooth, we'll extract him. And if the rot extends further, we'll just keep digging until every fool who had a hand in attacking me begs for death."

As Booth and Ayres left the building, trailed by half a dozen undead slaves, Booth said, "I thought he was just a coddled and privileged boy with power, but it seems he's a man, after all."

"He's more than a man," Ayres said. "He's a god."

"What I mean to say is—"

"Shut up," Ayres said. "Go stand with the other slaves."

Booth withdrew, but Ayres took no pleasure in the assassin's subjugation. He preferred being the vizier to a happy, rutting dictator. An angry Walking Death meant hard work for Ayres, and he was an old man, and behind on his sleep. *Still,* he thought, *raising a whole cemetery. That's the sort of act that leads to legends.*

"The wardrobe isn't here," Rondeau said. "It's normally *right here*!"

Beadle nodded. "There are still traces of the magic, but it's gone, and has been for hours, at least."

"Can you track it?"

Beadle shook his head. "I can only sense the spells because they sat here, on this spot, for so long, it's like a wine stain soaking into a carpet. Now that's it been moved . . . No. I have no idea where it's gone."

"Maybe Viscarro stole it." Rondeau paced around Marla's bedroom. "He's always coveted her artifacts. Or maybe Death recognized it as a threat and took it. But who knows?"

"So what now?"

"How should I know?"

"You're the leader," Beadle said, gently.

Rondeau stopped pacing. "Right. Yes. The leader." He considered. He pondered. He looked at the ceiling. "Shit. I don't know."

"All right. Let me know when you *do* know." Beadle glanced at his pocket watch. "But let me know soon. There may be repercussions from our assault on Death. We should be prepared for possible retaliation."

Rondeau groaned. Marla always said "plan" was a four-letter word for something that didn't work, but Rondeau hadn't really understood that; he'd been prepared for success. And he didn't have Marla to bail him out this time. He had faith she was out there somewhere, working an angle of her own, but he was the one in Felport, and he couldn't just wait for her to come charging back. "Okay," he said. "I've got an idea."

"What's that?"

"I'll tell you later. I need to check something out first." Which spared Rondeau from admitting he didn't really have an idea. But there was no reason to diminish the morale of his troops.

"I can't wait to hear it," Beadle said.

11

Marla, Pelham, and B drove into downtown Berkeley near midnight and parked on a side street not far from the nearby commuter train station. "Last train arrives pretty soon," B said. "Then the place closes down, and when it's deserted . . . assuming things work like they did last time I did this . . . the train will come along shortly. I had to slip by the tracks and hide halfway down the tunnel last time, and that was kind of terrifying. That was before I really knew about magic, though."

"Yeah, a look-away spell should be enough to keep the three of us from getting noticed," Marla said. "And it's lots more hospitable than crouching in a tunnel, hoping no late trains come along."

"May I carry your bag, Ms. Mason?" Pelham said as they got out of the car.

"Nope," Marla said, pulling the black messenger bag over her shoulder. She missed her battered leather satchel, which she usually filled with nifty ordnance for field operations, but B had loaned her this bag, and she'd raided Cole's office for a few items infused with magic. Cole was a seer, not a battle-sorcerer, so he didn't have much in the way of weaponry, but Marla had found a few useful tidbits, and glass and metal and porcelain clanked gently together when she shifted the bag. They walked into the train station, which was pretty much empty, and Marla cast a look-away spell, which was easier than true invisibility and just as effective; it simply kept people from noticing them. They slipped through the gate without buying tickets, then rode down the escalator and had a seat on a long, low, wooden bench. "I like escalators," Pelham said. "I never rode one until yesterday, at the airport. They're fun."

"The world's full of fun stuff," Marla said. "Let's hope we get to come back and experience more of it." The day had been full of big and little pleasures, and she might even have enjoyed herself, if not for her constant worry about Rondeau, Hamil, and Felport itself. She figured if the city burned to the ground or sank into the bay, that would make the national news, but otherwise, how could she know what was happening there?

"Anything I should know? About the train?"

B nodded. "I did think of one thing—time. When I rode that train before, the trip didn't seem to take much time, and I didn't stay down there long at all, but when I came back, it was nearly sixteen hours after I left."

Marla nodded. "Variable time. Gotcha. Supernatural stuff does weird things to your subjective time sense. Death and his minions can probably bop back and forth in an instant, but for living people, it's a more momentous trip. Time and space are probably pretty wonky down there."

"So how long do I wait to panic?" B said.

Marla shook her head. "A few days? Though I'm not sure what good panicking will do you. You can try calling Hamil every day. There's a spell preventing any news about me from getting into the city, so if you find yourself able to tell him about my plan, you can pretty much guarantee my plan failed, and I've gone from a tourist to a permanent resident of the underworld."

They waited. The last train, a short one of only three cars, pulled in, disgorged its passengers, and left. A transit employee walked through, looking under benches for who-knows-what, and Marla and company had to draw up their feet so he wouldn't feel them. Finally he left, and gates rattled closed somewhere in the distance, sealing off the station from the world above, and the lights went out.

Marla took her friends' hands and said, *"Fiat lux,"* and they all blinked at the sudden grainy brightness of their night-vision. "More waiting. I hate waiting."

"I know," B said. "I brought a deck of cards."

They played Oh, Hell for a while, with Pelham keeping score in his head. "What if it doesn't come?" B said.

"You dreamed about Pelham and a train," Marla said. "It'll come." B was an oracle-generator, a magical catalyst, and maybe the train to the underworld was just a ghost of a potentiality most nights, but B's presence here would drag it into immanence.

A distant whooshing sound filled the air. Pelham

efficiently picked up the cards before the onrushing train-wind could blow them away.

A headlight appeared in the dark, a strange pale light that made Marla squint, and then the train slid to a stop before them—a single car, the front compartment all dark glass, the driver hidden. The train was white, not the usual silver, and it was streamlined, organic, all of a piece, as if carved from the thighbone of a leviathan. The windows on the side were trapezoidal, and the doors, when they slid open, seemed to have tiny triangular interlocking teeth. "All aboard." Marla impulsively grabbed B and kissed his cheek. She glanced at Pelham. "Last chance to stay behind, Pelly." He shook his head, though his face was as white as the bone train.

"Be careful!" B said, but Marla didn't answer him, as it was hardly a promise she could make in good conscience. Marla and Pelham stepped onto the train. There were no seats, just gently curving walls, and instead of metal handrails, there were hooks of bone hanging from the ceiling. Marla and Pelham grabbed on, and a cold dry voice over the loudspeaker said, "Doors are closing." B waved at them as the doors hissed shut, and the train lurched and began to move forward. Marla and Pelham swayed for a moment, then Marla said, "I'm going to go talk to the driver."

"Are you sure that's wise?"

"Probably not. But as you get to know me better, you'll realize it's kind of a bad habit of mine." She walked toward the front of the train, where only a crack in the wall indicated the presence of what might be a door. She knocked. "Hey," she said. "I'm Marla Mason. Mind if I come in?"

The loudspeaker clicked on, but there was only silence for a moment, a blank hiss. Finally the voice said, "Door is opening," and the entryway to the compartment clicked open with a hiss, swinging inward half an inch. Marla glanced back at Pelham, gave him a nod she meant to be reassuring, and pushed through the door.

"Psst," Rondeau said from his chair in the corner. "Heh. I've always wanted to lurk in the dark and go 'Psst.' "

"You shouldn't be here, Rondeau." Hamil looked around the darkness of his bedroom. "How did you get in here?"

Rondeau shrugged. "For the security system, Marla gave me the code. For the dumb locks—hell, Hamil, I've been breaking into places since I got this body. Don't worry, I wasn't seen, I crept like a mouse. Been waiting for freaking ever for you, though."

Hamil sighed. "Yes, well, Death is howling for blood. Someone—I won't speculate—tried to blow him up today. Nice effort, by the way. He seems to be blaming Viscarro, which is good for our purposes."

Rondeau grunted. Part of him was glad his little group was still secret for the moment, of course, but another part of him wanted the credit. "Well, see, the big boom was mainly a distraction. We were planning to get Marla's cloak."

Hamil whistled and settled onto the edge of his bed. "That might be powerful enough to actually damage him. It's dangerous, though, that cloak—too many uses and you begin to go mad."

"I wasn't planning on wearing it every day," Rondeau said. "I've seen what it does to Marla—when I was a little kid, she ripped off my jaw while she was wearing that cloak. It made her so cold and crazy, she didn't see a little kid, she just saw a potential object of power, a jawbone she could use as an oracle. I've got no fondness for the cloak."

"Even with its healing powers, it might not be able to keep you alive if Death decides to stop your heart. He can kill any of us with a thought."

Rondeau shrugged. "I've seen Marla catch fire, take damage that should have reduced her to ash, and the cloak healed her. But yeah, he *might* kill my body, but not before I get a few licks in, and anyway, what's a body? I'm fond of this one, but push comes to shove . . ."

"If your mind goes looking for a new host, you'll oust someone else's mind," Hamil said. "That's murder."

Rondeau nodded seriously. "I'd accept the karmic debt. Besides, if I get killed, I'll try to take over Death's body—I know it's not his real form, that ultimately he doesn't have a body, but he's walking around in flesh-and-blood up here, and if he has a brain, I might be able to seize control of it. Wouldn't that piss him off? Makes me wish I could jump bodies at will, but I'm stuck in this one until it stops operating. If that doesn't work, if he's got some kind of god-condom on to keep me from stealing his body, Ayres is usually with him, so I'll take over *his* body."

"A good plan. When will you strike?"

"Ah. That's the thing. We went to Marla's tonight, and her wardrobe was gone. We heard Death summoned you last night, and we were wondering . . ."

"He called me to Marla's apartment," Hamil said. "Perhaps he saw the cloak, and recognized it as a threat? But it's not something you can burn or destroy, so he'd have to dispose of it some other way. He asked me to arrange a meeting with the Bay Witch."

"Crap. So you think, what, Marla's cloak's on the bottom of the bay?"

"It seems plausible, but I can't be sure."

"Can I talk to the Bay Witch? Is she with us?"

"I wouldn't count on it. She likes Marla, but she asked Death to kill off some invasive species that was taking over the bay, and he did so. I'm afraid he may have her loyalty now."

"Damn it." Rondeau stood up and paced a bit. "Hmm. Down by the docks, that's Honeyed Knots territory. Maybe they saw something, saw the wardrobe get transported? I'll put the word out. And if the Bay Witch did take the wardrobe away and hide it, well, a big fucking magical thing on the bottom of the bay, there must be a way to track that."

"And then what? You go down to get it with scuba gear?"

"I was thinking of making Langford infuse me with selkie blood or give me gills or something," Rondeau said. "But your idea is way simpler."

"Good luck. I'll try to keep Death from suspecting

anything, though that probably means blaming things on Viscarro."

"I never liked that moldy old troglodyte anyway," Rondeau said. "And he's not loyal to the cause. I say give him hell."

Rondeau crouched beneath an overpass near the docks and shared a few tokes on a pipe with a handful of Honeyed Knots. He didn't even know what he was smoking, but he'd smoked just about everything in the past, so it didn't much matter. "So, fellas," he said, "did you see anything like that lately?"

The Honeyed Knots were a more stylish bunch than the Four Tree Gang, most wearing beads and charms and fetishes, many with extensive facial piercings that reminded Rondeau uncomfortably of a cannibal witch named Bethany he'd had the displeasure to meet a while back. Though the Four Tree Gang outnumbered the Honeyed Knots by about three to one, the Honeyed Knots had a much higher magical skill level, consisting mostly of disgraced apprentices who'd been bounced out of their positions, though every one had a sob story about how they'd been unjustly persecuted. The Four Tree Gang was good if you needed somebody beat up, or a lot of equipment stolen out of the back of a warehouse, but the Honeyed Knots were better for more delicate work. One of Marla's most significant moves as chief sorcerer had been mediating a peace between the two gangs, and giving them a sort of quasi-official status in the city's magical underworld, retaining the leaders of both gangs as "consultants" and occasionally employing them in operations that needed warm bodies who wouldn't be totally confused if impossible things started happening. They were in awe of Marla, who'd kicked the asses of the best fighters in both gangs—her way of mediating a peace was, of course, somewhat violent—and Rondeau trusted the loyalty of the gangs, in the aggregate if not necessarily in the case of each individual member.

One of the Honeyed Knots, a guy named Mondrian with an elaborate abstract face tattoo and enormous pegs in his earlobes, nodded. "I was down by pier 14 yesterday morning, early, and saw some old guy leading a group of five or six people carrying a big bulky thing, it could have been a wardrobe. It was wrapped all over with chains. They went to the end of the dock, and the old guy said something, I couldn't hear what. Then the guys with him tossed the wardrobe, if that's what it was, into the water, and they all walked off."

Rondeau nodded. "That all?"

Mondrian grinned, showing sharpened teeth. "Nah. One man's trash is another man's treasure, right? The water's not real deep there that time of morning, so I figured I'd see if the package was anything worth salvaging. I went down to the water, and was just about to jump in when the Bay Witch popped out of the waves." He shook his head. "I always heard she was out there, but I've never seen her before, hot blonde in a tight wetsuit, pure surfer-girl, I couldn't believe it. I bet she's really a hundred years old and has seawater for blood. She looked at me like I was, I don't know, some kind of weird bug, and then she dove down. I couldn't see much under the water, it was sort of churned up and it was only just dawn, but I think she took off with the box, yeah. There was nothing there when I poked around anyway, and there were so many chains on it, the thing would've dropped straight to the bottom."

Rondeau clapped him on the shoulder. "Thanks, bro. That helps."

Mondrian nodded, sucked on the pipe for a moment, then said, "So, Marla. Is she, you know. Coming back?"

"We're working on that," Rondeau said. "And you just went a long way toward making it happen." He said his farewells and headed toward his current safe house, a utility shed near the little amusement park down by the esplanade. Being a revolutionary ringleader had its good points, but sleeping on cots next to old paint cans and broken carousel horses wasn't one of them. Not that he had much night left to sleep in. He opened his cell phone and made a call. "Hey, Beadle. We're going to need a boat, and some diving gear, and somebody who can do a little divination."

In the first glow of dawn, Ayres led a score of his newly exhumed zombies down the street, Booth walking stiffly at his side. Ayres had draped the zombies in illusions to make them look alive, and he'd made them all black, just to mess with Booth—except for one, which Ayres had decided to disguise as a young Abraham Lincoln, acromegaly and all. "It's this way," Ayres said, for Booth's benefit, and led his little army down the steps to the rocky strand of stinking beach, toward the entry to Viscarro's tunnels.

As he had suspected, the door was bricked up. Ayres clucked his tongue and moved aside, and his zombies stepped forward, lifting pickaxes and sledgehammers and banging in perfect rhythm against the bricks, smashing through them in a matter of minutes. Ayres rang the silver bell, and Death dropped down from above, apparently having leapt from the top of the sea cliff, or else simply materialized in mid-air. He landed in a crouch, then straightened. "Well, then, in we go."

"Why did you have us break the door down, sir?" Booth said. "Surely no wall can stand before you."

"I like to give you fellows something to do," Death said. "To make you feel useful. Hamil says one can rule as effectively with kindness as fear, and I thought I'd experiment." He paused. "Though perhaps telling you my motives spoils the effect? Ah, well. It doesn't really matter." Death strode into the darkness.

Ayres followed, and the little zombie horde came after them. When Death reached the unmanned gate, he reached out and tore the door off, tossing it behind him to clang on the stone floor.

"Viscarro!" Death shouted. "Your new master is here!" All the vault doors that had stood open when Ayres came—was it only a few days before?—were now sealed shut, but the god just spun their wheels and pushed them open, like a series of airlocks in a science fiction movie. Death paused, noticing the vaults along the side walls, too. "Come out, or I'll start opening your treasure chests and breaking whatever I find inside!

What I can't break, I'll eat, Viscarro! Come out, and stand before me!"

A crackling public address system came to life. "One moment," Viscarro's disembodied voice said.

The circular vault door before them swung open, revealing Viscarro and a dozen of his apprentices, all armed with rather outlandish weapons—pole-arms and morning-stars and axes and swords—probably taken from Viscarro's ancient armory. Viscarro himself was unarmed, dressed in a simple robe, unadorned apart from a gold-rimmed monocle. He bowed slightly. "My apologies for not answering your earlier messages, my lord. I was in the midst of an inventory." He glanced behind him, at his well-armed horde. "We were doing a thorough catalog of my hall of weapons when you arrived." Viscarro squinted and frowned. "That man behind you looks exactly like Abraham Lincoln."

Death crossed his arms and looked down on Viscarro. "Did you try to explode me?"

Viscarro blinked. "No, my lord, I did not."

"Mmm. You only tried to avoid me, then?"

"I . . . may be forced to admit that much."

"Why? Why not kiss my ring and swear fealty? I am a gentle ruler . . . unless I'm given cause to be cruel."

"I dislike conflict," Viscarro said.

The god reached out and caressed Viscarro's cheek. "Whether you're guilty of assaulting me or not, I think I need to make an example of you. I'm going to rip out your soul and send it to Hell now."

Viscarro's acolytes raised their weapons, but Viscarro lifted a hand to stay them.

"Facing death with bravery," Death said. "I hope you don't think that impresses me. I don't care if you go stoically or shit yourself in fear." He reached out, his hand passing through Viscarro's skin, disappearing to the wrist into his chest . . . and then he pulled his hand out again, in confusion. "What is this?"

Viscarro sighed. "Something wrong, my lord? Have you chosen to be merciful?"

"You have no life." The Walking Dead circled Viscarro. "You're a ghost haunting a body." He poked Viscarro in the back with one finger. "You're . . . oh, what's the word? A lich."

"I don't know what you're talking about," Viscarro said, but his acolytes milled in confusion and began talking low amongst themselves. Ayres smiled. The secret was out. How amusing.

"Hmm. Your life must be hidden here somewhere," Death said, "but I already grow bored with you, and the thought of searching these mounds of crap for the box that holds your soul is tedious. Still, you must be punished for your refusal to answer my summons, and for daring to cheat death."

"All sorcerers cheat death," Viscarro said. "I was simply forced to use a more inelegant solution than most."

"I don't care about everyone else. I care about you. You took your life out of your body, Viscarro." Death placed both hands on the sorcerer's shoulders. "I'm the only one who gets to do that." He looked at Ayres. "His body is a corpse, Ayres, and you are the master of corpses. Make him dance for us. Make him join your horde. Drag him up above. Put him on guard duty outside in the sun. Don't let him speak. He's your puppet now." Death strode away, apparently done with this business, shoving his way through the zombies and back toward the exit.

"Of course, my lord." Ayres crooked his finger, making Viscarro lurch forward. His acolytes, clearly confused, began to move to follow their master, and Ayres sent his zombies to push them back. The apprentices raised their swords and axes, but the press of undead, unfeeling flesh pushed them back, and they were soon disarmed and cowering. Ayres cleared his throat. "As the vizier of the lord of death, I declare these vaults and all their contents the property of Death. Any of Viscarro's apprentices who wish a place in the new regime may lay down their arms and remain below in an administrative capacity." He glanced at Viscarro, who looked wholly like a dead thing now, except for his eyes, which were cold and furious and terrified. "Call out if you're interested!"

Most of the apprentices were willing to switch allegiances. Those who weren't provided more bodies for Ayres's undead army. As they departed Viscarro's catacombs, Ayres glanced at Booth, who walked along morosely, head down. "Feeling a bit useless, Booth?" Ayres said. "If you ever get tired of your pointless existence, say the word, and I'll send you back to Hell, where you can do something useful, like be tormented for your crimes."

"If I decide to depart this mortal coil, you will be the first to know, sir," Booth said, but didn't look up.

* * *

There was only one seat in the driver's compartment, so Marla had to stand. The window showed only blackness, and despite the glare of the pale headlight, she couldn't even see tracks before them, just nothingness. "So." Marla tried not to look directly at the driver, staring into the darkness instead. "How long have you been driving this route?"

"Forever," the driver said, three syllables carved in ice, doused in liquid nitrogen.

"Since before the invention of subway trains?" Marla tried for a light tone. She glanced at the driver again, and what she saw was so horrible it made her stomach clench and her head throb, so she looked away, and instantly forgot what he—what *it*?—looked like. The same thing happened every time she looked at him. She knew the human mind was incapable of truly remembering the sensation of extreme pain; it muted the memory in order to spare further agony. Perhaps looking at the driver was like that. Marla tried to keep her eyes firmly on the dark ahead.

"Not always a train," the driver said. "Sometimes a boat. Sometimes a car. Sometimes a mule-cart. Sometimes only a guide on a trail leading up a mountain, or down from one."

"How many passengers do you get?"

"Many. Always. I am ferrying hundreds at this moment, simultaneously, but not contiguously." He paused. "You and the one in back are the only ones who are alive. And you are the only one in a long time who has come to talk to me for any reason other than pleading or screaming."

Screaming. Yeah. She could understand that. "So, am I supposed to pay you two pennies or something?"

"That's for a one-way trip. Round-trips cost more."

Marla felt a chill. Every transaction with beings like this had a cost, and it was usually steeper than you hoped, and nonnegotiable. "Care to tell me how much this ticket will cost me?"

"Varies. But it's payable on return. Maybe you won't return. Then you won't have to pay. I take people down alive, sometimes, like you. Some of them come back. Most don't."

"You're cheerful, aren't you?" Marla said, but the driver didn't answer her.

A moment later, he said, "Door is opening."

The door behind Marla clicked open again. She could take a hint. "Thanks for the ride." She slipped out. The door closed behind her, and Marla was annoyed to find she was trembling a little. Death hadn't bothered her as much, but he was pretending to be human, wearing a normal, if artificial, body. But that thing in the front of the train was undisguised, utterly and completely . . . whatever it was. A force of nature with a face. Not that she could remember its face. Which was probably for the best.

"What was he like?" Pelham asked.

Marla shook her head. "Terse. Not mean, exactly, but . . . he's definitely seen it all."

Pelham laughed. "He's seen an attempted invasion of the underworld before?"

"I didn't go into all that. I was afraid he might back the train up, or just stop here in the middle of nowhere and toss us out. I was hoping to ask him for directions to this throne room Cole mentioned, but I didn't get the feeling he wanted to be a tour guide, so I . . . ah . . ." *Chickened out,* she thought. "Decided discretion was the better part of wisdom."

"Of course, Ms. Mason. What do you think we'll see down there, when we arrive?"

Marla shrugged. "A gate guarded by a three-headed hellhound? An arch inscribed with the words 'All Hope Abandon, Ye Who Enter Here'? A long line with a supernatural bureaucrat at the end of it ready to assign you to the sixteen chambers of heart-gouging or the upside-down prison? I've read about so many underworlds, Pelham, I'm a little terrified that we're going to get a big syncretic sampler-pack underworld experience. Cole says our subconscious decides how we perceive the underworld, and my subconscious is primed with images of the underworld from pretty much every mythology you've ever heard of, and a few even *I* hadn't heard of three days ago. There's no telling what we'll get. Maybe a little bit of everything."

The train slowed, and they swung on their handgrips. Bright lights poured in through the trapezoidal windows. "Guess we'll find out now." Somehow, she'd expected their first sight of the underworld to be dark.

"Underworld station," the voice on the loudspeaker said. "Doors are opening."

The doors hissed open, and Marla stepped out into the brightness, Pelham following. She shaded her eyes and looked around. And then, quite without intending to, she let out a low moan.

Because what she saw wasn't any underworld she'd read about, not the cold city of Hel, not the howling chasm of Druj, not the fields of Elysium, not the cool shade of the cosmic tree in Yaxche.

This Hell was made from a place in Marla's past, which was, after all, the only mythology she truly believed in.

12

I've been thinking about our current situation," Booth said.

"Silence." Ayres led his zombie army along the esplanade, much to the confusion of early-morning joggers who passed them by. "I'm enjoying myself. Don't spoil it with your blather." The day was already warm, and the chill that eternally seemed to grip Ayres was fading. Life, after all, was sweet. He was the greatest necromancer who had ever lived. He had power. So what if he sometimes still smelled rot, if the people around him appeared waxy and dead when he saw them from the corner of his eye? They *were* mostly dead, after all, and when the Cotard delusion asserted itself too strongly, he could use the therapeutic techniques Dr. Husch had taught him to overcome the sensations.

"I feel our accommodation cannot be sustained," Booth said.

"Shush." If Death didn't periodically voice his preference for Booth's continued presence, Ayres would have disposed of him by now.

"Ayres. Look at me."

Annoyed, Ayres stopped, the zombies around him lurching to a pause as well. He turned.

Booth had one arm flung out, extended so close to Ayres's face that, for a moment, he couldn't recognize the item in Booth's hand. The smell of metal and oil made it click for him; Booth held the gun he'd taken from the would-be mugger a few nights ago, the snub barrel pointed at Ayres's face. "What—"

"Thus, always, to tyrants," Booth said, and without hearing a sound, or feeling a thing, Ayres's whole world went silent and black.

The revivified mummy of John Wilkes Booth lowered his pistol and looked at the crumpled body of the man who had brought him to life. Ayres, head fatally pierced, lay among the collapsed bodies of his zombie army, and they had all lost their illusions, so they were nothing but bones and rot and ruin. Booth looked at his own hands, and whimpered; they were brown and black, shriveled, wrinkled. The illusion of his old flesh had died along with Ayres. Booth supposed the only reason he still stood while the other corpses had fallen was because he had his own spirit inhabiting his body, and had been more than a mere marionette controlled by the necro-mancer.

"Well done, young man," Viscarro said, and Booth turned, surprised, having almost forgotten about the subterranean sorcerer, but by then Viscarro was racing away with surprising speed, robes flapping as he went. Booth began to give chase, but knew he couldn't overpower the sorcerer—he'd only been able to stop Ayres thanks to surprise. He wondered if Death would be angry, if he would send Booth back to Hell. Booth decided that would be all right. He had always contended that he would rather die free than live a prisoner. Still, better to know one way or another than to suffer uncertainty. Booth knelt, felt around in Ayres's jacket, and found the tiny silver bell he'd used to summon Death. Booth rang it.

Death appeared from an alleyway and cursed. "What the hell happened here? My troops are fallen! Where's Viscarro?"

"Escaped, my lord," Booth said. He thought about blaming the death of Ayres on Viscarro, but didn't like the idea of others receiving credit for his deeds. "I shot Ayres, sir. I could no longer tolerate his cruelty and disrespect."

Death sighed. "Damn it, Booth, he was useful." Death moved his hand, and the zombies rose up, clothed again in their old illusions, and Booth was pleased to see his own artificial flesh returned as well—this time, he even had the tattoo of his initials on his hand, an improvement over the illusion Ayres had provided. "I could restore his spirit to his body but his complaining and bellowing would be endless. He already had some confusion over whether he was alive or dead, and I don't want to hear him playing Hamlet, in an agony of uncertainty, do you? Fine. All right. You'll have to make yourself twice as useful to make up for killing him, Booth."

"I shall try to give satisfaction, sir," Booth said.

"Good. Though this won't satisfy *you*. I'm sending you back to the underworld."

Booth shivered, though he felt no chill, except a mental one. "Sir, I am sincerely sorry for—"

"Quiet," Death said, which angered Booth—so peremptory!—though Booth knew he could not dispatch this tyrant as easily as he had Ayres. "I'm not sending you back to whatever tiresome torment your mind created for you. I'm sending you on a mission, not as a spirit, but in this body you're wearing now." Death placed both his hands on Booth's shoulders and looked into his eyes. "I've just received word that Marla Mason has entered my kingdom. I have no idea what prompted her intrusion, but I don't want her there."

"It is your realm, sir. Can you not simply expel her?"

"There are rules concerning living pilgrims in the underworld. I cannot strike her directly, but you—you are half of the world of the dead, and half of the world of the living. The rules that bind me will slide around you, your twilight status providing a certain freedom of action."

"What would you have me do, sir?"

"Stop her before she reaches the heart of my realm. Kill her, if you must, and I'll try to wrest my dagger from whichever sorcerer replaces her—Hamil, I suspect. He will be scarcely more tractable than Marla was, but I doubt he would try something as audacious as sneaking in the back door of my realm. Your intercession may not be necessary—my realm has many terrors and dangers for those who enter unprepared. But, just in case . . ."

"How will I find her?"

"You'll wait, like a trapdoor spider, in the corridor before my throne room. If she never arrives, fine." He shrugged. "I'll hear of it if she dies, or goes mad and becomes trapped wandering in my realm. But if she does enter that corridor . . ."

Booth drew his knife and his pistol. "I shall dispatch her, sir."

"Good man." Death frowned. "Well, horrible, small, vicious, arrogant man, actually. Better to say 'useful man.' You are that, at least."

Booth's anger began to rise again, but he bit down on a sharp retort. "'I must obey: his art is of such power,'" Booth said, and bowed low. "How shall I journey to—"

But before Booth could finish his question, he fell through space, and landed with a crash in a narrow corridor of dusty gray stone. He struggled to his feet and looked up and down the length of the corridor. It seemed to stretch on forever, but it was lined with little niches, some of which held ancient statuary of men with the heads of animals; or men with beards, sitting on thrones, or banker's scales, or miniature boats. Some few of the niches were empty, however, but for plinths, and Booth found one such, and sat down. He knew he might be waiting a long time—such was the nature of the underworld. But he knew how to occupy himself. Booth began to recite *Romeo and Juliet*, all the parts, but in a whisper, so as not to startle Marla, should she come along. Perhaps she would arrive at the moment when Juliet took her own life. There would be a certain poetry in that.

Rondeau burst from the water and hauled himself up the ladder into the boat. He wanted to flop on his back, but the oxygen tank made that impossible. Lifting his mask from his face, he shook his head at Beadle. "No good," he said. "Are you sure it's down there?"

Beadle, who in his neat suit looked strangely out of place aboard a fishing boat, nodded. "It's hard to pinpoint. Salt water dulls the divination, I think—salt is traditionally used to confuse spells, you know." He pointed to the topographical map of the bay, circling one spot with his finger. "It's just down there, probably."

"That's great." Rondeau opened a bottle of water and chugged it down. He'd been given a crash course in scuba diving by Langford, but he wasn't an especially powerful swimmer, and the waters of the bay were cold, even in summer, even through his wetsuit. "It's tough to know where the hell I'm going when I'm down there, though, it's so murky, and it gets dark faster than you'd think. I could use a beer."

"I don't believe beer and scuba diving mix."

Rondeau squinted at the sky. "We're going to lose the light. I feel like we're wasting time." He sighed. "But I don't know what our next move is if we don't get the cloak. I feel like we didn't even dent the Walking Death with that explosion."

"I think we made a dent in his sense of well-being. I

hear he led an attack on Viscarro's vault this morning, but I haven't heard how it went, as I've been out here on this boat with you all morning. Oh, I wanted to show you this." Beadle reached into his jacket and withdrew a thick cream-colored envelope. "Since you're damp, I'll just give you the salient details—I've been invited to the Founders' Ball at the Chamberlain's house this weekend. A grand masque, to be hosted by the new ruler of Felport, the Walking Death."

"It says that?" Rondeau said. "About the 'new ruler of Felport'?"

"Oh, yes. Langford and Partridge were invited as well, along with every notable person in sorcerous society. All the members of the ruling cabal, their better apprentices, and noble freelancers like myself. You, of course, were not invited."

"Hell," Rondeau said. "I hear it's a great party, if a little stuffy. I really thought I'd get to go this time." He sat in a swivel chair bolted to the deck and squinted at the sky. "You know, maybe I should go anyway. Crash the party."

Beadle was silent for a moment, though Rondeau imagined the faint sound of flywheels spinning and gears meshing and ticker tape unspooling. "Hmm," Beadle said. "Elaborate, please."

"If the ghosts of the founding fathers get pissed off, they can make big trouble for the leader of the city, right?"

"They can make big trouble for the *city*, a symptom of which is trouble for the city's leader, yes."

"No, hear me out. I figure, the ghosts probably don't

like Death much anyway. I mean, hell, they've avoided going to his realm for decades. I bet if something fucked up the Founders' Ball but good, they'd blame Death, and make things tough for him. If nothing else, they'd cause so much trouble in the city that it wouldn't be fun for Death anymore. They could stir up such a ruckus that a little thing like being exploded would start to feel like a fond memory."

"The kind of 'trouble' the ghosts could cause in the city might be more than you're counting on," Beadle said. "Only one Founders' Ball has ever been skipped, during the disastrous war of succession when Candlewick fought Butcher for possession of the dagger of office, and that was the year of the Great Fire of Felport. Much of the city was destroyed. You can still see burn marks on some of the stone structures in the historic district."

"I'm not talking about *skipping* the party. The party will still happen. I'll just sneak in before it's over and spoil Death's fun. If we can spin it right, if we can direct the attention of the ghosts toward Death in particular as the reason the party went bad . . ."

"That's a lot of ifs," Beadle said.

"I thought your whole talent was turning ifs into definites?"

"I'll examine the idea further," Beadle said. "It's a bold plan, certainly. Decisive."

"Marla says the Founders' Ball is the social glue of the sorcerers' world. It's where alliances are made, displeasure shown, rewards given out, all that. It's where a leader shows how rich and awesome and powerful and suave she is. If we let Death throw the party, and it goes well, I think he'll be more deeply entrenched than ever, and he might make *real* allies, instead of just people who are afraid of him. What if Marla can't ever come back while he's here? What if Death doesn't get bored and go away, or if he only gets bored on *geological* time scales, and he stays in control of the city until we're all old? I don't want that. I can't allow it."

"All right," Beadle said. "I'll examine the idea *very carefully*. Fair enough?"

"Yep."

"Good. Get back in the water. Whether you crash the party or not, things will be a lot easier for us if you're wearing Marla's cloak."

"True." Rondeau put his tank back on. As he slipped into the water, he knew he'd already decided. He was the leader of this miniature resistance, and the ultimate choice was his. He was going to crash the party and wreck up the place. He was going to make a fool out of Death.

"What is this place?" Pelham said, as the train behind them—their only link to the world of the living, apart from their own beating hearts—pulled away.

Marla crossed her arms and surveyed the platform, illuminated by floodlights, the only obvious form of egress a spiral staircase with copper pipe rails. "It looks like the Tenderloin Station. A secret subway stop underneath San Francisco."

Pelham sighed. "So it didn't work, then? We just

took a train to some station in San Francisco? All that darkness was the tunnel under the bay?"

Marla shook her head. "Tenderloin Station isn't connected to any other rail lines. The only track here runs in a circle. It's like a toy train set writ large. It was the lair of a sorceress named Bethany. No, this is the underworld. It just looks like a place I've been before." Marla had been prepared for any number of Hells, but not for one based on her life story. "I don't know what's waiting for us up those stairs, but I think we'd better go."

"All right." They started for the stairway, and somewhere deep beneath, the station machinery ground to life, and the spiral stair began to twist widdershins with a terrible whine, turning like a barber pole or the point of a drill, unspooling downward. Marla swore, but by the time she reached the stair it was turning eye-blurringly fast, an apparently infinite spiral she couldn't possibly climb, and when she squinted upward, it only disappeared into deeper darkness anyway.

"Okay," Marla said. "This isn't exactly like the Tenderloin Station, then. There must be another way out of here." There was precious little on the platform, just a transit map and a blank train schedule, because Bethany's train came and went as it pleased, and there were no obvious ways to escape. Marla considered going into the tunnel to look for some sort of maintenance exit, but what if a train came and squashed them?

"Perhaps it's a puzzle," Pelham said. "Mr. Cole warned you that the dead would try to trick and befuddle you. Tell me, this Bethany . . . is she dead?"

"She'd better be. I killed her. I killed her here, or in the real-world equivalent of this place."

"Ah." Pelham swallowed. "It was self-defense?"

"Well, broadly. Bethany was allied with a serious enemy of mine, and if I hadn't killed her, she would have made trouble for me, yes. And she did try to kill me first." Bethany had been strong, decisive, sardonic, and Marla had liked her, until her betrayal was revealed. "She wasn't a very nice person, Pelham. She was a cannibal."

"Good heavens."

Marla shrugged. "It was a magic thing. She only ate the willing—believe it or not, there are people who want to be eaten, it's their kink—and I was going to let that slide, disgusting as I found it, but when she tried to kill me . . ." Marla shrugged. "I did what I had to do. I don't know why I'm here." She kicked a wall. "We need to move forward. Shit."

A rumbling arose from the tunnel, and Marla cocked her head.

"Is that the bone train, coming back?" Pelham said.

"I doubt it."

A train screeched into the station, an engine of black metal and stainless steel with smoked windows, followed by a similar passenger car, the whole thing an elaborate techno-fetishist fantasy. Bethany was a builder, a creator, a modifier, and she'd fabricated her own train by hand. Only this was a ghost of that train, or an illusion of that train, or . . . or something.

"Should we get on?" Pelham said. "Maybe it will take us out of here."

"Maybe," Marla said, and then the doors whispered open, revealing an inviting golden light inside the car.

"*Marla.*" The voice had the timbre of a whisper, but was very loud. "*I've been waiting for you.*"

"Oh, fuck." Marla hadn't known Bethany long, but she recognized the voice. Bethany had been into extreme body modifications, and in addition to the subdermal implants in her forehead that gave her stubby goatlike horns, the multiple body piercings, the scarification and brands and tattoos, she'd also bifurcated her tongue, making it forked like a serpent, and that gave her voice a distinctive quality. "Hey, Bethany," Marla said. "Fancy meeting you here."

"*I will eat you. Then I will live again, I will have life inside me, I will assume your life.*"

"Oh, dear." Pelham stepped back, partly behind Marla.

Marla wondered if Bethany had somehow become the train. She was a fabricator, a lover of elaborate and strange machinery, and perhaps in the afterlife she got her wish and became a built thing rather than a born thing. "I don't think so, hon," Marla said. "I killed you once. I'm not afraid of you."

"*Only one of us can die now,*" Bethany said, and then, dashing Marla's theory that she had become the train, she emerged from the open doors of the carriage.

She had to stoop to get out, because she was much larger than she'd been when she was alive, and she wasn't human anymore.

Pelham whimpered. Marla couldn't blame him.

Bethany's bodily modifications had continued after

death, and she'd transformed herself—or been transformed—into a monster. Her stubby horns had grown, bursting from her bloody forehead as great curling pointed horns, and she had wings now, of leather and wire and gleaming bolts. Her upper body was much the same, though she was bare-chested, her nipple rings glinting, the tattoos on her chest revealed as elaborate abstract designs. But her lower body was no longer human at all. She was like a centaur now, but with the elongated body of a clockwork lizard, all scales of hammered brass and spines of wickedly sharp volcanic glass, metal seams releasing little puffs of steam when her tail twitched. Her face was different, too, her jaw a hinged thing of blue glass and silver joints, her teeth stainless steel triangles, but her eyes were the same, yellow with horizontal slits. "*Marla. You did this to me. But I am a greater predator now than ever before.*"

"Too bad there's nothing to hunt down here," Marla said, with bravado she didn't really feel. "Except, what, the ghosts of rats?"

Bethany slithered forward, her mechanical legs pistoning smoothly, and then rose to a great height, looking down on Marla. "*Who is the little man? My little appetizer.*"

"Don't touch him—" Marla began, but Bethany spun impossibly fast, swiping out with her spiked tail and smacking Marla across the room. Marla landed hard, groaned, and sat up, then jerked back when she almost stuck her hand into the spinning spiral staircase. If Bethany had smacked her with a little more English on the blow, Marla would have hit the stairs and been transformed herself, into a bloody red cloud of fragments. "You're still a bitch." Marla rose, but then she screamed—actually screamed—as Bethany flashed her a grin and proceeded to eat Pelham.

She *ate Pelham*. Bethany's jaw unhinged, unfolded, expanded to impossible size, and she snapped downward, Pelham disappearing into her now-vast mouth with only a little squeak. Then Bethany rose up again and Marla's valet disappeared, feet waving, down her throat. Her jaw folded up to human proportions again. Bethany's throat was still human-sized, Pelham should never have been able to fit, but . . . but . . .

But this was the underworld, where physics were, at best, a convenience. Still, underworld or not, some things were constant.

Marla drew her dagger, and Bethany belched a gout of steam. "*You next*," Bethany said. "*Shishkebabed*." From somewhere on her body Bethany retrieved a steampunk crossbow, an oversized thing of elaborate flywheels and tiny humming engines, loaded with half a dozen bolts as long as a forearm and thick as the fat end of a pool cue. She fired, the bolts launching with little percussive noises like champagne corks popping, and Marla dodged and dove and rolled, trying to think—how to fight a dragon?

The same way you fight anything. Hit it where it's sensitive. She rolled again, closer, coming perilously near the metal talons on the ends of Bethany's mechanical legs, and then lashed up with her dagger, slicing neatly through the overlapping white armored plates of Bethany's belly. Bethany screamed like a steam whistle and reared up, trying to escape, but that only exposed more of her belly to Marla, and so Marla rose from her crouch and kept cutting, dragging the blade down, parting metal as easily as cloth.

"Ms. Mason!" Pelham said, and yes, he was in there, she could see him through the slash she'd made. He clung to a metal lattice, face sweaty and streaked with soot, eyes wide.

"Get back!" Marla said, and when he retreated as far as he could, she lashed out with her blade, slicing away a dozen plates of armor. Bethany staggered back, and Pelham fell out of the hole Marla had made. Before Bethany got out of range, Marla went for the wires and tubes and hydraulics at the ankles and knees of her front legs, severing connections and spilling hot dark oil all over the station floor.

Marla grabbed Pelham and dragged him away as Bethany fell. The dragon-witch began dragging herself backward with her functional rear legs, eyes fixed on Marla, crossbow forgotten on the floor. "*You killed me,*" Bethany said, retreating into her train. "*You did this.*"

"We've established that," Marla said, breathing hard. "Now stop the staircase from spinning, or I'm coming onto the train after you. You remember what happened last time I boarded your train, right? I might not be able to kill you again, but I can force you to spend the rest of your eternity repairing all the damage I'll do."

Bethany hissed and vanished into the train. The spiral stair slowed down and finally stopped.

"Okay," Marla said. "Let's get the hell out of here."

She retrieved her bag, the contents of which hadn't done her much good, but might serve her better in the future.

"I've never been eaten before," Pelham said, voice trembling. "It was most unpleasant."

"Just be glad she didn't have stomach acids. Come on. Upward and outward." She hoped Bethany wouldn't start the stair spinning again when they were halfway up. "I'll lead. Who knows what we'll find up there." Marla stepped onto the stair, which, in the real world, led up to one of San Francisco's rougher neighborhoods. It would lead elsewhere here, she was sure. "Unless it's somebody else I killed. I hope that isn't the theme for this visit." But she knew just *thinking* that increased the likelihood it would be. They were unlikely to encounter any of Pelham's personal demons, assuming he had any—he was magically bound to her in a subservient position, and she guessed that her own ghosts would take precedence.

"How many people *have* you killed?" Pelham said from the stairs below her.

"With my own hands? Not that many. I mean, too many, even one is too many, but not as many as most people probably think. There was Bethany. A guy named Joshua, who killed a friend of mine." *And broke my heart.* "Somerset, but he was *un*dead when I killed him, so maybe he doesn't count. A jungle sorcerer named Mutex who tried to destroy the world, but he was complicated, too—I only killed his body, his mind was somewhere else at the time. Then there was a guy I knocked off a rooftop in my misspent youth—though that was an accident, we were fighting and he fell. I atoned as best I could for that, made offerings at his grave, tried to obviate the bad karma. . . ." She paused. "And, ah, when I was about fourteen, there was this guy, and he . . . hell. This is going to be hell."

Rich emerald light burst in, and Marla emerged from the darkness into a new and—thankfully—unfamiliar place, a lush green wet jungle filled with the calling of birds and the screeching of monkeys. The humid air smelled of wet leaves and sickly sweet flowers. The stairway jutted surrealistically up from a tangle of vines and undergrowth.

Pelham came after Marla as she gazed at the canopy of branches above. "If it's not too forward, may I ask, whom did you kill in a place like this?"

"Nobody. I've never been to a spot like this before. I don't know where—"

"Marla Mason." Mutex emerged from the trees, hands clasped behind his back. He looked as he had in life, dark skin, dark eyes, bare chest, wearing a short iridescent cape woven of insect wings. "Welcome. I will cut out your living heart." He smiled, and his teeth were little obsidian chips, and when he showed his hands, his fingers were knives of volcanic glass, the same kind of knives he'd once used to cut out the hearts of half a dozen sorcerers before Marla stopped him.

"I just kicked Bethany's ass," Marla said. "Do you think you can—"

The jungle behind Mutex stirred. Something vast and green approached, trees snapping and falling as it came.

Marla's mouth went dry. *"Run."*

But before she could run, Mutex sprouted several long shafts from his chest. He stared down at himself, puzzled, and fell backward. The vast thing behind him paused, then drew back, retreating before it fully showed itself, leaving Marla with the impression of a walking green cliffside.

She turned, to find Pelham holding Bethany's clockwork crossbow, which now held only two bolts. "I thought the weapon might be useful," he said, almost apologetically, and Marla hugged him.

"Good man." She released him. Mutex groaned and began trying to pull one of the crossbow bolts out of his chest, crying out in frustration when his razor-sharp fingers cut right through the shaft. "We'd better go before he gets up again," Marla said.

"That enormous thing that followed him. What was it?"

Marla brushed hanging vines away and kept her eyes open for snakes and poisonous frogs. "Mutex was a priest of the old Aztec gods. He killed people and cut out their hearts as sacrifices, hoping to bring his gods back to life. Some of those gods are *nasty*. That thing behind him . . . I think it was one of those gods. Or at least Mutex's own personal version of one of those gods. Either way, it could have hurt us badly, but knocking Mutex down was enough to make it pause. I don't want to give it a chance to catch up, though. Something that big can cover a lot of ground. Thanks for thinking fast. My usual response is more fight than flight, but when I saw that thing coming out of the jungle, buggering off seemed best."

"That's two, then," Pelham said. "Of the people you've killed. Do you think we'll have to face them all?"

Marla sighed. "Yeah. Probably. I mean, I do think so, which means it will almost certainly happen, damn it. I guess deep down I knew I'd have to answer for the things I've done, no matter how justified those actions seemed at the time." And the worst was yet to come, though Marla didn't want to scare Pelham. Somerset was terrifying. Joshua had been her lover, before she murdered him. And the last one, the boy from her hometown, from before she ran away from home, from before she knew magic . . . That would be hard. They would all be hard. Cole had told her there was always a cost to visiting the underworld. She hadn't thought the cost would involve ripping the scabs off her own history of violence.

13

Marla and Pelham trudged through the sticky jungle, alert to every rustle and roar and screech in the distance, afraid Mutex and his pet god would catch up to them. Eventually they emerged into a clearing, where they were confronted by a crumbling step pyramid, all dark vine-crusted stone, with a human-scaled stairway leading to the top. Long gutters ran down either side of the stairway, stained the dark reddish-brown of old dried blood.

"Do we go up?" Pelham said.

Marla nodded. "We climbed stairs to get out of the last place. Going up seems counterintuitive in a place like this, but like Cole said, direction is more a courtesy than a fact down here."

"Who do you think we'll see next?" Pelham puffed a bit as they began the long climb. The distances they were crossing might be imaginary on some level, but the energy Pelham and Marla were expending was real.

"Hopefully nobody. An empty throne room. But if

we're not that lucky, I don't know. I killed Bethany before I killed Mutex, so we're not going in reverse chronological order. If there's a pattern, I'm not privy to it." They paused halfway up the pyramid to rest, and Marla took a bottle of water from her bag and shared it with Pelham. A millipede scurried up the face of the pyramid, pursued by tiny green lizards, and Marla wondered if they were the ghosts of an entomologist and a herpetologist in their ideal forms, or if they were just part of the scenery, the illusion of jungle and pyramids that Mutex had made. The air smelled wet, and faintly of coppery blood and sweet flowers. "All right. Up we go."

They reached the top of the pyramid, where Marla had expected to find a slab of stone for human sacrifices. Instead, there was a metal door, like the access to an interior stairway from a rooftop. Marla turned and looked back the way they'd come, shading her eyes against the sun, and there was nothing but jungle as far as she could see, except for one green hill—

—which began moving toward her, knocking down trees as it came. She swore. Not a hill. "Time to go." She tugged on the handle of the door.

It didn't open. Marla kicked at the door, but even with her magically reinforced boots, it wouldn't budge. "Shit. Shit, shit, shit." She looked behind her, and the green hill was still approaching, a creature bigger than the pyramid they stood upon, and hungry, surely hungry.

"Allow me to try." Pelham drew a thin leather case from the inside of his dirty suit jacket. He opened it, revealing a row of thin metal devices.

"Lockpicks? You're a lockpick?"

"There are 145 different types of locks in the Chamberlain's mansion, Ms. Mason, and I was trained to open them all. This resembles the door to the pantry. I often helped myself to midnight snacks there, I confess, and opened it more often than the others."

"You seem remarkably calm, considering," she said, as Pelham bent and began working on the lock, fiddling little bits of metal into the door handle.

"I don't know what you saw, Ms. Mason. I chose not to look. I further choose to believe I will open this door before whatever you saw reaches us."

"That's the spirit." The green thing was closer now, and she could see Mutex on top of it, like a man standing on the deck of a rocking ship. She could also see the green thing's eyes. They were as big as the Ferris wheel down by Felport's esplanade.

"There." The door clicked open and swung inward.

Marla looked through the door at a dark street, surrounded by tall buildings. Far behind them, something roared, a sound like the Earth cracking apart, and Pelham rushed through the door, taking the lead for once, and Marla followed, kicking the door shut behind her, suddenly glad that she hadn't been able to break the lock. Because now the door latched and locked securely, whereas, if she'd broken it down, a passageway between *this* place and *that* place might have remained open.

Pelham gestured at the buildings, the rain-slicked streets, the dirty alleyway off to the right. "Is this—"

"Felport. Yeah." Marla's voice was steady. It took some effort to keep it that way. "But not exactly the one we left. See there?" She pointed to the distant spire of the

Whitcroft-Ivory building, the tallest skyscraper in the city, which was all girders and scaffolding for the top few floors. "That building is still being constructed. Back home, it's finished."

"So, then, when are we?" Pelham said.

Marla shook her head. "Work on the building was stalled for a couple years. But that was at least five or six years ago, back when I was a freelancer. And this isn't time travel. There are no people here, no cars, no traffic sounds, no radios, nothing." This felt less like Marla's city and more like the set of a postapocalyptic movie. "I bet it's Somerset. We fought on a night like this. Though I'd expect great clouds of pigeons in that case. He was a vermomancer, among other things. Let's keep moving."

"Vermomancer?" Pelham followed her down the sidewalk, in the direction of the Whitcroft-Ivory building. "I'm unfamiliar with the term. A sorcerer of . . . worms?"

"Vermin. Somerset used rats and roaches, but he especially liked pigeons. Rock doves are all over cities, you know, and nobody takes notice of them, but send five hundred pigeons after somebody, each one weighing about a pound, with talons out and beaks stabbing and wings flapping, and when they're done, you'll find nothing left but a bloody pecked-up mess." She stepped around a pile of rags and garbage on the sidewalk. "He was a nasty guy, Somerset. Besides his magical ambitions, he was a slumlord, and he used to drive out tenants with swarms of roaches and rats, then raise the rents before new people moved in. The city was a polluted, unpleasant mess under his leadership, at least for a lot of people, but he made the sorcerers under him rich, so there was a lot of loyalty there." She looked skyward. "But I don't see any pigeons."

"Watch out," Pelham said, and she stopped short, realizing she'd almost stepped right on another pile of refuse, this one bigger than the last, and more fragrant. Marla started to go around it, and then the pile of garbage reached out a hand, grasped her ankle, and moaned her name.

Marla jerked back, drawing her knife, but the thing on the street didn't attack her, it merely shifted and half rolled over. She could make it out now, just, as a human being wrapped in torn rags, body broken, folded, spindled, dampened, splattered. A rather beautiful green eye rolled into sight and gazed at her.

Pelham vomited.

"I didn't die for two days," the thing on the sidewalk said, and Marla's own stomach rolled over. "After you threw me from the roof."

"I'm sorry," Marla whispered. "It was nothing personal. I was working for someone. You were working for someone else. They should have fought each other. We fought instead." She didn't even know this dead man's name. He'd been an apprentice, Marla a mercenary in someone's temporary employ, and they'd fought on a rooftop for possession of a deck of cards wrapped in a silk scarf that their respective masters both wanted very badly.

"I suffer for the things I did." The thing on the sidewalk coughed wetly. "You will suffer, too, when you are like me." It tried to drag itself toward her. "I will make you like me. I will pull you down here with me, and we will run into the gutters together when it rains."

"I'm sorry," Marla said again, meaning it, but knowing it was empty. "Can I—could I—put you out of your misery? A knife in your brain, would that give you peace, even here, for a little while?"

"Die with me. That's all I need." It inched itself forward again, the remnants of its fingernails breaking off on the pavement.

"Ms. Mason," Pelham said. "We should go. Forward, remember? Ever forward."

"He was like me." Marla stared down at the dead man. "Just doing his job, trying to take something from me, but I fought him off, I knocked him over, he fell."

"You threw me." The thing's voice was more ragged now from its efforts at locomotion. Marla knew she would dream of its pursuit forever, that her occasional nightmares of being chased would change to nightmares of this thing—this *man*—pulling himself along after her, endlessly, implacably, tirelessly.

"Ms. Mason," Pelham said again, and then, more loudly, "Marla!" She heard him, distantly, but mostly she looked at the streak of red left in the wake of the man she'd killed, the blood left behind as he dragged himself after her, and wasn't that just like her life, too? She moved forward, and left a trail of the dead behind her? A streak of blood on the pavement of her past?

Pelham slapped her face, and the shock made Marla gasp. He reared back to slap her again, and she grabbed his wrist, twisting it and dropping him to his knees.

"I'm sorry, Ms. Mason, I was losing you, you haven't

moved in nearly ten minutes, that thing wouldn't stop *whispering* . . ."

Marla released his hand abruptly. "Pelham, I didn't know, I . . . it's fine. You did right." She looked down again at the broken man on the pavement. If Pelham hadn't been here, would she have been mesmerized, trapped here until the thing reached her and pulled her down? "I left flowers. I poured whiskey on the grave. I *tried*."

"Not for years. You have not left those offerings for many seasons."

And it was true. Marla had let time heal her guilt. Killing this man accidentally had taught her not to kill casually, to murder only when her own life or the fate of her city was at stake, but while she'd remembered the lesson, she'd forgotten the man who inspired it. "When I get back, I will again. I promise."

"Die with me," it said again, and Marla could only shake her head, and turn away, allowing Pelham to guide her from the mess she'd made.

Pelham and Marla took a construction elevator, partially open to the wind, up the Whitcroft-Ivory building. The air was so cold their breath puffed, but when they reached the top level, there was a walkway that led to a wooden door. This time Marla led, and this time the doorknob turned easily in her hand. Marla took a deep breath, pushed it open, and stepped into a perfect replica of her own office, with her high-backed desk chair turned to face away from her.

"Hello, Joshua," she said. The chair swiveled, and her dead lover tried to nod at her with his broken neck.

* * *

Rondeau spat the regulator out of his mouth. "Fuck this." He pulled himself up the ladder. "Two fucking days of this, and not a goddamn—" He stopped. Beadle sat hunched in the far stern of the boat, and the Bay Witch was in one of the swivel chairs, staring at Rondeau quizzically.

"Fuck what?" she said.

Rondeau got onto the boat, legs shaking. The Bay Witch was weird, but powerful, with titanic forces at her beck and call. Marla said the witch could've given her a run for chief sorcerer, if she'd had any political ambitions. Nobody knew what the Bay Witch's ambitions were, if she had any, and Rondeau had no idea how to talk his way out of this. "Hello, ma'am. I'm just . . . frustrated. Nothing you need to worry about."

"You work for Marla," she said. "I like Marla. When does she come back?"

Rondeau glanced at Beadle, who shrugged miserably. "Ah, she's been banished by the Walking Death. You know, that guy who killed all the zebra clams or whatever?"

"Yes. Marla is still banished? Sad. I like Marla. I like your boat. I like boats."

This is like talking to a six-year-old. Only a six-year-old who could drown you with a gesture. "Thanks. It's a good boat."

The Bay Witch rose abruptly. "What are you looking for? Tell me what you're looking for."

"I was just going for a little swim—"

"Don't lie. Liars get turned into chum. Into cut bait.

Don't lie!" She was right up in his face now, shouting, and her breath smelled like raw fish and salt. Rondeau couldn't back up without falling off the boat into the water, and going into the water wouldn't make him any safer from her.

"Okay! I'm looking for Marla's cloak."

"Cloak? No cloak. Not in my bay." She sounded puzzled, and strands of wet blond hair hung clumped in her face, giving her a slightly deranged look.

"The cloak is in a box. A wardrobe. I know you took it."

"Oh. The box. Yes. The death man asked me to take it deep, where no one else could find it, as a favor. I owed him a favor. For killing the zebra mussels."

"Okay. I understand. But that's what I'm looking for."

"You'll never find it. No one but me ever will. That was the favor."

Rondeau spread his hands. "I have to try. For Marla. To help her."

"Oh. Why didn't you ask me for help? To find it?"

Rondeau stuck his pinky in his ear and wiggled it around. There was water in his ear canal, but he could hear okay. "What? You hid it. Why would you help me find it?"

"You would owe me a favor. Better, no, wait, yes, better if *Marla* owed me a favor. You can owe me a favor from her?"

"You . . . want me to promise Marla will do a favor for you? If you help me find the wardrobe?"

The Bay Witch nodded vigorously.

"But aren't you loyal to Death?"

The Bay Witch frowned at him. "He did me a favor. I owed him a favor. He asked me for a favor. I did him a favor. I owe him nothing now. Even-steven. He never said I couldn't bring the wardrobe *back*."

He didn't know he had to, Rondeau thought, and right then he could have kissed the Bay Witch right on her bizarrely literal lips.

"Yes," Beadle said, rising. "Will you do this favor for us? And keep it a secret, and tell no one?"

The Bay Witch looked at him, then at Rondeau. "This man can make a favor for you for Marla?"

Rondeau thought he followed that. "Listen, yes, I can promise Marla will owe you a favor when she comes back, if you get the cloak for us. But we'd like you to keep it a secret. And, um, don't take it away from us or anything later on, even if somebody asks you to. Is that okay?"

"Okayfine," she said, all one word, and then, "Wait here." She dove cleanly into the bay and vanished from sight.

"Guess we should have asked her in the first place," Rondeau said.

Beadle sighed. "Some people defy rational analysis."

"So if she pops up with this cloak . . . we hit the party tomorrow night. Agreed?"

"Let me lay some charms of deflection and misdirection on you, and, tentatively, yes. Partridge and Langford are on hand to provide distractions. We have to be careful, to spoil the party without harming the guests. The cloak might make you . . . unpredictable, yes? Likely to attack bystanders?"

Rondeau shrugged. "Marla says it's tricky, that you sort of lose control, but she said it's like steering a really big boat, you have to be steady and guidance is slow, but it *can* be guided."

"We'll try to chase the party guests out anyway, to be safe. Langford is working on a potent stink bomb that works psychically as well as olfactorily. It shouldn't affect Death—or, alas, the ghosts of the founding fathers—but it should clear out the rest of the guests, and give you a free hand to face our opponent. He really might kill you, you know, oust your psyche, force you to find a new body. And now that Ayres has dropped out of sight, you won't be able to seize his body."

Rondeau shrugged. "There's risk, I know. But it's for Marla. For the city. It's gotta be done." He sat down. "That's crazy about Ayres disappearing. You think he's dead?"

"Probably all the excitement got to his heart. No one has seen the mummy Ayres raised, either, the one that claimed to be John Wilkes Booth. Being in Death's employ seems a hazardous enterprise."

The water rippled, and the Bay Witch surfaced, along with a box wrapped in chains. She climbed the ladder one-handed, carrying the heavy wardrobe by a chain wrapped around the fingers of her free hand, and she swung the box onto the deck, where it landed hard enough to make the whole boat rock. "Okay," she said. "Marla owes me a favor. Good-bye." She vanished into the water, then emerged again. "Wait." She seemed to be thinking something over very hard. "Will you be at the Founders' Ball?"

"We will," Rondeau said.

She nodded. "I will see you then." Looking pleased with herself—for managing a simple social nicety, perhaps?—she dove back beneath the waves.

Rondeau and Beadle stood on opposite sides of the wardrobe. "All right, then," Beadle said. "Let's get these chains off."

"You've looked better, Joshua," Marla said. "Death doesn't agree with you." She was trying to be strong and cold, but seeing him again whipped her emotions into a whirlpool with a sucking funnel of darkness at the center. There was hate in there, sure, and she tried to focus on that, but there were other feelings, too. Joshua had made her happy, for a little while, before he turned to poison, but the happiness had been real, even if his motives had not.

Joshua had been a lovetalker, a Ganconer, a man with supernatural charisma, capable of seducing anyone. He'd bewitched Marla, but all along he was working for one of Marla's enemies. At the end of their affair, he'd murdered one of her friends, right in this very office, and then tried to kill her. She'd killed him first, breaking his neck, but she had still been so thoroughly under his spell that killing him had been like ripping out her own heart and grinding it under her boot heel.

"Marla," Joshua said. His broken neck made his head cock at an angle, giving him a quizzical appearance, like a little boy lost. "I know I don't look my best. Forgive me. You look beautiful."

"I have nothing to say to you." Marla crossed her arms, trying to separate out the hate from the churn of her feelings, trying to isolate and distill that fury until she felt nothing else. It was like trying to separate the whiskey in a glass from the water. "You're a betrayer, Joshua. Ever read Dante's *Inferno*? In his vision of Hell, betrayers get chewed up for eternity in Satan's mouth. You should be there with Judas and Brutus, gnawed forever."

"I was never much of a reader." Joshua swiveled back and forth in the office chair—*her* office chair, right down to the squeak. "Is this your new assistant? The replacement for Ted? I never liked Ted. He liked me, though. Everyone did."

Marla instinctively maneuvered herself between Pelham and Joshua. "He's my friend. And he's none of your business."

Joshua shook his head. The broken bones in his neck ground together audibly. "You don't have friends, Marla. Not really. There's no room inside you for anything but yourself and your duty. Your *city*. Nothing but ashes in the hearth of your heart."

She gritted her teeth. "Fuck this. Pelham, look for a door out of here."

"You don't leave until we're done," Joshua said, gently, gently. He rose from the desk, and he had a kitchen knife in his hand, the same knife, still wet with Ted's blood. "Which means you don't leave at all, because we never had closure, you and I. I was your lover. You took me into your arms, your bed, your confidence. Into your heart—I thought. I was closer to you than anyone. And what did you do?" He looked down at the knife in his hands, then back up at her. "You killed me. I know you loved me until the end. I saw it in your face, in the tears just starting to well up in your eyes when you snapped my neck and sent me here. What kind of woman are you, Marla? What kind of person kills what they love?"

Marla licked her lips. "I don't . . . you didn't . . . you were going to kill me. You killed Ted. I had no choice."

He shrugged. "I never loved you. I was a liar. I acted true to my nature. But you . . . you did love me, and you snapped my neck anyway. What's your nature? Ashes. A heart full of ashes." Joshua put the knife down and came around the side of the desk, head lolling, eyes fixed on her.

"I had no choice," she whispered.

"Please. You could have incapacitated me. Twisted the knife out of my hand, dropped me to the ground, knocked me out. I was no match for you. I was a lover, not a fighter. But you don't hold back, do you, Marla? Erased me like a mistake on a blackboard. Because I was inconvenient, and complicated. Because I embarrassed you, tricked you. Isn't that right?" He stepped toward her, put his hand on her cheek, and gazed into her eyes. She could smell him, the scent of honey, vanilla, just a hint of male sweat. Even without his supernatural glamour, he was still beautiful, her beautiful boy, and he was a monster, yes, of course; but wasn't she a monster, too?

"We're both monsters," he whispered, and she wondered with a jolt if he could read her mind, or if their thoughts simply ran on parallel tracks. "Two monsters. We may as well be monsters for each other, and leave everyone else out of it. You and I, together forever, here in this room. Just one thing to do first. To make us match. I'll give you what you gave me. One little twist." He put his hand on her chin, and Marla just waited for what she knew must come next: the hard twist, the break of her neck. She deserved it. She'd killed Joshua, and she'd never allowed herself to feel a moment's regret or remorse for that act. But he was right. It had been easier to kill him than to cope with him alive, knowing he'd played her for a fool. She hadn't faced that fact. Righteousness had been her armor. Until now. Now it was all rising up, and a broken neck was only the beginning of the penance she owed.

But Joshua staggered away, reaching behind him, flailing, and suddenly Pelham was there, taking Marla's arm, tugging her away, saving her. Marla's eyes slowly came back into focus, and her fuzzy head cleared. "What—Pelly? What?"

"I stabbed him with his own knife," Pelham said grimly. "Just like he stabbed your friend Ted. It seemed only fitting. I apologize if I overstepped my bounds, Ms. Mason, but he was going to hurt you."

Joshua sat down on the edge of the desk, still trying to reach the knife Pelham had jammed into him. He began weeping, blinking tears from his beautiful eyes. "I was alive," he said, voice harsh, no longer a lover's whisper. "Damn it, I was alive, you loved me, you should have let me kill you, I'm supposed to be the one who's alive."

"The door is this way, Ms. Mason." Pelham led her

by the arm to the far end of the room, to a door that didn't exist in her real office.

Marla let herself be led. "I had to do it," she said, not sure if she was talking to Pelham or Joshua. "It was him or me. He tried to kill me, I had no choice. Isn't that right? I had to do it."

"Of course," Pelham said, and opened the door.

A heart full of ashes, Marla thought.

They entered a gray stairway, and after Pelham closed the door, Marla sank down to sit on a step and put her head in her hands. "This place is getting to me, Pelham. If you weren't here, I'd have been lost two or three times by now."

"It is not a pleasant journey for me, but it is . . . less personally tailored to my experience. I think I am better able to cope. These women and men and monsters are all strangers to me. I have never, myself, killed anyone."

"I don't recommend it. It's bad for your soul. Even if you had the best reasons in the world, it eats at you. Maybe not right away, but eventually. The best you can hope for is to die yourself before all the shit you've pushed down comes welling up again."

"But . . . we're almost done, aren't we? Not much farther now?" Pelham's voice was hope layered on top of desperation. He'd done some fighting down here, hadn't he? That was new for him. Like B said, you couldn't go to Hell without the experience changing you.

Marla stood up. "Yeah. The only way out is through. Let's go upstairs." She had to focus on the task at hand. To repress everything else. It was the only way to continue.

They emerged onto another rooftop—it was the roof of the club, Marla realized, on a warm summer evening—and faced a twisting tornado of gray feathers, white shit, and harsh cries. The buildings in the distance were all liberally spattered with bird shit. "Pigeons. Somerset's turn, I guess." She opened her shoulder bag and took out a good hunting slingshot with a molded grip, and a couple sacks of ball bearings. "Get Bethany's crossbow ready. If Somerset appears—he'll be the thing that *isn't* a pigeon—hit him. I'm going to get his attention."

"You seem eager to confront him."

Her relationship with Somerset had been unambiguous: he was her first great enemy. There were none of the treacherous depths she'd run into with Joshua. This would be simple and direct. Just what she needed. "Fighting Somerset, putting him down, made my name in this city. It's how I became chief sorcerer. It was also the hardest, best fight I've ever had." She loaded the slingshot with a steel ball, drew back, and let it fly. A tiny portion of the tornado of pigeons fell, and Marla started whistling as she loaded up another shot, and another, plinking away at the birds. "Better than fish in a barrel." After she'd fired two dozen times, the tornado finally began to shift, twist, and open up, birds parting like curtains, revealing a figure hanging in the air in the center of the vortex.

"There he is," Marla said. "Hit him!"

Pelham raised the crossbow, took aim, and fired. Marla half expected the birds to fly in and intercept the bolts, but both struck Somerset true, in the chest. He didn't plummet from the sky like a stone, though. He flew forward, and Marla saw now that some of those dirty gray feathers were attached to his back. Like Bethany, Somerset had grown wings in the afterlife, though his were enormous bird's wings. He seemed to dangle from the wings like a spider from a thread, and as he slowly flapped his way closer, he looked just as gangly as always. He wore only a ragged loincloth, and his skin was the same gray shade it had been in his undeath, when Marla killed him.

Somerset glided down and landed on the rooftop, unconcerned with the bolts sticking out of his chest, and folded his dirty wings behind him. "Marla Mason." His voice like something that scuttles in the night. "Why have you dragged me here?" His eyes seemed to spin like dirty pinwheels, almost hypnotic.

Marla blinked. "What?"

"I was having a perfectly pleasant afterlife when I heard you calling. Ruining the solitude I've made." He gestured at the guano-stained cityscape before them. "I can't create any *people*, but to be honest, people only got in the way. I'm happier here than I was alive. I always liked the inside of my own head better than the outside world anyway. The outside was so resistant to being shaped."

"Aren't you supposed to be psychotically attacking me?"

Somerset shrugged. "The dead often go mad in the presence of the living, I'm told, but after you've been brought back to life and sent back here again, something changes. You realize that life, real life, is no longer an option—just a false life, as an undead thing, skin numb, like your whole body is wrapped in leather. No taste, no smell, no real pleasures. It takes the edge off the blinding jealousy a bit. It helps you accept your fate. Normally, the dead can't change, but being brought back to life provides another little window for learning experiences to slip through."

"But I killed you," Marla said.

Somerset frowned. "Hardly. You couldn't have killed me. You were an upstart. Sauvage killed me, and took over the city. And I killed him for that when I came back to life, which is how you took control, I suppose. Don't look surprised. I still hear things down here, sometimes. I have many connections. But no, you didn't kill me, Marla. You just . . . put me down. Helped me rest again. I know I resisted you, but being raised from the dead made me crazy, ambitious, violent, desperate for things I could no longer have. I'm happier here, in my own little empire of the dead and the gray. And if this meeting has fulfilled whatever strange subconscious longing you had to see me again, I'd just as soon you moved along. You're spoiling the whole milieu."

"Um, sure. That's . . . sure."

"I imagine you're a terrible chief sorcerer." Somerset turned away. "But I do still respect the office, you know. Good luck regaining your place." He jumped off the roof and flew away, disappearing into his cloud of pigeons again.

"That was not what I expected," Marla said. "This place is fucked up."

"There's a ladder here, Marla," Pelham said from the edge of the building. "Leading down."

"Good. Down is good."

"We're nearly there, aren't we?"

"Nearly somewhere, Pelham. Though I'm worried this place has saved the worst for last."

"What do you think we'll find down there, Ms. Mason? You said something about when you were younger. . . ."

Marla glanced back. Somerset had taken his flying horde off into the distance, so maybe they could linger unmolested for a few minutes. She was not eager to head down this ladder if she was going to find a facsimile of rural Indiana at the bottom, and the remains of the man—the *boy*—she'd killed there. "I grew up in the country, in Indiana. We had a trailer on a big dusty lot, backed by some trees, and there wasn't much around but farms and a garbage dump."

"I'm surprised, Ms. Mason. You seem so firmly a creature of the city."

"By choice, Pelly. Because I didn't much like being a creature of the country. Back then, in junior high, I only had a few friends, mainly two girls, Amy and Carol. We all three liked climbing trees and playing kickball more than wearing makeup and hanging out in the mall, which made us sort of outcasts, but we were outcasts together, so it wasn't so bad. We hung around together, caught a lot of hell, people talked about us, called us dykes, whatever." Was that a little Hoosier accent creeping into her voice, overpowering the carefully neutral accent she'd cultivated after she ran away? "I think Carol might have actually been a lesbian, though back then, around there, she'd never have said so, not even to her best friends." Marla looked over the ledge, wondering if she'd see stubbly cornfields below, but it was only a guano-spattered street. For now. "Carol got attacked," she said flatly. "And then Amy got attacked. They were both too ashamed to say anything about it—Amy actually went out on a date with the guy, though it wasn't really a date, just a walk after a school dance, but anyway, she blamed herself, said she had it coming. Bullshit, but young girls, in situations like that, don't necessarily understand where blame belongs. Dwayne. His name was Dwayne Sullivan. Older kid, by a couple of years, so maybe sixteen? In our grade still, more because he was lazy than stupid, I think. Always had a cigarette tucked behind his ear, and had a little fuzz of a mustache, and sometimes his voice cracked. He hung around with the kind of guys who think the height of comedy is snapping a girl's bra strap, but there was always something different about Dwayne, more intense, more patient, more serious. But kind of alluring, too, in that way dangerous older guys can be alluring when you're young and inexperienced."

She glanced at Pelham, who seemed rapt, and she supposed a story like this, all sordid and messy, was as alien to his experience as walking on the moon, or windsurfing off the Great Barrier Reef, or choking to death on poisonous gas in a coal mine. "Carol didn't even go out with Dwayne, didn't go near him. But her walk home from school was along kind of a back way. Mostly we walked with her, since we lived farther down in the same direction, but after Amy got hurt she was out of school for a week, and me . . . I just wasn't there one day. Something stupid. My mom wanted me to pick up a loaf of bread before I came home or some crap. Next day Carol wasn't in school, and the story was someone hit her on the back of her head and tore off her clothes and left her in a ditch. Carol went to the hospital. They thought she was going to die. Everybody—*everybody*—in school knew Dwayne had done it. He didn't brag, exactly, he was too serious for that, too careful in his own way, but he must have told one of his cronies, because word got around. Suddenly I was alone. I didn't have my friends with me. I didn't have anybody. I was just another poor white-trash kid, nobody and nothing. My brother was only two years older than me, but he'd dropped out of school by then, so he wasn't there to protect me. One day Dwayne came along and pressed up close to me when I was standing by my locker. He whispered in my ear. He said, 'Two out of three.' And then he just walked off. I stood there, Pelly, shivering, and terrified. Amy, he raped. Carol, he raped and beat. Me, I was no great shakes in math class, but I figured there was an exponential progression there: come my turn, he would kill me.

"So I told my brother." She went silent. She didn't think about her brother much—though, in a way, he'd helped make her who she was now. He'd taught her to fight, and to fight dirty if that was the only way you could possibly win.

"You mentioned him, when I asked you about your family," Pelham prompted. "Your brother."

"Yeah. Back then, I could still ask him for help. Back before he was a bad guy—or at least when he was a bad guy who happened to be on my side. I told him what Dwayne had done, and what he'd threatened to do, and my brother said, 'Do you want me to take care of it, Marlita?' He always called me that. I thought about it, and I said, 'Can you teach *me* to take care of it?' So my brother taught me what to do. I still don't know where he learned it all. Some of it was just bar fighting, and sure, there were bars in the county that would serve a sixteen-year-old, if it was the right sixteen-year-old. Some of it was dirty tricks. The spots to hit to inflict maximum pain, and the other spots to hit to do maximum damage. How to make speed count more than strength. How to forget everything I'd ever heard about playing fair or fighting honorably. I wondered back then if my brother had ever killed anyone, or if it was just bravado." If he were down here, how many ghosts would he have to confront? Maybe none. Maybe you didn't have to see the ghosts if you didn't have any guilt, and her brother had never suffered from an excess of conscience. "But after he taught me that fancy shit, pressure points and nerve clusters, he told me it was better if the other guy never got a chance to throw a punch at all. If you wanted to take somebody out, there was no percentage in giving them a sporting chance. Ambushing, he said. Bushwhacking. Sucker-punching. So anyway, before Dwayne could get me, I got him instead." A cold wind blew, and the great pigeon tornado began to drift their way again. "We'd better go down, Pelham."

"I am sorry for what you went through, Ms. Mason."

"It could have been worse." She swung over the ledge and started climbing down the ladder. "Hell, I'm young. It still could be."

14

The morning of the Founders' Ball, Rondeau strolled from his safe house under the bandstand in Fludd Park—there was a whole *apartment* down there, totally unknown to Granger, the sorcerer who ran the park—toward the Wolf Bay Café. Beadle had undone the bindings on the wardrobe in just a few hours. They were hastily, sloppily done, unlike Marla's original safeguards. The cloak was now rolled up and wrapped in a paper sack under Rondeau's arm. They'd make their final battle-plan arrangements today; it was going to be quite an evening.

As he started down the alley that led to the café, he noticed a larger-than-usual crowd milling around on the sidewalk, every street-side table occupied, even though it was only just dawn. Odd. Maybe they were having a two-for-one croissant special or something. The people didn't look like tourists, exactly, more like working stiffs with that zombified look ordinaries with day jobs sometimes got at the end of a hard week. They were all black, which wasn't so odd for this neighborhood.

Except for that one white guy, sitting alone at a little round table. The tall one, with the beard. He looked . . . exactly like Abraham Lincoln.

Rondeau veered off, pulling out his cell phone and dialing Beadle's number. It went straight to voicemail. He tried calling Partridge, and got only line static, but that didn't mean much—sometimes Partridge accidentally melted his cell phones. The pyromancer was a little unreliable, which was why they hadn't told him about the cloak, or the full extent of their plans—as far as Partridge knew, they were just planning on breaking up the Founders' Ball with a stink bomb. Rondeau dialed Langford, who answered and said "You're an idiot. Position 5A." The line went dead, and when Rondeau dialed it again, frustrated, he got the hum of a dead line. Shit. Position 5A. That was from one of the contingency plans Beadle made up, right? Which one was it?

Oh, right. The we're-fucked contingency plan. And when you were fucked, where else should you go, but the erotic bookshop Marla—or one of her shell companies—owned? Rondeau ducked into an alley and took out a Polaroid photograph of a blandly smiling white guy in a sports jacket. He chanted the words Langford had taught him and took out his metal butane lighter, the kind rich potheads at the college used, which looked like a miniature blowtorch and burned at 1,300 degrees centigrade. He flicked on the flame and burned the photograph, inhaling the smoke, though the chemical odor made him gag. Probably poisoning himself and shortening his body's life, but it was worth it if it got him through the streets safely. The photo had been enchanted, and Rondeau brushed a boyish lock of blond hair out of his eyes—he was now draped in illusion, and looked just like the man in the photo, a male model from another state who'd had no idea what he'd been posing for. The illusion would protect Rondeau from casual discovery. Death would probably see through it, but if Rondeau ran into him, he was double extra fucked anyway.

Their little gang had apparently been found out. If Rondeau hadn't heard the stories about the one zombie Ayres made look like Abraham Lincoln, he would have been screwed. Good thing Death wasn't conversant enough with American history to know how conspicuous that particular zombie was, and Ayres wasn't around to warn him.

Rondeau hopped on a bus and rode downtown. On the way he passed his nightclub and felt a pang for the place, and for lost income, though it was good to see Death hadn't made good on his threat to torch the place. After he disembarked, Rondeau strolled into the bookstore and into the back room, where Langford waited, disguised as a drag queen with an elaborate wig and a sheath dress. It would have been funny if they hadn't been in fear for their lives. Langford flipped open a pocket compass and set it on a rickety desk heaped with porn movies and glossy smut magazines. "We were found out," Langford said, then gestured at the compass. "Dampens surveillance. We can speak freely."

"It can't have been Beadle," Rondeau said. "Partridge must have fucked up."

Langford nodded. "He was very excited about the stink bombs we were building. I think he must have said something to someone, and word got back to Death. . . ." He shrugged. "Partridge must have given up Beadle. Some of Ayres's zombies came to my laboratory this morning. I slipped out through an escape tunnel. They didn't know where to find you."

"They were waiting at the café. Almost scooped me up." Rondeau sighed. "So. What now?"

Langford frowned. His pancake makeup made him look ghastly, almost like a dead thing himself. "Well, that's up to you. The stink bombs are made. I presume that's the cloak under your arm. We can assume that Partridge gave up what he knows of our plan. Beadle may be holding out. He told me that he's resistant to interrogation."

"So the cloak could still be a surprise," Rondeau said. "Huh. The stink bombs, though . . ."

Langford shrugged. "They're already hidden in the ducts in the Chamberlain's house. She's a Marlista sympathizer, but she'd never go along with a plan to disrupt the Founders' Ball. Fortunately, one of her apprentices was less scrupulous. I gather she's been forced to scrub the ballroom floor one too many times. I doubt Death will cancel the party over the chance of stink bombs. Besides, he probably thinks he stopped us. So, leader— do we proceed, or abort?"

Rondeau chewed his lip. Beadle was the planner. He was supposed to arrange for Rondeau to get onto the grounds of the mansion, to slip in unnoticed, to time things just right so he could pounce on Death by surprise. Without him, Rondeau would have to improvise. He'd always considered his improvisational skills one of his strong points, but Marla said his main skill was devising new and unheard of ways to fuck up.

But Marla wasn't here, either.

"We're on," Rondeau said.

"Good. Because if we don't win, I'm a dead man. I don't have the luxury of your immortality. So what's the plan?"

Marla descended into a harvest moon evening in familiar farm country. She walked with Pelham down a wooded trail, keeping her eyes and ears open, wary of a possible ambush. If something jumped her from concealment, that would be poetic justice, after all. It was the way she'd attacked Dwayne.

"There," she said, pointing.

Pelham squinted up. "Is that a tree house?"

"Deer stand. Hunter hides up there and waits for a deer, then, pop. But during the off-season, teenagers used to go up there, get drunk, have sex sometimes. That's where Dwayne took Amy." Marla walked beneath the deer stand and gazed up at the weathered wooden boards. "When I asked my brother's advice, he told me about leverage, how even a girl as small as I was could break a man's arms and legs using some rope and a good solid stick. But as much as I hated Dwayne, I couldn't bring myself to do that, to torture him." Though later in life, she'd been less scrupulous about using such techniques. "I mean, if there's a rat loose in your house, you don't torture it, you just kill it. Dwayne was . . . vermin. So one night I made a sort of basket from an old burlap sack tied to a rope, and I hauled the biggest, most jagged rock I could lift up into the tree. The next day I came here and waited for Dwayne. I cut class early so I could get here before him. I was up in the deer stand, and I called down to him, told him I was waiting, that I'd always liked him. I let him get about halfway up the ladder, and then . . . whoosh, I dropped the rock. It hit him right in the face. Knocked him down. Messed him up bad." Thinking back, remembering, Marla saw herself hurting Dwayne from the outside, as if it was an act she'd observed, not committed. "I climbed down and looked at him. He was still breathing for a while, though not very well, because I'd messed up his nose and his face, and there was a lot of blood in his mouth. He was conscious, I think, in terrible pain. I talked to him. Told him I'd done it for my friends. I didn't say I was really doing it because I was afraid for *myself.* I waited with him until he died. The first man I killed.

"My brother tidied things up for me. Nobody suspected us. Everyone assumed Dwayne just ran off. Poor kids did that. But after that, I couldn't look at the world the same way. Even when Amy came back to school and Carol got out of the hospital, I couldn't talk to them. What I'd done—what I'd made myself capable of doing—set me apart too much. Even my brother looked at me differently. And though I didn't like killing Dwayne, the knowledge that I could defend myself was comforting.

And the next time one of my mom's asshole boyfriends tried to press his body up against me in the hallway of our trailer, I thought, very clearly, 'I could kill him.' I knew just how. I could think of half a dozen ways how. So I packed my shit and I left town, Pelham, and went to make a new life for myself. But this is where it all began. This is where I became the woman I am today. The woman who does what's necessary."

Something mewled then, up in the deer stand, a whistling, pitiful sound. "He's up there now," Marla said. "That's him, trying to breathe through the mess I made of his face. I could have covered his airways and suffocated him, let him die more quickly, but I didn't show him mercy. For a long time after that, I lost all capacity for mercy, and thought the whole world deserved to be punished for what I'd gone through, for what I'd been forced to become. Sometimes, when I let my self-control slip, I still feel that way."

"Should we go up and see him?"

"No," Marla said. "This was the beginning of something, a long time ago, but I know what's up there. I can see it every time I close my eyes. A thing I made. Two wrongs failing to make a right, but at least putting an end to some few future wrongs. Let's go, Pelham. Keep following this trail, and see where it takes us."

They set off, and up in the tree, behind them, the shade of a dead boy wept in relief at Marla's departure.

They found an old storm cellar, all that was left of a house that burned to the foundations. "Down again,"

Marla said, pulling open the door, and leading Pelham into the dark.

They entered a long dim corridor lined with little alcoves holding bits of statuary and bas-reliefs, with dusty skylights overhead providing a sort of tentative illumination. "Where's this?" Pelham said.

"Nowhere I've ever seen before. So maybe we're finally getting somewhere." She set a brisk pace down the corridor, glancing left and right occasionally. Apart from the alcoves, there were a few open archways, but none led to anything like a throne room, just catacombs, pools of black water, mausoleums, looted treasure chambers. Up ahead, at the faraway end of the corridor, torchlight flickered, and as it grew nearer, Marla broke into a trot. She'd been down here too long, stirred up too many old ghosts, but she was finally back on mission, and the throne room was there, ahead of her, she was sure of it.

Behind her, Pelham gasped, and Marla paused, turning, half expecting the corpse of the man she'd knocked from the roof to be there, pulling himself along, or for Bethany to slither out of a side corridor.

But instead it was the mummy of John Wilkes Booth, pointing a gun at her, an expression of terrible smugness on his face. She could reach for a weapon in her bag, or just throw the bag itself at his face, but not fast enough.

Pelham was behind Booth, though, and he didn't hesitate, just grabbed the man's gun arm and kicked the back of his knee. Booth dropped, and Marla crowed, but of course Booth didn't feel pain, so he turned his fall into a spin, pointed the gun up at Pelham, and fired. The angle of the shot was steep, and for a moment Marla thought the bullet had missed, or maybe just grazed Pelham, but then he widened his eyes. "Ms. Mason," he said. "Marla. I'm shot." Then he sagged against the wall and slumped down.

Marla started forward, ready to stomp Booth's face in with her boot, but the dead assassin raised his gun again, muttering something about Rathbone, about people getting in the way of noble acts. As if killing Pelham was noble. Ah, fuck, Pelham. Such a good guy. He'd tried so hard. And she couldn't even avenge him.

Booth didn't fire. He sort of *twitched,* and then the gun fell from his fingers, and though his lips moved, no sound emerged.

Marla didn't bother to question why her attacker had stopped. She rushed to Pelham, thinking, *This is Ted all over again,* that being in her employ was a good way to get murdered; she was poison, wasn't she, she was *cursed.*

But Pelham was alive. She checked him for wounds, and found a bullet entry on his thigh and an exit wound higher up, but it looked like the slug had missed the femoral artery. Really just a flesh wound, and though she hated to imagine what kind of bacteria lived in the underworld, he would probably be okay. Thank the gods. Pelham's eyes fluttered. "Am I killed?"

"No." Ayres emerged from one of the side rooms. "I am the master of the dead, and you are not dead."

Marla picked up Booth's gun. She wasn't fond of guns, but in this case, she was prepared to make an exception.

Ayres prodded Booth with his walking stick. "Are

you real, Marla, or another vision sent to torment me? Booth is real—he is dead, and so falls under my sway, and I can confirm his reality, I can—but you, you I can't tell."

"Ayres. What are you doing in Hell?"

Ayres frowned. "Don't torment me, demoness. I know this isn't Hell. *I* am not dead. Though I smell my own rot, though I look into myself and see no spark of life, I know it is only a delusion, a sickness, and I have learned to overcome the lies my senses tell me. I *live*. Death has betrayed me, thrown me from his circle, cast this illusion of the underworld around me, but I do not believe I am dead. I sensed Booth, doubtless sent to torment me, and I made my way to him, through many dark corridors, and I *ripped his spirit out*." Ayres tapped his walking stick on the stone floor. "I sent his soul back to its torments, and left this empty husk of a body. Can you believe he tried to kill me? I am the greatest necromancer who ever lived." Ayres walked a few paces down the corridor, toward the throne room, revealing the horrible wound in the back of his head, caked with dry blood, revealing shattered bone and ravaged brain.

"Ayres," Marla said. "Ayres, you're dead this time, you're really dead." He still had his powers over the dead, it seemed, though he was one of them now himself.

"Nonsense," Ayres said. "I was cured."

Marla decided trying to reason with the dead was a lost cause—and why wasn't Ayres freaking out at the sight of her? Probably because he didn't *think* he was dead, so had no jealousy, or resentment, or rage, just his perpetual annoyance. "Can you get up, Pelly, if you lean on me?"

"I will try, Ms. Mason."

As she helped Pelham to his feet, she said, "Ayres, if Death is torturing you, do you want to help me get back at him?"

Ayres shrugged. "I suppose deposing him might break the spell of this cursed illusion."

"Can you lead me to the throne room?"

"It's there. Just there." He gestured down the hall. "But none of this is real."

"That's fine," Marla said. "Can I borrow your stick? Pelham could use a crutch."

The three of them set off down the corridor, into the flickering torchlit splendor of the throne room. It was a cavern of sorts, the walls seeming to shift from stone to smoke and back again, and torches burned at intervals with pulsing white and yellow light. Vaguely human shapes shimmered in the corners of Marla's eyes, flitting forms that fluttered like moth wings as they moved. *Shades*, she thought. *Servants of Death*.

There were two thrones: one small, and one large. The larger throne was huge, carved from a single gemstone that seemed to sparkle emerald, ruby, sapphire, and onyx in the firelight. But the throne was not empty. A man sat there, pale as ice, with a neat black beard and eyes like the blue part of a flame. He leaned forward, smiling, nodding. "Welcome, visitors to my realm," he said. "I am the Sitting Death."

* * *

Back in his old familiar Hell, John Wilkes Booth leapt from the balcony of Ford's Theatre, landing on the stage awkwardly, but in the thrill of the moment, he barely felt the impact. Sometimes when he jumped he broke his leg, and had to make his escape in agony. Other times, like this time, he was unharmed by the leap, but would later claim in his diary that he'd broken his leg, because it made a better story. He shouted *"Sic semper tyrannis!"* this time—other times he shouted "The South is avenged!"—and set off through the backstage area of the theater he knew so well, pursued by Major Henry Rathbone and others. Booth wanted desperately to turn and face his attackers, to make a last stand, to avoid the scenario he'd endured so many times, but he could not; he had to play the part, of course, to the bitter end. In his real life, his *original* life, Booth had not been cornered in a barn, had not been surrounded and burned out—oh, no, he'd faked his death, escaped to the West, lived many years. Though, he'd been forced to keep his identity a secret, telling only one man the truth—a lawyer who later had him mummified, and took his body on the sideshow circuit as a traveling curiosity.

But here, in Hell, Booth took part in a sort of fictionalized historical drama, living over and over the fate the history books said he had endured. He was pursued. On the run. Treated discourteously. Always hungry, sleeping rough, living in the woods for days on end. Finally cornered in a barn in Virginia, where he was sometimes shot by a man named Boston Corbett, and where he sometimes shot himself. Sometimes his last words were "Useless, useless." Sometimes he had no last words at all. For twelve miserable days he would be hunted, and in the end, he would die, spinal cord severed by a bullet.

And then it would start again, with the leap onto the stage. Not even the thrilling moment of shooting Lincoln in the back of the head, of striking a blow for higher ideals and home and God—no, that was denied him. Each time his torment repeated, it was with the leap, falling through space, landing on the stage, never knowing if this time his leg would snap in agony or if he would be all right. At this point, Booth couldn't even remember whether he'd really broken his leg or not, the first time. Still, he'd almost grown used to it, bored rather than tortured by his fate, until this last reprieve, this brief return to the world, to life, to new and unpredictable events. Now that he was back in the old familiar pattern, it was as if his suffering had begun anew, and he would have wept, and screamed, and cursed Ayres and the Walking Death and even God if he could have, but he could only say his same old lines, with their same old variations.

Booth leapt. He ran. He died. He leapt.

Thus, always.

"Okay," Marla said. "I'm not too proud to admit when I'm out of my depth. You say you're the *Sitting Death*?"

"I do," the man—or whatever—on the throne agreed. "I am." Then he tittered, a high-pitched sound that made Marla's skin crawl. He was certainly regal in his way, but one of his eyes was drooping, as if he'd had a stroke, and his mouth twitched as he smiled. He gripped the arms of his throne as if he thought he was in danger of falling off, and Marla could see the places where his clenched fingers had actually cracked the precious stone. There was something *wrong* with him. The room smelled not of dust, as the hallway had, but faintly of sewage, corpse flowers, drying blood.

"Don't believe him, Marla," Ayres said. "He looks like the old Death, but he is dead and gone, replaced by the Walking Death, and this is all mere illusion."

The Sitting Death squinted at Ayres for a moment. A little trickle of blood ran from the Sitting Death's right ear and dripped, adding to a crusted stain on his shoulder. "I know you, shade. I knew you when you were alive, I think. And . . . you have power over the dead? I did not grant you that power. It is too much for a mortal." He gestured, and Ayres staggered and almost fell. Could dead people break their hips? Probably not.

Ayres sat down on the stone floor and began to weep into his hands, and Pelham started toward him, perhaps to comfort him, then stopped. Marla was glad. Ayres might have helped her out a tiny bit in the past few minutes, but he still didn't deserve any comfort.

"He is dead, but you are alive," the Sitting Death said. "Living people almost never reach my throne room." He leaned forward and sniffed, loudly, closing his eyes and inhaling deeply. "I smell deaths on you. You've sent men and women to my realm. Well, well. Well done, very well done." He opened his eyes. "I will hear your petition."

"My petition?" Marla stepped around Ayres, a little closer to the being on the throne. His skin was pale, like stone, and now that she looked, there were tiny cracks in his face, as if he were a statue that was starting to crumble. "Look, a guy calling himself the Walking Death came to my city. He banished me and took over. I came here to give him a taste of his own medicine, to usurp *his* throne. But now you're sitting in the chair I came to take." She drew her knife. "Maybe you'd better think about getting up."

The Sitting Death squinted. The cavern walls shifted and groaned, and stone dust sifted down from the ceiling. "That knife," he said after a moment. "I lost it, to a sorcerer, in a game, long ago. Hmm. The Walking Death, you say? I wondered what he'd gotten up to since I sent him away. My *son,* I suppose, or close enough. I'm sorry if he's caused you inconvenience. That sort of behavior is just the reason I can't, in good conscience, retire and let him take over." He tittered again.

Marla sheathed her knife. "So that's it. You're supposed to move on, and make way for the new blood, but you refuse to give up your seat, because . . . what?"

The Sitting Death smiled. His teeth had fine cracks, too. "I don't answer to mortals, but you made it all the way here, you *impress* me—yes, you do, no one's made it this far in ages—and tradition says if you make it here I should extend every courtesy, so . . . yes. There are seasons in Hell, and my season is, technically, at an end. But you've met the Walking Death, as he styles himself. He is vain, egotistical, irrational, impulsive. . . ." He shrugged, and the throne room groaned again. "Not fit to rule this realm. And when the time came for me to shuffle away into whatever waits beyond this world for my kind, I resisted. I refused to give up my chair. I *clung.* The Walking

Death attempted to oust me, but he couldn't hurt me—I'm too old, I'm too smart, and I'm sitting in the seat of power. You rule a city, Marla Mason, don't you? Would you give up your position to some intemperate upstart?" Now his droopy eye was twitching, in counterpoint to his mouth.

"I didn't realize this was optional for you. I thought it was like gravity, or inertia, a law of nature. A rule. I thought you guys had to follow rules?" Breaking the rules seemed to be taking a terrible toll on the Sitting Death. He was going crazy, falling apart, and his realm was showing wear, too. What happened if Death went totally mad? Would things stop dying? Or would everything die at once? Would Hell disgorge the dead onto Earth again? Or something even stranger?

"If I rise from this chair, I abdicate, yes," the Sitting Death said. "But I have not moved from my throne. Nor will I. And I won't be forced. The Walking Death can't make me. He has some support in the outer fringes of my realm, perhaps a few informants scattered here and there, and he's created some creatures to follow him, but without possession of the throne, he can't really challenge me."

Pelham came up beside her, leaned close, and whispered in her ear, "The dagger, Ms. Mason."

Exactly. "Your boy, Death Junior, he didn't pick my city at random. He came because he wanted my knife, and he's holding my city hostage until I give it to him. I didn't understand why before. But now I think maybe I do. So what do you think, Sitting Death? Should I go give my blade to him? Take my city back, and let him do . . . whatever he needs to?"

The Sitting Death was very still. The flittering shades stopped flittering, and Marla got her first good look at them, alabaster women in white garments, very clichéd. Or maybe that was just the way she perceived them.

Then the Sitting Death sighed, and glanced to his right, where the smaller throne, carved of turquoise, sat dusty and empty. "The king of death traditionally has a queen, did you know that? She has certain token responsibilities, having to do with the seasons, mostly. They're ceremonial—the queen doesn't have to do anything, she just has to exist. Each new incarnation of Death goes walking in the world until he finds a mortal woman to take as a bride. She gets immortality, of a sort, and other powers." He got a faraway look in his eyes, and the shades all withdrew, as if his expression heralded some disaster.

"Sexist bullshit," Marla said. "There's never a Lady Death?"

"You might be surprised," the Sitting Death said, and Marla supposed that was possible. "But my bride chose to go on to the next world, when our son . . . emerged. She didn't agree with my decision to retain control. She called me a number of cruel names, actually. Told me I was mad. And why? For wanting to preserve what I've built? But I didn't start to fall apart until she left." He shivered, and gripped the throne, and it cracked a little more. He was squeezing hard enough to splinter diamond. "I miss her. But Marla, my bride was wrong. I am a good leader. I am wise. I am not cruel. I believe in balance. I do not torment the dead beyond whatever torments they devise for themselves. Do you understand? The Walking Death delights in cruelty. He is vile. He is like I was when I first awoke from the dark and took my place on this throne. I remember the depths of my own viciousness. I won't let such dark days come again."

The rebel becomes the establishment, always, inevitably. People in power come to believe their power is deserved, and not just a quirk of luck, and they convince themselves that power equals wisdom. This guy was violating the laws of the universe because he thought he *knew* better, and who knew what the ultimate consequences would be? The scary thing was, Marla could see where he was coming from. She didn't think there was anybody more qualified to run Felport than herself. But as nasty as the Walking Death was, this was supposed to be his throne, his realm, and if he were here, he wouldn't be aboveground, fucking with her city. "Listen, this is nice, but I'm going to take off. I'll miss the knife, but at least now I know what the fuck is going on. He's not messing with Felport just because he's bored, or because he's pissed that some mortal has his family heirloom. It's about his life and his future and his place in the world. I can respect that. If the Walking Death gets this dagger, he can come back here and kill you, can't he? It will transform into a sword in his hand, a terrible sword, and I've heard about that sword. It can slice out hope. Carve up dreams. Even kill Death. It won't work in my hands—I'm only human—but if I give the dagger to the Walking Death, you're lunch meat, am I right?"

"Don't threaten me." His voice was a cold wind.

"You're supposed to extend me *every courtesy*, right? Then give me the courtesy of an elevator back to the world of the living."

The Sitting Death laughed—not a creepy titter, just a laugh. "Oh, you're wonderful, Marla Mason. I wish you'd been alive when I first went looking for a wife. You're as sharp as my bride was. I didn't go looking for her, you know. In all my travels, I never found a suitable wife, but my bride fought her way down through the underworld to ask for a boon, and I fell in love with her straightaway."

"What boon did your wife ask for?" Marla asked, genuinely curious.

The Sitting Death's face changed. All the liveliness and vigor he'd just shown drained away, and his expression was like the abyss staring back, all emptiness and void. "I don't remember," he almost whispered. "When she left, when she moved on, I lost so much, so much of her . . . I only remember that I miss her." He shook his head, looked at Marla, and began to nod. "Perhaps we can make an arrangement. I think we can each provide something the other needs."

"I'm listening."

"Good. Good. Marla Mason, will you consent to be my bride?"

Marla blinked. "Why the hell would I want to marry you? So I can be first lady of Dustville here?"

"Because if you marry me, you would heal me, I think, and help stabilize things. I might be able to stand up from this chair again in a few years, if you were seated in your throne beside me."

"Bully for you. What's in it for me?"

"If you became my bride, you would be something like a god," he said, sounding saner than he had before. "And your dagger of office would transform into the terrible sword of Death in your hand, and you could use it to return home and slay the Walking Death."

After Marla's initial shock, and her understanding of what he was really offering, and why, they negotiated. It took hours, but they finally agreed to terms.

Two pale shades of women emerged and erected a screen of some dark substance that looked like woven smoke, and—though she was no more modest than an alley cat—Marla went behind it. The shades presented her with a pale gray wedding dress and tried to strip her, but she shooed them away and said Pelham would help her dress.

Pelham assisted her with the spiderwebs and moonbeams and dust—it itched, of course it fucking itched—and murmured congratulations. "It's not how I imagined ever being proposed to," she said. "Back when I was, oh, ten years old, and occasionally imagined such things."

"It is certainly a good match," Pelham said. "Not a love match, no, but an advantageous one, a strategic one, and sometimes people in positions of power like yours must make such decisions."

"Preaching to the choir, Pelly. But you do know he's *crazy*, right?"

"Perhaps he only needs the love of a good woman to set him right," Pelham said.

"And you think that's me? Right. Let's get this over with."

Marla took her place on the hard, unspeakably uncomfortable turquoise throne beside the Sitting Death. Maybe the seat wouldn't be so uncomfortable once she was, ahem, like unto a god. A shade glided out of the darkness and placed a crown of silver wire and tiny gemstones upon her head.

"Ready, my dear?" The Sitting Death tittered again, and now his other ear was bleeding, too. Marla figured this was a bad idea, but she was faced with a set of difficult choices, and this seemed like the best option at the moment.

"Yes, my . . . uh, you."

Pelham and Ayres stood as witnesses for the living and the dead, respectively—though Ayres still insisted he wasn't dead—and the Sitting Death performed the ceremony himself, intoning words that slithered into Marla's head and then promptly vanished. Having the bridegroom do the officiating seemed questionable to Marla, but she supposed he made the rules. When the words were done, the cavern rang with thunder, and Marla didn't feel any different at all.

"Say 'yes,' " he prompted.

"Right. Yes."

"Now you are my wife," he said, and after a long moment's deliberation, he lifted his right hand from the throne's arm. The world didn't end or anything, and he reached over to take her hand. His fingers were incredibly cold. "Marla Mason"—she'd insisted on keeping her last name—"queen of the underworld."

"In absentia." Marla hopped down from the throne and rubbed her numb ass. She didn't feel a bit like a newly minted demi-goddess. "As we agreed. I'm not interested in staying down here with you, not even for six months out of the year."

"But at your moment of death, Marla Mason, in the fraction of a second before your life departs, I will come for you, and bear you back here, and you *will* sit at my side, for all eternity. Until then, your mere existence will be enough to keep the seasons running their courses. The first night you join me here, we will consummate our union, and that will be the lushest spring in human memory."

Consummate. Marla wondered if the rest of him was as cold as his hands. "That's the deal." Kind of a terrible deal, but you play the cards you've got, and make the best hand you can. "Now, how do I get back to Felport?"

"I will arrange transportation."

"And the banishment won't work on me anymore?"

The Sitting Death waved his hand. "You are the queen of the underworld. You cannot be banished by your"—he smirked—"stepson, the Walking Death. Would you like a cohort to ride out with you?"

Marla considered. Riding out with Hell at her back sounded good, at first, but then again, was that really the best place to stand in relation to Hell? She thought about how Rome fell, sacked by barbarian mercenaries who were once in the city's employ. Bringing a horde of hell-spawn to Felport seemed like a bad idea. "No, just me and Pelham. Is there anything I, ah, need to know about . . ."

"Try it," the Sitting Death said. "You are not mortal anymore. At least, not *only* a mortal. You are family."

Marla took the dagger from its sheath, and it changed in her hand, the blade lengthening, the hilt thickening, and now she held a sword in her hand, a long slender shining rapier tipped with a single drop of some yellowish venom. The weapon was beautiful, but simple, the hilt still wound with bands of purple and white electrical tape. It was no heavier than the dagger had been. Marla wasn't much of a swordswoman, but she thought she'd be able to do some wicked things with this blade.

"With that sword, you can kill the Walking Death, and secure my reign—our reign—forevermore," the Sitting Death said. "The sword will give you an edge, but my son—our son—is still formidable. Be careful."

Marla snorted. "I'm not worried about beating him. I could carve a better man out of a banana."

"I wish I could go myself, but if I leave my throne while the Walking Death lives, he will flow into this spot like air rushing into a vacuum, instantly. So it must be you, my love."

"Shut up about love, or I might just try cutting *you*." It was a tempting idea. Widow herself and get the crazy guy out of power. But if she killed the Sitting Death, the other Death would take over, and he was an evil, entitled little fuck. Should she support the old, mad, stagnant regime, or the new, violent, nasty one? Neither one appealed, but she'd made her choice. "Let me get my *real* clothes back on, and then you can send me home." She swung the blade through the air, and it hummed. She'd go to Felport. She'd kill the Walking Death and let her—shudder—husband retain his power. And then she'd sit down with Hamil and have a very, very serious talk about life-extension. She'd never feared death, not as a concept, but she wasn't too keen on the notion of sitting forever on a throne made of jewels next to a guy who was, even for a god, pathologically megalomaniacal. Better to put that off as long as possible.

Pelham helped her get dressed, and as she was tying her boots, he whispered, "I knew you'd become an aristocrat."

"I like you, Pelham. I do. But you better cut out that aristocrat shit, or I might leave you down here."

Ayres shuffled toward them. "Take me with you, please," he pleaded. "I don't like this place. The smell . . ."

"Nope," Marla said. And then, after a moment's reflection, she added, "Fuck you. This is all your fault anyway, Ayres. I'm glad you're dead." Not very queenly, she supposed, but she'd resisted the urge to kick his ghostly ass, and that was a little bit genteel, wasn't it?

15

"How do I look?" Rondeau struck a pose as best he could, given the fact that they were standing in a damp steam tunnel.

Langford eyeballed him. "Like a man in a white-and-purple cloak. So a bit like a gay Latino Elvis."

"I like you better when you don't make jokes." Rondeau adjusted the silver pin that held the cloak closed at this throat. The pale white side was showing now, the purple lining inside, but with a mental command he could reverse the cloak, and make the purple show. That would turn him into . . . well, into a badass killing machine, more or less, one capable of soaking up tremendous amounts of damage and dealing out absolutely hellish punishment. He'd seen Marla destroy an armored car with her bare hands once while wearing this cloak. He wouldn't be able to use it with as much finesse as she did, but he figured he could get the job done.

"I joke when I'm nervous. I get nervous when death is imminent."

"Just give me, oh, fifteen minutes, then set off the stink bombs, okay?" Rondeau put on a black Zorro mask and shot the cuffs on his ruffled tuxedo. The Founders' Ball was a grand masquerade this year, which made matters of disguise easy anyway. The cloak was recognizable, but after Marla first became chief sorcerer, when she wore the cloak all the time, several of the suckups in sorcerous society had commissioned similar but nonmagical garments, so if anybody noticed, they'd probably assume he was some upstart sorcerer wearing his master's hand-me-down knockoff. "You think they have those little crab-puff things at this party? I love those things."

"Perhaps you'll survive to eat one again someday," Langford said, which was probably as close as he was going to come to wishing Rondeau luck.

Rondeau proceeded down several branches of the steam tunnels, up a ladder along a vertical shaft, through a hatch, and into a by-god escape tunnel that one of the founding fathers had built from this mansion—more intel from the Chamberlain's rogue apprentice. The tunnel was well maintained, but currently unoccupied, which was good. Invited guests weren't likely to pop out of the false back of a coat closet. Rondeau figured once he got mixed in with the milling mass of Felport's finest, he'd be less noticeable. He hoped.

Rondeau came out of an empty closet and carefully closed the false panel behind him. He wasn't familiar with the Chamberlain's mansion, but the party was in full swing already, so he just followed the noise, going down marble hallways until he encountered a group of young apprentices lounging in a corridor. They were dressed in fine garments and small masks, except for one, who'd gone for a full feathered-and-sequined carnival mask that covered his whole face. One of them, a woman in a lemon-yellow mask and a slinky dress, berated the others. "Don't you idiots read? It's a reference to 'The Masque of the Red Death' by Edgar Allan Poe. The whole party, with the rooms draped in blue, purple, green, orange, violet, and black. The red-tinted windows in the dark room. 'The prince had provided all the appliances of pleasure. There were buffoons, there were improvisatori, there were ballet-dancers, there were musicians, there was Beauty, there was wine.' You know?" The other apprentices looked at her blankly.

"I've read that story," Rondeau said. He'd spent several months reading all sorts of things, in an effort to impress a smart woman he'd had a crush on, and he'd discovered a certain pleasure in the experience. "A prince throws a big party for all his nobles in a fortress, while outside everybody dies of a plague, the Red Death. But then there's an uninvited guest at the party, a guy dressed in a gray robe and a mask of a dead guy's face. Turns out, he's the incarnation of the plague, and he kills everybody at the party."

"Finally, somebody here who knows something," she said, still cranky.

One of the other apprentices glanced at Rondeau. "He doesn't know much about fashion. That cloak, really! Unless you mean it ironically, since Marla Mason has been deposed. Is that it? Is it irony?"

Hipster apprentice. Rondeau ignored him.

"Anyway," the woman said, "my point is, we should all take off as soon as it's halfway polite to do so. That guy in there is *Death,* and he's decorated the place to look like the setting of a story where all the party guests *die.* Aren't you even a little worried about that?"

One of the other apprentices belched. "You worry too much, Cherie. Nobody would be dumb enough to spoil the Founders' Ball, especially not the guy throwing it. The ghosts would never forgive him. I'm gonna hit the punch bowl." He beckoned, and his friends followed him back toward the party.

"It's your funeral!" Cherie called. "I'm leaving!" She glanced at Rondeau. "You?"

"Nah, not yet. If there's going to be a plague of blood-sweating instant death, I need a little free champagne first."

She looked at him quizzically. "So whose crew are you with?"

"I'm freelance at the moment." Rondeau excused himself, following the other apprentices so he wouldn't accidentally wander into a bedroom or something. They led him straight to the ballroom.

The vast space had been subdivided by immense cloth hangings that draped the walls and hung in swoops and arcs from the ceiling, and the first room was sky blue. Medieval-sounding string music drifted in from deeper in the ballroom, and the smells of sweat and incense and rich food mingled in the air. Dwarves in tasseled costumes jumped and tumbled on a stage, and a crowd of living people stood at one end watching, while at the other end, a good selection of the ghosts of the founding fathers watched them, too, with deadly seriousness.

Rondeau had never seen the ghosts before. He'd been expecting a sort of spectral version of the cast of the musical *1776,* all waistcoats and spectacles and beards. There were a couple of prosperous-burgher ghosts, but others looked more like thugs in nice suits, faces craggy and scarred. The women wore enormous skirts. Why the hell did nobody ever mention the founding *mothers*? They were here, too. The ghosts all looked a bit like figures in a fog—grayish, not exactly translucent, but fuzzy at their edges. Marla said that even those rare ghosts who retained consciousness and sense of self were still basically forced to assemble their ectoplasmic forms constantly from memory, and after so many years of death, their mental visions of themselves got a little frayed. The dwarves executed an impressive series of flips, crossing one another in the air, and a couple of the female ghosts clapped, and the men gestured with what appeared to be real cigars. How the hell did they hold them? Ghosts were supposed to be immaterial, except maybe for dampness, or slime. Did they get extra physical definition on the night of the Founders' Ball?

"You shouldn't be here." Hamil appeared at Rondeau's elbow, pretending to watch the dwarves. He wore a mask, of course, red and black, but his size made him unmistakable. "It's dangerous."

"Not as dangerous as it will be," Rondeau said.

"He must know you're coming," Hamil said. "Even the theme of his party, the Masque of the Red Death, it's as if he expects an unwelcome visitor. Striking here, now, it's not wise."

"Yeah, but it's happening. He doesn't know I have the cloak, at least. Go on. You probably shouldn't be seen with me, in case I fuck things up and get caught."

Hamil started to move away, then paused. "Be warned. In the last room, the black room, two of your associates are . . . on display." He hailed someone across the dance floor and moved away.

Shit. On display? What did that mean? Heads on pikes? Rondeau hurried through the other rooms, noting that the servers moving about with trays all wore costumes that matched the colors of their chambers. He almost paused by a groaning buffet heaped high with delectable-smelling food, but decided to move on. He saw the Bay Witch—who had a clump of seaweed sitting on top of her head, which was maybe her idea of a costume? Someone who might have been Ernesto, wearing an elaborate mask of hammered metal. The Chamberlain herself, standing by a troupe of musicians, laughing with a crowd of ghosts who seemed to be having a merry time. For now. Rondeau moved on, weaving among the dancing, chatting, eating people, and finally reached the black room.

This is like being on the inside of a cancerous colon. There were slits in the black cloth, with crimson light pouring through. And there, suspended above the center of the room, right in the intersection of three beams of red light, were two metal cages. Beadle's cage was an asymmetrical tortured teardrop of metal, all eye-wrenching curves and angles, probably covered in symbols of chaos magic. He lay at the bottom of the cage, pale and weak, and he was probably responsible for the puddle of vomit on the floor below. Partridge's cage was square, but rimed with ice, and Rondeau saw the pyromancer's teeth chattering, and puffs of cold air coming from his mouth. They were both hung just high enough that Rondeau couldn't quite touch the bottom of their cages, and they were guarded by a row of undead, including the Lincoln zombie. This room, perhaps because of the prisoners, perhaps because of the color scheme, was nearly empty. The only people here were a few dozen ghosts. . . .

And, way in the back, almost hidden by overlapping folds of black cloth, Death. He seemed incredibly bored, and sat on a throne made of something glittery and black, with a number of pale, dark-haired goth girls in black lace and shredded white wedding dresses sitting at his feet, gazing up at him. *Guess none of the guests like hanging with the host.*

Rondeau started to turn and leave the room, unwilling to be spotted, but then he heard a scream in one of the other rooms, and the sound of people gagging and retching. He didn't smell anything—with his nose *or* his mind—but then, his mask was enchanted to protect him from the psychic stink bomb. Sounded like people were stampeding out there. He worried briefly that someone might get trampled, but these were sorcerers, or at least apprentices, and they could probably protect themselves. Those who couldn't, well, call it sorcerous Darwinism. Magic was a tough business.

"What's happening?" the goth girls said, and then gagged, and fled the room. Partridge and Beadle, in their cages, seemed oblivious, their binding spells making them numb to the world, no doubt. The zombies guarding the cages didn't even twitch, but Rondeau wasn't too worried about them. If they came at him, he could cut them up like a chainsaw through rotten logs. The ghosts were also unaffected by the psychic stink bomb, though they frowned and gestured in a little clump. That was too bad. Rondeau wasn't thrilled to have an audience.

Okay. Moment of truth. *Viva la revolución.* Nothing to lose but everything.

"Hey, Death!" Rondeau called. "Nice party!" The ghosts all turned and looked him.

"Finally." Death stepped down from his throne. "I didn't think you'd ever show up. The leader of our local revolution in miniature. I've got a cage all picked out for you. It causes pain without killing. It's wonderful. I'll clean out this stink and then bring all the guests back, so they can throw things at you for spoiling the party." He came around the cages and got his first clear look at Rondeau. He went even paler, if that were possible. "What . . . what is that on your *back*? Where did you get that?"

"This old thing?" Rondeau said, and reversed the cloak.

Though there was no apparent way in or out of the throne room besides the door they'd entered through, a fine carriage pulled by four black horses came rolling in. The driver was the same man, or thing, who'd driven the bone train, and now Marla could see him for what he truly was, without the knowledge skittering out of her brain right away. Such vision was part of being a goddess, she supposed—seeing the truth of things. The driver was a terrible being, but he had a certain dignity, too. Pelham carefully avoided looking at him.

Marla glanced at her—oh, crap, really—husband. "A limo might have been more inconspicuous."

"Why not make a grand entrance?" the Sitting Death said. "The carriage will take you to the Founders' Ball, which is a grand masque this year, I'm told. There are costumes in the coach."

Marla swore. "It's the Founders' Ball already? We were down here that long? So, wait—the *Walking Death* threw the party?"

"Indeed."

"Huh. I'll have to thank him before I kill him. That's something I won't have to worry about for another five years."

Pelham opened the coach door for her. He was limping a little, but his leg was bound up in a bandage, and he didn't seem too bad off.

"Come give me a kiss good-bye," the Sitting Death said.

"Save it for the honeymoon," she said, and got into the carriage, followed by Pelham.

The inside of the carriage was bigger than the outside, as big as a good hotel suite, complete with a bed and a couch, Tiffany lamps, a bathroom, and a walk-in closet. Though there was some vague sense of motion, it was mostly as steady as a good train ride.

"Costumes here," Pelham said, and Marla went to

examine the clothes hanging in the closet. Nothing too objectionable. She'd seen how men of a certain age liked their trophy wives to dress, and she wasn't going to put up with that shit. Her outfit was more swashbuckling than slutty, all black silk trimmed with silver, a white shirt with lace at the throat, a black-and-silver domino mask, and a hat with a giant red plume. It would go well with her black-and-silver cloak, too. There was even a sword belt and a sheath that fit her terrible sword perfectly. There were elaborate boots with heels too high for her liking—she would keep her own battered work boots with the magically reinforced toes. "It's a pirate pimp look, I guess." She ripped the feather out of the hat. She had her limits. Pelham's own costume was very simple, a tuxedo with tails and a black mask. They each got dressed, then sat down as the coach rocked and swayed.

"I bet you'll be happy to be home," Marla said after a while.

"Actually, Ms. Mason, the past few days have been the most wonderful of my life. Even when I was terrified, it was wonderful, in its way. I was never terrified when I lived at the estate, you know. That was a new experience."

Marla laughed, and there was the sudden sensation of slowing, and the driver's voice, from a concealed speaker, said, "Doors are opening." Pelham swung open the door, and Marla slipped out. They were in the driveway before the Chamberlain's mansion. *Quick trip.* She was achingly grateful to be home, but she had work to do.

One of the Chamberlain's lackeys stepped in front of the door as Marla went up the steps. "Invitation, miss?" he said, bored.

She lifted up her mask. "I'm Marla Mason, you idiot."

His eyes bugged out, and he stepped aside, tripping over himself to apologize. "Of course, but, ah, that sword. You aren't supposed to . . ."

"What?"

"Nothing, ma'am. Go on in."

"I will. Don't mention I'm here. I'd hate to spoil the surprise. Tell anyone I've arrived, and *you'll* get a surprise. A nasty one."

He swallowed and nodded, and Marla swept past him, Pelham following. She remembered the route to the ballroom, and when she entered the first room, which was blue, she was annoyed to see so many familiar faces, sorcerers of high and low standing, milling around, eating, chatting, and having a fine old time. None of them recognized her. Wasn't anyone fighting against the Walking Death? Had they all just rolled over in the past week? She saw Hamil, and Ernesto, and Nicolette, and wanted to beat the crap out of all of them just for being here, but she had work to do first.

She'd only made it to the green room when people started screaming and running. Marla looked around for the source of the disturbance, but couldn't find anything. She grabbed Pelham and swung him out of the way, behind a giant ice sculpture of Death, so they wouldn't get trampled. Pelham doubled over, gagging. "The smell," he said, "it's in my *head,* it's awful."

Marla smiled. So, somebody *was* doing something on her behalf, then, ruining the party with some kind of psychic stink. That would piss off the ghosts, which would be big trouble, but she was heartened just the same. "Get out of here, Pelly. I don't smell anything. I guess that's one of the Sitting Death's wedding presents."

"I should stay," he said, and then doubled over, retching.

"No, get out of here, find the Chamberlain, tell her I'm back, and sorting things out, would you?"

Pelham nodded and scurried away, joining the last of the fleeing guests. Marla tore her mask off. There was no one left in the room but some of the ghosts of the founding fathers, gray (and fuzzy) eminences all, and Marla said, "Hey, fellas! It's me, Marla. Sorry for the disturbance. Want to come watch me kick Death's ass?"

The ghosts consulted. One, with muttonchops and a unibrow, nodded. "Indeed. He's in the black room."

Marla set off, sword swinging at her belt, grinning so hard it made her cheeks hurt. She picked up more ghosts on her way, until she had a good crowd coming after her, but when she entered the black room at the end of the ballroom, she saw there was already an event in progress.

Rondeau was there, fighting with Death. He leapt around with fiendish dexterity, struck out with incredible ferocity, cackling all the while, and he seemed to be holding his own against Death, who bled from a cut on his cheek. But Marla scarcely paid attention to the fight. She was focused on the *thing* clinging to Rondeau's shoulders. It was a monstrous flap of grayish-green skin, a ragged gangrenous beast with leprous patches and hundreds of rheumy red eyes, and teeth like straight pins, and it clung to Rondeau's neck and shoulders with those teeth, fastened into him, seeming to feed on him, swelling up like a tick engorging itself. And, gods, it *reeked*, like something half-digested and rotting.

Marla blinked, and blinked again, consciously trying to dispel the strange new sight she'd gained since marrying the Sitting Death, and in a moment, she saw Rondeau with normal vision—he was wearing her purple-and-white battle cloak. But that hideous monstrous form, she knew, must be the cloak's *real* shape, a parasitic thing that pretended to be clothing, the way the venom-dripping sword of Death had pretended to be a simple dagger. She'd let that thing fasten onto her intermittently for years, and now it was fastened on Rondeau. He was fighting for her, but now that she knew what the cloak was, she had to stop him.

"Rondeau, get back!" she shouted, and even in the grip of his battle fever Rondeau heard her voice, and turned, and then suddenly the cloak reversed itself, the purple cloud around him replaced with pure white, and he collapsed, unconscious, the cloak's healing energies tending to his injuries. Marla, briefly, stepped up her goddess vision, and the cloak was still a horrible thing, but now its red eyes were slowly drooping closed, one after another, as if it was dropping off to sleep. Maybe it was only really awake when it was being used to fight, and for a short time afterward. That explained the way its malign intelligence lingered in the mind for a few seconds—or even minutes—after battle.

"Marla Mason?" The Walking Death struggled to his feet. "You—this can't be. I banished you."

"Yeah. About that. I came back. Son." She drew the sword, and Death actually hissed, like a cat. "I came to cut you down."

"You met the Sitting Death, then. I was afraid you might discover my secret, that my predecessor still reigns, when I heard you went to the underworld. Clearly Booth failed to stop you."

"He tried. Just like you tried to take my city. Remember how I told you that was a mistake?"

"The throne should be mine," Death said, anguish in his voice. "I emerged from the darkness, knowing my purpose, knowing my place, but I was attacked when I entered the throne room. He should have stood up, shaken my hand, wished me well, but instead he threw me out. You allied yourself with that monster?"

"You should've told me what you needed the dagger for. I might have agreed to help you."

"It was not mortal business," he said frostily.

"But you had to be an asshole instead. Frankly, I don't like the idea of letting *either* of you rule down there. You're an asshole, and he's pretty much insane."

"The land of the dead is fragmenting," Death said. "Some of the spirits are developing their own autonomy. There are regions of the underworld that are not safe for *me*. And my father cannot leave his throne to take those regions in hand—he cannot rule, because he is too busy protecting his reign. But his reign is already over. It's dead. It's rotting. I just needed the dagger—the sword—to cut him out. He is a cancer, and reality will suffer if he's not removed. Even his marriage to you won't stabilize things completely, not for long. Please. It's not too late. Give me the sword."

"You're cruel, vain, vicious, and egotistical." Marla glanced at the cages hanging from the ceiling. "You display your enemies like party favors. You don't deserve to lead, either."

Death snarled and attacked her.

Marla lifted the sword, and using powers she didn't quite understand, she cut through time itself, and made her enemy hang in mid-stride, much as he'd suspended her before banishing her, though Death was not conscious, as she had been. Marla walked around him. One clean blow. Strike off his head, fulfill her arrangement with the Sitting Death, get her city back, and try not to think about what awaited her after death.

But she'd just traveled through the underworld. She'd faced every life she'd ever taken. Some, she felt guilty about. Some, she felt justified in. But all of them troubled her, more than she would ever let anyone know. Did she want to kill again? She was now the queen of death, but the idea of spilling more blood did not appeal.

The sword hummed in her hand, and she thought about what Cole had said. The sword could cut through *anything*.

This Death was a bad guy. *I could carve a better man out of a banana*. She didn't want the Walking Death, cruel and vain as he was, to win. But maybe . . .

Maybe I can just cut out the bad parts. Marla let her goddess vision fill her. She could see now a series of overlapping auras, in colors as diverse as the rooms at the ball. His cruel sense of humor, red. His insecurity, green. His sadism, black.

Carefully, with deft strokes, Marla began to cut out the most terrible parts of his character, carving away his hatred and his smugness and his villainy, like cutting the bad parts out of an apple, the moldy spots off a block of cheese. She couldn't *add* things—not kindness, not wisdom, nothing—but perhaps, like pruning back a tree, he could grow stronger, better, and more healthy after she was done. Finally she stood back, examined her handiwork, and nodded. This sword . . . she could do amazing things with this sword. Go to the Blackwing Institute and cut the crazy out of the inmates there. Cut up the hatred in her enemies and make them support her. Slice off threats before they even became threats. Eradicate pedophilia, pyromania, and the more annoying forms of political dissent. She could make the world in her image, and it would be good.

She waved the sword, and time resumed, but Death did not attack her. He swayed. "You changed me," he said dully. "You . . . you . . ."

"Made you suitable to rule," Marla said, and tossed him the sword. He caught it, hilt first. "Take it. Go down there and kill the Sitting Death. It's just a loan, though. I'll want that blade back. I have plans for it."

"I can't bring this sword back to you," Death said.

"The fuck you can't. You have to. It still belongs to the chief sorcerer of Felport. I'm not relinquishing it."

"You must relinquish it," he said, gently. "You changed me, Marla. You made me better. You made me a better person than *you* are, and you know it. If you had this sword in your hands, here, in the world . . . you would have the powers of a god, but you are still a mortal, and so you would not be bound by the rules of a god." He shook his head. "I can't believe my father gave you such power. It proves he's gone mad. Why, you could use this to change people, to change whole populations, to make the world your slave."

Marla shifted uncomfortably. "I don't want slaves," she muttered. "I just wanted to make some adjustments."

"You know what absolute power does. I will keep this. I will have a dagger made for you, which has the same powers this did, in human hands—to cut through ghosts, to cut through all matter, but without the true sword's terrible capabilities." He leaned forward then and kissed her full on the lips, and though he'd startled her, Marla didn't draw back. "You have your city, Ms. Mason. Be good to her." He bowed, and then stepped sideways, through nothing, away.

Marla stood, stunned, for a moment. It had worked. She wished she'd kept the sword a little longer, made some fixes, but . . .

Around her, the founding fathers (and mothers) were clapping. She'd forgotten they were there. The fiercest-looking one of the bunch came up to her and shook her hand, which was a bit like shaking hands with a skinned eel, all slipperiness and give. "We like a good fight," he rumbled. "And we like a good kiss. Best Founders' Ball in years. All those pompous asses running around like fools. Ha! Good show. Good show."

"Thank you," she said, then added, "sir." The ghost clapped her on the shoulder and sauntered away, and the other ghosts went with him, right through a black-draped wall. Marla went to Rondeau, who was just waking up. "Hey there, kid. What've you been up to?"

"Marla?" He smiled up at her, and she'd missed that smile, she really had. "I was a revolutionary. I kicked *ass*."

"I bet you did. You'll have to fill me in on everything I missed. But first, let's get this nasty cloak off you, what do you say?"

16

"I t was good of you to pardon Viscarro," Hamil said, sipping a glass of brandy.

Marla looked up from the mess of reports on her desk. "Are you kidding? I *had* to pardon him. He's the only one—including you—who never swore loyalty to Death. Granted, he hid in his spider hole out of cowardice, but he didn't outright betray me, like nearly everyone else did. I don't like having that thing in my highest councils, and if he ever gets that crazy vacant my-humanity-is-gone look in his eye, I'll have him exterminated. I made him give me the phylactery that holds his soul. He'll be on his best behavior, believe me." She shuffled the papers before her. All the sorcerers had submitted explanations to her in writing, trying to cover their asses. She'd had an amazing number of secret conspirators, it seemed—*everyone* was really just spying on Death on her behalf, waiting for contact from the revolutionary force, or acting as sleeper agents, and none of them were actually collaborating with the occupier—oh, heavens, no.

Marla had decreed a general amnesty for all collaborators with Death, in a spirit of forgiveness and goodwill—and also because if she'd banished or jailed or executed all the collaborators, she'd be damn near the only sorcerer left in town. Then she'd gathered a few of the sorcerers she had special concerns about and reminded them that it never, ever, ever paid to back her opponents. Ousting the god of death had given Marla tremendous cachet. Even the irreverent chaos magician, Nicolette, was in awe of her now. None of them knew exactly what she'd done to get rid of Death, but the ghosts of the founding fathers spread increasingly outrageous stories of an epic battle among Rondeau, Marla, and Death, and Marla let the rumors fly. They only enhanced her legend. For the ones who'd actively helped her cause—Rondeau, Beadle, Partridge, Langford, and in their advisory capacities, Ernesto and Hamil—she saved special rewards. Taking a page from the Bay Witch, she offered each and every one of them a favor. That might come back and bite her in the ass at some point, but they'd all risked their lives for her (and Partridge had lost two toes to frostbite), and they deserved boons. The Chamberlain, for her part, was content with the way the party had gone, psychic stink bomb and all, because the founding fathers had enjoyed it—though she was irked that they wanted to see gladiatorial combat incorporated into the next Founders' Day ball. That, she'd suggested darkly, was going to be *Marla's* job to organize.

"Things are back to normal, then?" Hamil said. "For our usual values of normal?"

"Pretty much. Except for the goat shit. We forgot we left Ayres's goat in the conference room. It crapped everywhere and ate the phone. I'm making Rondeau clean it up, but he thinks that should be Bradley's job, because apprentices live to get dumped on, he says."

"Ah, yes. Bowman is coming next week, correct?"

"Unless he comes to his senses before then."

"It will be interesting to meet him, after hearing your stories." He appeared to contemplate the contents of his brandy glass. "And, of course, though I expect you to rule for many more years, it's never too early for you to start grooming a successor."

Marla tapped her fingernails on her desk blotter. "What makes you think I've got B in mind for that?"

Hamil shrugged one of his eloquent, tectonic shrugs. "I find that brushes with mortality tend to make chief sorcerers contemplate their legacies."

"Well, Felport could do worse than B, once he's all trained up, which will take a while anyway," Marla said, unwilling to outright confirm Hamil's suspicions. "He's kind, he considers things carefully, he's brave, and after being trained by both a seer like Sanford Cole and an asskicker like me, he should be pretty well-rounded."

"As I said, I look forward to meeting him, and helping you any way I can. He *will* be your first apprentice, so if you ever need advice on the care and feeding of such—"

Rondeau came in, carrying a long box. "Marla, this package—the, ah, return address here is pretty messed up."

She looked at the package. She sighed. "Hamil, Rondeau, will you two excuse me?" They withdrew, shutting the door and leaving her alone, and she considered the box. The return address said "Hell," and Marla figured that didn't mean Hell, Michigan. She opened the box, and there was her dagger—or, at least, something so similar to her dagger that she couldn't tell the difference . . . and neither would anyone else. She tested the edge against an industrial diamond in her desk drawer, and it sliced through the stone neatly. Death had promised it would have the same properties and enchantments as the old dagger. She missed the terrible sword, but maybe she was better off without it.

There was a letter in the box, along with the dagger, written in a rather childish hand. Marla read it. Then she read it again, and swore. She pulled open another desk drawer and rooted around until she found the silver bell the Walking Death had given her when he first banished her. She rang it furiously.

"I was hoping you'd call." Death strolled in from a door that didn't usually exist. "Ayres is driving me mad. He still insists he's alive, even though I got a mirror and showed him the wound in his head. Compliment your Dr. Husch on her cure. The man is fixed in his delusion of life. I'm thinking of sending him to a perfect facsimile of Felport and letting him wander among illusions of all of you, just to calm him—"

"Shut up," Marla said. "I don't care about Ayres. Now, what the fuck is this about us being *married*?" She shook the letter at him.

"You married the Sitting Death, Marla."

"Yes, and I'm a very sad widow woman, since you killed him."

"The Sitting Death is a title, Marla, not a person. I was the Walking Death when I wandered, but when I took the throne, I became the Sitting Death. As in the *presiding* Death, you see. And, yes, by the laws of the gods, you and I are married. My father and I are, shall we say, magically identical. We were never meant to overlap the way we did. That's why I couldn't give you back the dagger when I was done. It's too dangerous in your hands. You are still the queen of the underworld, though it's strictly a ceremonial position, for now, while you're above. Apart from the power to see through illusions at will, you have no more powers than you did before. I think it's better that way. The arrangement you made with my father stands. At the moment of your death, you will be taken to the underworld, there to rule by my side." He went down on one knee. "I would have asked for your hand in marriage anyway, if my father had not done so first. You made me what I am today."

"I don't want to be the queen of the underworld, a pretty ornament in an uncomfortable chair. I don't care if spring is especially lush—I like the winter better anyway."

"My father was not truthful with you, Marla. The position of queen of the underworld is far more than ceremonial. He told you it was a role of no consequence because he was so jealous and possessive of power. You will have great strength, and great responsibilities."

"Like what?"

He told her. It took a while, and he had to repeat

parts of it several times because of her interruptions. When he was done, she stared at him. "You . . . you're serious? All that?"

"Yes. But you'll forget what I just told you, I'm afraid. It might weigh on your mind otherwise. You're still mortal, for now, and it's not right for mortals to know such things."

"Okay," Marla said. Already the details were fading, but the job was important, she knew—she clung to that—so very important. "I guess I accept, gods-damn it."

He gave her a charming little half smile. "That's good. Because the laws of the underworld don't recognize divorce. If it's any consolation, though, infidelity is okay. I mean, we have a long-distance relationship, and we're married, not *dead*."

"How did you get a sense of humor?"

"I always had one. You just cut out the part of it that found ripping the legs off frogs funny. I have one other question. About that *thing* you thought was a cloak—"

"I'm taking care of it," she said. "Putting it someplace way more remote than the bottom of the bay."

"I could attempt to destroy it with the sword," he said, a trifle doubtfully.

"Do you think it would work?"

"I am the death of everything that lives in this universe, but the cloak seemed . . . wrong to me. I think it might come from someplace else. Someplace *older*." He shook his head. "What if stabbing it didn't kill it, but only made it angry? Perhaps you're right. Seal it away somewhere until this universe ends."

"Consider it done." She fingered the hilt of her new dagger and sighed. "I went from having two artifacts to having none."

"Now, now. That dagger of office is still an artifact. It was forged from eldritch metals in the fires of one of those godawful hot Hells you humans have favored for the past several centuries. It counts." He took her hand, bowed low, and kissed it. "Farewell, Marla."

She looked at him, and tried to decide if he was handsome. It was tricky, because she could see him with her goddess vision, too, and he didn't look much like a man at all when she saw him that way. He was something far more icy, remote, and beautiful. "Well, just don't come around here all the time. I've got my own life."

"You rang *my* bell, Mrs. Death," he said, and slipped away.

Marla put the bell back in her desk drawer, gently, so it wouldn't ring.

Someone knocked at her door. "Come," she said, and Pelham entered, dressed in archaic gentleman's traveling attire, complete with a little hat.

"Your Majesty," he said.

"I told you not to call me that." No one but Pelham knew about her marriage . . . and even he thought she was a widow now, though he insisted she was still royalty, technically, and she'd gotten tired of arguing. "You all packed?"

"Yes, ma'am. And the . . . item in question . . . is secured. I had Beadle triple-check the bindings, though I didn't tell him what was inside."

"Good," Marla said, coming around the desk and

shaking Pelham's hand. "You stay gone at least three years. Longer if you need to. Find a place where the cloak will never, ever be found. Tell no one where you've hidden it. You know the spells to cloud minds and obscure memories, so even guides to remote places won't remember you. *I* don't want to know where it is, under any circumstances."

"It's a great responsibility, Ms. Mason. I thank you for trusting me."

Marla put her hand on his shoulder. She'd noticed a certain restlessness in him in the days after they returned to Felport, and she understood—he'd never left home before, and on his one outing he'd seen the joys of California and the bizarre, horrific majesty of the underworld. Now he was supposed to go back to folding shirts and brewing tea? He was willing, but clearly, having glimpsed the world outside, he wouldn't be happy close to home. She'd considered firing him, but was afraid the trauma would upset him too much—they were magically linked, after all, and it would result in some serious separation anxiety. So she'd hit on the idea of sending him on a mission, to travel to every place in the world he could think of until he found the perfect place to hide the cloak, preferably forever, or at least until the Earth burned to a cinder when the sun went nova. He was utterly trustworthy, and this way, he'd get to see the world without feeling like he'd abandoned his duty. "Be careful, Pelham. Send postcards. Let me know if you run low on funds." She kissed him on both cheeks—it was the way the Chamberlain said farewell to her friends, and she thought it would mean something to Pelham.

"Hamil will get you a ride to the train station." He said good-bye, and there were tears in his eyes. She'd never seen him happier.

Marla dropped into her desk chair and swiveled back and forth a few times. Then she opened the bottom drawer of her desk, lifted up a pile of dusty black books, and stared down at the white softness of her neatly folded cloak. The cloak Pelham had wrapped up in all those magical bindings was just an old bedsheet with a glamour cast on it. She wished she could get rid of the *real* cloak, but despite her deeper knowledge of its true nature, it was simply too valuable to put away forever. She also had the terrible suspicion that even if she did send it away, it would find its way back to her. Marla was the one who'd found the cloak in that thrift store for a reason. The cloak had some horrible destiny in mind for her, and she didn't think it would give up hope that she might someday fulfill it. Still, she now believed it was better to let everyone think the cloak was well protected and gone forever. She'd temporarily lost her city to a man who wanted one of her artifacts. Maybe letting people know she possessed items of such power wasn't such a bright idea. Plus, the mission got Pelham out of the house. He'd return to her with a greater understanding of the world and human nature, still with all his competence and dependability, but without a tendency to break down in airport bathrooms.

"Good night, you old bitch," Marla said, and closed her desk drawer, which was as impregnable as any of Viscarro's vaults; she'd ordered him to design the drawer just last week, after all. She hoped she never had to take the cursed cloak out again, let alone put it over her shoulders. Those red eyes, those needle teeth . . . she shuddered and put the cloak out of her mind.

Things were sorted, more or less. For now. As for what would happen to her after death, well, there was plenty of time to worry about that, and anyway, there would be advantages, like, ah . . . the advantages escaped her. Something about the duties and powers of the queen of the dead. She *remembered* that she'd forgotten something, which was a thousand times more annoying than forgetting alone.

Before she had time to worry the thought any further, Rondeau appeared. He was frowning. "Marla. There's this guy here to see you."

"What, an ordinary? What for?"

"He says . . ." Rondeau looked over his shoulder. "He says he's your brother."

Marla sat still for a moment, then her hand crept, almost of its own accord, toward the hilt of her new dagger. "Okay. Send him in."

Looking anxious, Rondeau departed. *Maybe it's a lie,* Marla thought. *Or an assassination attempt. Or a trick. Or—*

A man entered. He smiled, and the smile was dazzling and familiar. "Hello, Marlita."

Still gripping the dagger, Marla rose. She didn't smile. "Hello, Jason."

ACKNOWLEDGMENTS

Writing a book about Death has the potential to be a sad and lonely business, but I was lucky enough to have a lot of help and support. Thanks first to my lovely spouse, H. L. Shaw, who is my most steadfast supporter and sounding board; to the rest of my writing group (Lisa Goldstein, Darrend Brown, David Ira Cleary, Susan Lee, Lori Ann White), who read the whole book in its rather lumpy first draft and provided invaluable feedback; to other fearless first readers, including Jenn Reese, Greg van Eekhout, Michael J. Jasper, Susan Marie Groppi, and Sarah Prineas, who helped make this a much better book; to my cover artist, Daniel Dos Santos, who makes such beautiful pictures from these stories; to my copy editor, Pam Feinstein, who saved me from a couple of monumental continuity errors; to my agent, Ginger Clark, who lets me concentrate on the writing by taking care of all the pesky business-related stuff; to my dauntless editor, Juliet

Ulman, who consistently pushes me to write better; and to all the other friends and family and coworkers who've had to endure my babbling and complaining and thinking aloud about this book. I couldn't have done it without you.

ABOUT THE AUTHOR

T. A. Pratt lives in Oakland, California, with partner H. L. Shaw and their son, and works as a senior editor for a trade publishing magazine. Learn more about your favorite slightly wicked sorceress at www.MarlaMason .net.

THICKER THAN WATER

"Marlita," the man said again, standing just inside the door to her office. He regarded Marla with an expression of mingled admiration and delight, and extended his arms, beckoning for a hug.

Marla Mason—ruthlessly pragmatic chief sorcerer of Felport, a woman who'd recently outwitted the avatar of Death, who'd once kicked a hellhound across a room, who'd thwarted the king of nightmares, and who had even killed a god (admittedly, a very implausible one)—stood behind her desk and stared at him, this man who was not quite a stranger, but almost. She'd already said his name once. She didn't think she could bring herself to say it again just yet. There was a dagger in her hand—when had she picked that up?—and she gently put it down. "You. Here. Why?"

"Eloquent as always, little sis."

SPELL GAMES
by T. A. Pratt

Look for the next exciting Marla Mason adventure in spring 2009 from Bantam Spectra.